Barefoot Lake

KIM SWIZZ

Copyright 2024 by Kimberly Swiszcz

ISBN (trade paperback) 979-8-9910534-0-2

ISBN (ebook) 979-8-9910534-1-9

Cover Art by Ink and Laurel

Interior book formatting by Grace Elena

Developmental editing by Megan Lally

Copy and line editing, proofreading by Cassidy Hudspeth

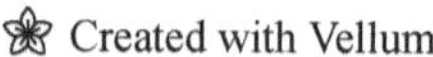 Created with Vellum

For everyone who thinks it's too late to start over.
It's not.

Playlist

"Peace" by Taylor Swift
"Keeping Your Head Up" by Birdy
"If You Go Down" by Kelsea Ballerini
"Stick Season" by Noah Kahan
"The Road" by Jonah Kagen
"What Ifs" by Kane Brown (feat. Lauren Alaina)
"Willow" by Taylor Swift
"Simple" by Florida Georgia Line
"It Will Come Back" by Hozier
"You've Got the Love" by Florence + the Machine
"Good to Be" by Mark Ambor
"Shower" by Becky G

Author's Note

Barefoot Lake is intended for adult readers over the age of eighteen and contains explicit language and intimate scenes.

Some readers prefer to dive into a story without any hints about where it may go, while others prefer a heads-up regarding certain topics. There is no right or wrong way to read a book, so readers can find full content warnings and a spice guide at the back of the book after Acknowledgements.

CHAPTER 1

Alice

I drive with the front windows down and can feel the very start of fall the further north I go. I should call my best friend Piper and tell her what happened but decide to wait until I get to the lake house. This drive — this escape — is just for me. I put the reason for my departure and my brief stop along the way out of my mind.

I turn on the radio and find a station that loves 90s and early 2000s hits as much as I do.

I know I'm getting away from any big cities when the speed limit kicks up to seventy-five miles per hour. Both sides of the highway are lined with lush green trees, and I can only imagine how gorgeous the drive will be once the leaves have changed in a few weeks. I smell damp earth, and my lungs can finally expand fully.

I've spent all of my adult life in a city. Before that, Mom and I lived in a condo in a suburb just far enough outside of Boston to not be hit with the full price hike of a New England city. I love the accessibility of everything in the city, the countless places to just wander and sit. I don't even mind public transportation — sitting on the T and reading can be nice. Of course, I won't deny the downsides. Sharing walls is the pits, not all parts of the city are pleasant, and sometimes the T is full of unruly passengers who sneeze without covering their mouths (among many other disgusting habits). But all in, Boston has been good to me.

At the same time, I'm excited when I exit the highway and slip further away from civilization with each turn. The little town center for Wilcox Grove is about fifteen to twenty minutes from the house, but in between is quiet. Roads get narrower and more winding. Streetlights disappear, and trees arch over the road like a canopy.

I'm driving under a sheet of confetti with the way the sunlight flashes between the leaves overhead. I even pass a house with chickens in the unfenced front yard. I notice the birds stay far back from the shoulder, even without a barrier keeping them in. I guess they learned about the dangers of the road the hard way. Yikes.

I know I'm almost at the house as soon as I turn off a paved street and find myself bumping along on a dirt road, the ping of pebbles tapping against the underside of my car echoing around me in the quiet. I've only been here once: when I picked Mom up for her move down to Boston and dropped some of my things off for storage. She had already sold her car in anticipation of moving in with me, and I was happy to come get her. I slow down to avoid missing the turn into the driveway.

I miraculously spot the narrow gap in the trees and crunch along the gravel toward the house on the right. At Barefoot Lake, the houses are paired off, with two in each opening around the lake. Mom's (my) house and the one to its left look similar. They're both two stories and have dark brown exteriors, so they blend with the trees around them. While the "front" of each house technically faces the gravel lot I'm currently in, there isn't much flourish on this side of either home. Each has a small grass lawn (mine is chaotically overgrown) but nothing more. All the excitement is around back, between each structure and the glistening water.

I park in front of my closed garage, situated on the far side of my house and set back from the gravel lot, so my car is tucked next to the house. The neighbor's garage is to the left of their house and there is an open gravel area between the houses that leads straight back to a ramp at the lake, presumably to allow for vehicle access if either of us needs to take our boat out of the water. I make a mental note to figure out what to do with Mom's boat during the winter before it gets too cold.

I didn't meet Mom's neighbor — I guess *my* neighbor, now, who I've now affectionately named "Neighbor" — last time I was up here, but I'm grateful nobody comes out of the house when I arrive today. I'm not in the right headspace for any introductions right now. I check my phone again. Still nothing from Reid, but there's a text from Piper.

PIPER

I love you. Call if you need anything.

There's another from a number I don't have saved but recognize nonetheless.

1 (617) 555-0910

It was good of you to come see him today.

I sigh and slip the phone into my pocket, getting out of my car.

As I approach the side door to the home in an opening by the front of the garage, my throat is suddenly thick. I know Mom will be present all over this house.

I take a deep breath before I unlock the door. I push on the door, but it doesn't budge. I'm sure I turned the key in the right direction for both locks, but I try again, jiggling the handle, rattling the door, and throwing my body against it with all my might. It still won't budge.

Come on, house. Don't be like that.

I dramatically groan as I walk around the home and across that overgrown little lawn to the front of the house to try another door. I climb the few wooden steps up to the door, frantically grabbing the banister as the plank of wood on the second step lifts on the opposite side from where I plant my foot. It noisily slaps back down as I right myself, the sound echoing in the otherwise quiet woods.

Smooth, Alice. Well done.

With my heart now racing from the near-fall, I say a silent prayer before unlocking the door. It opens. Praise be…

My excitement melts away and is replaced by a solemn feeling as I step inside and close the door behind me. I toe off my sandals and slip them under the bench behind the door. Most of the first floor of the lake house is one open space with the living room toward the front of the house and the kitchen toward the back, and a table sitting between the two spaces. Off to my left are a small bathroom, which also houses a washer and dryer, and Mom's library. I know the upstairs has a full bathroom and two bedrooms.

I sigh quietly as I look around. The couches are covered in sheets, and the countertops are bare. Mom meticulously cleaned everything before she left. The space is more sparsely decorated than I remember, but I hadn't been here very long last time. Some things are exactly how I remember them, though, including Mom's extensive collection of Disney movies in her TV stand and a couple of pictures of us throughout the years. She was adamant about printing out her favorite ones, even once everything went digital. There are some more recent pictures, too, of her and people I don't recognize.

I trail my fingers across the back of the big sofa and gather up the sheet. I drop it in a pile on the floor and quickly check the side door to see what was wrong with it. The cheeky thing swings in with ease.

I see how it's going to be.

I set my purse on the table, intending to go out to my car and unload it before I lose whatever motivation I'm pretending to have, when I spot a folded piece of paper with my name on it. There's no question as to who it's from. I'd recognize Mom's handwriting anywhere, and my eyes immediately fill with tears.

I fall into a chair and slide the page toward me.

Baby Mine,

If you're reading this, we both know what happened to me. Don't cry, sweet girl. I was living on borrowed time and I'm so lucky to have spent it with you. You are and have always been my greatest pride and my best friend.

I'm sorry. I tell you not to cry, and then I get sentimental. This isn't meant to be a posthumous good bye. I just couldn't imagine you coming here without me being here to welcome you, even if just on paper.

The house itself is still a treasure, and so is this town. The lake is beautiful, and the people are good — you'll be hard-pressed to find many better. Let them love you, trust me.

The house itself is... well, it's weird. I hope you love it while you're here, the same way I did. If you decide to sell, make sure you say the house has "charm." That's the polite way of saying it's old and temperamental.

I've left some sticky notes around with tips on how to handle the quirks of the place, but I'm sure you'll figure it all out with time.

Oh! The side door sticks. I didn't leave a note on that because I have no suggestions on how to make it behave. It's just a crotchety old curmudgeon of a door. Some things can't be changed.

I bought this place to find peace and it delivered. I hope it can do the same for you.

I love you always,

Mom

I set down the letter and wipe my hands across my wet cheeks as I lean back in the chair.

I miss my mom.

CHAPTER 2

Alice

I weasel my phone out of my pocket and call Piper. She answers after a single ring.

"Hey. Are you ok?" Her voice is softer than usual, like she's talking to a baby animal.

Piper is always loud, like an explosion of happy, so hearing her be so gentle with me tugs at my heartstrings. When Piper cares, she cares with her whole being.

"I'm at the lake house," I blurt. There's a beat of silence on the line.

"WHAT?!" And that's the volume I know and love from Piper. She pauses maybe half a second at most before her voice flips to absolute venom. "What did he do?"

"He did nothing, Pipe. He did nothing." I sigh and carry on. "I got home, and he wasn't even there. He said that since I spread her ashes in the ocean already, it wasn't even a real funeral, and he didn't get what the big deal was."

Her gasp is audible. "He did *not*!"

"Well, technically, he said I 'dumped' her in the ocean, so…"

"That walnut-brained fucker." The way she huffs tells me she has many more things she'd like to call Reid. "Damn. So, what exactly… you know… happened?"

"We fought, again. It was bad. He — it doesn't matter. It was bad. I told him to get out, and he left."

"And you're at the lake house because…?" Piper sounds hopeful.

"He didn't come back, and I haven't heard from him. He wouldn't answer my calls. So, I woke up this morning, packed what would fit in my car, and left."

"Are you going back?" Piper is being gentle again.

An irrational laugh barks out of me. "I left the ring on the nightstand and shoved the key under the door after I locked up. I'm *never* going back there."

Cheers explode from the other end of the phone line, and the two of us descend into a fit of giggles. Piper has *never* liked Reid, so her reaction isn't unexpected. I'm a bit surprised laughter already comes so easily for me, but if I'm being honest, I haven't felt any positive emotion toward Reid for a while.

As I compose myself, I feel the relief that comes from not being shamed for making a life-changing decision. My logical brain knew there was no chance Piper would ever judge me for leaving Reid, but hearing her support means the world.

"I'm so proud of you, babe," Piper gushes. "But you should have sold the ring. Why did you leave it behind?"

"Pipe. I *hate* that fucking ring. He designed it for himself and was going to put it on the finger of whoever agreed to marry him. It was never mine. It was his."

"I *guess*… but a rock that size could have gotten you a lot of new books! Speaking of books — do you need me to go over there and get anything for you?"

"The things I left behind are things I'm willing to lose. Reid can keep his overpriced plates and fancy sheets but thank you."

"Alice, you are an icon."

It feels good to let her pull another laugh from me.

"So, did you move up there forever?" Piper asks.

"Just for now. I need to be back in the spring for work. The department only gave me the fall semester off."

"Well, enjoy it. You can reclaim Boston whenever you want."

She promises to come visit as soon as she can to get all the details and leaves me to explore my new home.

I push myself up from the table and look around. I glare at the evil side door as I pass it, knowing it's going to be my nemesis, and spot a shock of bright yellow on the fridge — the first of Mom's notes. There's an elegant script J and a phone number. The note doesn't say anything more about who the number belongs to, but I save it in my phone, nonetheless. Mom thinks they're important, and that's enough for me.

When I open the fridge, it's dark and warm. The only thing inside is another sticky note from Mom with the name and address of a grocery store on it. Closing the door, I spot the plug taped to the backsplash of the adjacent counter and plug the fridge in. I'm relieved when I immediately hear the whir of the compressor kicking on.

The water runs clear from the tap, so I'm counting my wins. It takes a while for the hot side to come out hot, but we eventually get there. As I'm standing at the sink, I get my first glimpse of Barefoot Lake. The trees cocoon my house and Neighbor's on the sides, but the backs of our homes have a straight shot down a slope to the sparkling water.

I turn off the faucet and move to the back door, feeling like

I'm in a daze. The door sticks a little but swings in with a little bit of persuasion. The air is heavy with humidity — it smells like it will rain later today — but I think the start of fall is pushing summer away. It's still early in September, but I cannot wait to see this place in all its fall and winter glory.

I tear my eyes away from Mom's boat, shifting lazily in the lake by the dock, and turn back to the house, but I leave the inside door open. Until it starts pouring, I might as well air out the place. I move through the home, opening doors and seeing how Mom left things.

In addition to the kitchen and living rooms, the house had been built with a bedroom on the first floor, which Mom had always used as a library, and a half bathroom. I flick the light switch by the library door and see she set it up with a long wall of bookcases but note they're almost completely empty. Two of the squashiest-looking chairs I've ever seen in my life are at the back of the house by a gigantic window with a great view of the yard and lake.

I turn on the two standing lamps by the chairs and get to work prying open the window. I blame the humidity and not my complete lack of upper arm strength for the struggle I face. Huffing and puffing, but admiring my success, I move to the center of the room and pull the chain to turn on the overhead fan. The motor hums softly before abruptly going silent as the room plunges back into shadow.

Did I already blow a fuse?

Apparently, yes. I turn off all the light switches and go looking for the fuse box. After some searching and another battle with the side door to get out of the house, I find it in the garage. Another of Mom's sticky notes is stuck to the metal door over the panel of switches.

Be prepared to blow a lot of fuses.

I smile wistfully at experiencing the same struggles she had in this home because here she is, still helping me figure it out. I flip the master switch and look at the carefully labeled diagram inside the box, trying to keep track of which circuits are separate so I can prove Mom wrong.

Comfortable with my level of studying, I close the box and turn on the garage light. My pile of boxes is right where I left it near the door, but I notice others further back in the garage that I must have overlooked when stacking my things last time I was here. Each collection is labeled with more sticky notes: books, clothes, junk, records, and one note with a phone number that says:

Keep what you'd like and call Denise to pick up the rest

I feel a wave of sorrow as I look at the piles, knowing Mom had been planning for me to come back here without her months ago. Still, in the face of her own mortality, she thought about me and how to make things as easy as she could. I feel a sharp pain in my chest and decide I'll start on her boxes tomorrow.

As I turn to go, I spot a trash can next to what looks like a moderately sized cooler — at least it's some kind of sealed metal box.

Place to keep bodies immediately pops into my head before I remember this was Mom's house and not some serial killer's. Then again, she was a spicy woman…

I shake my head to clear out the nonsense and spot Mom's next note.

This box is for any foodstuff trash. NEVER FORGET TO SEAL IT SHUT. EVER.

Wow, Mom. Think we're being a little dramatic?

The note also includes the town dump's address. It sits beside another note with recycling information. Given the narrow road leading to the house, I guess it makes sense that a garbage truck can't come by.

I stop by my car to grab the bag of food I'd brought with me and head back inside. I drop the food in the kitchen and go upstairs.

Both bedrooms are mostly cleaned out and packed away. I poke my head into the bathroom.

A plain sheet covers towels and linens in the bathroom closet, protecting everything from dust. New bottles of shampoo, conditioner, body wash, shaving lotion, and hand soap are lined up on the sink. I find cleaning supplies in the cabinet underneath and get to work. Mom did a great job protecting as much as possible, but the whole house still needs vacuuming and a good wipe-down.

Downstairs, I start a load of the random sheets she had used to cover things and get to work. I spend the day snacking and cleaning and am thoroughly exhausted by the time evening rolls around.

I step outside to finally get some more bags from my car, hopefully including one with pajamas, but screech and fling myself back inside when I see a raccoon launch from under my back bumper and into the woods. I always thought I liked raccoons and would react well to seeing one in the wild, but here we are, likely both nursing pounding hearts.

After heaving and hip-checking windows and doors closed so none of nature can get inside, I frantically bolt up the stairs and change into a robe I found in the bathroom. I flop on the bed and fall asleep right in the middle of the stripped mattress, oblivious to the pouring rain starting outside.

Funnily enough, it turns out Mom is right even after death. I blew a fuse four more times today.

CHAPTER 3

Alice

I wake up early the next morning to the shockingly loud sound of birds chittering among themselves and a soft whistle from the breeze outside. I always imagined homes outside of the city to be quiet without blaring horns and Diesel engines growling past the windows at all hours of the night, but I guess there's just a different kind of symphony out here.

Surprisingly invigorated, I hop right in the shower before remembering that it takes *time* for the water to warm up. If I wasn't awake before, I certainly am now.

After showering and putting the robe back on, I try unloading my car again. Today, I lose the battle with the side door. There's no chance it's opening after a night of rain. Instead, I go out the front door and come face-to-face with a surprised deer on my front lawn, no more than two feet away from me at the base of the steps. I freeze, and my mouth pops open.

Where the heck AM I?

The deer overcomes its shock much quicker than I do and lazily walks away, disappearing into the forest.

Sorry for interrupting your breakfast, Bambi.

Maybe they'll come back for some more grass later, so I don't have to figure out how to mow a lawn. I've never had my own yard to care for before.

I take a few very quick trips to unload my car, extremely aware that I'm only in a robe. Thankfully, Neighbor's house stays quiet, and no other animals come by to say hello.

I leave my bags in the living room for now and take pride in the fact that I only stepped on the broken step once, and when I did, I still didn't fall.

I throw on jeans and a sweater from one of my bags but leave unpacking for later. Food is a must, and there's nothing in the house. Mom's note, pleasantly cooled from sitting inside the fridge directs me to the grocery store. I punch the address into maps on my phone, and take off. A quick glance at Neighbor's house as I turn through the trees toward the road tells me there's still no sign of life over there and no car out front.

On my way to the grocery store, I stop at the post office to check the PO Box. Yet another note in a kitchen drawer informed me that, in addition to not getting trash service, the lake house also doesn't get mail service. I wait in line to speak with somebody about picking up my mom's mail and getting my name added to the box. An older woman with kind eyes summons me forward after a few minutes. Handing over my license, I ask about the PO Box.

"Alice McDermott… you must be Rain's daughter, then?" She has a light southern drawl, not a common accent in New England, and her name tag says *Bets*.

"Yes, ma'am," I say hesitantly. I'm not used to anybody knowing anything about anyone. The Boston metro area has almost five million people, and everyone goes about their own business.

"I'm so sorry for your loss. She's good people." Bets gently pats my hand on the counter between us. I bite hard on the inside of my bottom lip to keep from crying and give a jerky nod in appreciation. Apparently, I don't mind strangers knowing my business when they're warm like Bets and still use the present tense when talking about Mom. Who knew the post office could get me right in my feelings?

She gives my hand a light squeeze before leaving to go get Mom's mail.

"You're Rain McDermott's kid?" a gravelly voice comes from my right.

The voice comes from a tall, lanky man with long, white hair tied back in a low ponytail. He's wearing a black, long-sleeved shirt with jeans and work boots, but it's his denim jacket that catches my attention, covered with patches from seemingly everywhere. I quickly spot one from the Marines, one from the library, and half a dozen with what look like black and white ducks on them. Thin old people usually seem frail, but he's got sharp eyes and seems sturdy. Honestly, he could be anywhere between sixty-five and a hundred years old.

I realize I've been silently gawking at him when he holds out his hand.

"I'm Grateful Bob. I live a few houses down from Rain's old place. I really enjoyed having her around, and I'm sorry she's gone. I assume the house is yours now?" He smiles kindly and looks sort of over my shoulder like he's remembering her. Mom had mentioned Grateful Bob before, but her description of a "kind old man" didn't do him justice.

"Yeah, it's mine now. And thanks. She talked about you a lot. It's a real pleasure." Mom told me he makes up a new explanation for his nickname every time somebody asks, and I'd be doing her a disservice if I didn't get my own answer.

"How'd you get the nickname Grateful Bob?"

He laughs, and I expect he's guessed Mom warned me about his antics. "I got it from my Mama. My first word was 'Thanks' and the second one didn't come for another three months, so I was a real grateful baby."

I immediately like Grateful Bob.

Bets comes back at that moment to hand me a roll of mail held together with a thick rubber band and tells me she's added my name to the PO Box. Thanking her, I slip the bundle into my bag.

"I like your ducks, Grateful Bob," I say as I turn to leave.

"They're loons! Greatest birds on this planet," he exclaims before saying at a normal volume, "If you need anything, just you ask. If you don't need anything, come by anyway. I'm old and bored, and you're the biggest change to this town since your mother moved here."

I head back to my car and finish my journey to the grocery store. The trip takes far too long, and I swear I buy half the store while I'm there. You don't realize how many staples live in your pantry until it's time to stock an empty one.

I'm proud of myself for thinking to grab a bundle of firewood from the front of the store. One of Mom's notes warned me that the heat isn't great and that I should keep a stock of firewood for the stove in the living room and the fireplace in the master bedroom upstairs. I noticed the rack outside the house was empty before I left, and I expect Mom donated any she had left over from last winter before leaving. I don't know how much I'll need, but the one bundle feels like a good start.

Like Bets had, the cashier quickly identifies me as Rain's daughter after a glance at the name on my credit card. They introduce themselves as Jordan and also offer their condolences before singing Mom's praises and poking fun at the insane size of my food haul, asking if I was sure that I hadn't forgotten anything.

They have a point; a shy teenager has to help me push my *second* cart out to the CRV, and I could be imagining it, but it sounds like the car whines a little louder during the uphill parts of my drive back home. It's possible that I bought way more food than a single person could eat in a month, but I came to the grocery store hungry, and I no longer need to buy only food that Reid, the pickiest eater ever, will eat. Plus, ninety percent of it is non-perishable. It's fine. This is fine.

The gravel crunches noisily as I turn back toward home, but there's still no visible movement from Neighbor's house. After I park in front of my garage, I decide it's probably best to try to introduce myself before it's suddenly been too long, and it gets weird. I decide to go over and say hi after unloading the car.

It's hard not to notice the juxtaposition of their lawn compared to mine as I step along the clearly visible stone pathway to the wooden steps that don't double as a booby trap before the door. The home has that empty, quiet feel, and I know nobody will answer even before I knock, but I try anyway.

Since I'm nosy — let's not lie about it — I peek in the front window beside the door. The sheer curtains obscure some of my view, but the layout seems to be the same as at my house, and Neighbor seems like a neat person. Not wanting to get caught with my hand in the cookie jar if Neighbor suddenly pops up, I head back to my side of our little lot.

As I'm walking, I feel my phone buzz in my pocket. I fish it out and see Reid's name on the screen. I consider letting it ring until voicemail picks up, but I want him to know I saw the call. With a deep breath, I press ignore and continue into my new sanctuary.

CHAPTER 4

Alice

I manage to stay extremely busy for the next couple of weeks, mostly going through Mom's old things and getting settled. Sifting through her boxes is bittersweet. One will be filled with random notepads she collected and never used, but the next will have sweaters that smell like her, and I'll suddenly feel like I've been punched in the stomach.

It's difficult to let anything of Mom's go, but I do my best to respect her wishes and only pick the most important keepsakes to hang onto. It turns out Denise from the sticky note volunteers at a domestic violence shelter, and Mom wanted her things to go where they could do the most good. I'm not surprised by the gesture and feel unworthy of somebody who would continue to try to do good after she's gone.

As I unpack my own things and put them away around the house, I wonder if it's even worth the effort. My time in Wilcox Grove is temporary. I'll have to go back to my life in Boston in a few months.

Then, I remind myself that Boston is a problem for later. For now, Wilcox Grove will be my sanctuary.

I've also spent a lot of my time on the back patio looking out over Barefoot Lake and enjoying the solitude. The townspeople have been kind, but I haven't made an effort to get to know anybody too well, and I haven't seen even a shadow from Neighbor's house.

After my first few days at Barefoot Lake, Reid stopped calling. I feel stupid now, looking back on our relation-shit and wondering how I'd given so much of my life to him.

We met through friends in college, and right off the bat, I pegged Reid as a dreamer. He had huge aspirations and stars in his eyes. It was romantic and thrilling. He was motivated and smart enough to back those dreams up. He graduated at the top of his class in five years with degrees in finance and accounting and an MBA. He was impressive, and I was completely under his spell.

I won't lie. He was and still is unfairly easy on the eyes. He's tall and lean and possesses maybe three percent body fat. As an adult, he looks like a finance guy from a corporate TV show with wavy dirty blond hair that swoops just right, and an ass that makes a suit grateful it has the honor of being on his body.

As time passed though, it felt like I saw Reid less and less, even after I'd finished my PhD program. He was always reaching for something higher. He went to work early and stayed late. When he wasn't in the office, he was at happy hour with the head honchos or client dinners, or brunches, or vineyard tours, or football games, or baseball games, and I was *never* invited, even to events I know his coworkers' spouses attended. When I tried to talk to him about it, he'd get incredibly defensive. Somehow, he would twist the situation and pick apart my concerns until I was apologizing to him. I always left the inevitable argument feeling like a burden, the ungrateful nag he told me I was.

I didn't realize it at the time, but Reid made sure I thought he was the best I'd ever get. I was *lucky* he put up with me. Every day, I made more changes in my life and hid more of the loud parts of myself to try to earn the love Reid told me I didn't deserve. Reid and I were never partners. If there was a give-and-take, it was because I gave and he took.

I'm enjoying a cup of coffee and one of my thought sessions on the back patio when I hear tires on the gravel out front. Has Neighbor finally shown up? Still nosy, I walk around the corner of my house and up the pathway between our houses to take a look. I'm surprised to see a red pickup pull beside my house and come to a stop, but my face splits into a smile when I see Grateful Bob behind the wheel.

I hurry up to his car as he opens the door and steps out. "Grateful Bob! What brings you here?"

"Just wanted to welcome you properly," he says, holding out a tiny paper shopping bag. I take it and find a Barefoot Lake fridge magnet inside. It showcases one of his beloved loons on the water.

"It's perfect! Thank you. I was just having some coffee out back. Would you like a cup?"

Grateful Bob accepts, and we end up enjoying each other's company for a couple of hours. He's lived in Wilcox Grove his entire life, and he's seen a lot of the townspeople grow up around him. He won't tell me how old he is, but he'll admit he's over sixty. He used to work in construction but is long retired. He has kids and grandkids, grown and scattered, but they visit from time to time. He and his wife divorced decades ago, and she moved away, but there's no ill will.

I tell him a bit about my life back in Boston and how I worked in the English department at a large university, but I had a planned sabbatical for this semester because I was taking care of my mom. I tell him I needed to lose some dead weight back in the city, and Wilcox Grove called me up.

He gives me a knowing look out of the corner of his eye and

simply says, "I have kids. I know what it means when somebody doesn't appreciate what they've got, and he didn't appreciate what he had with you."

Grateful Bob seems to know something about everything. He offered to help with Mom's boat once it comes time to take it out of the water and shared some stories about people I haven't met, the old gossip.

As I'm walking Grateful Bob around the house and back to his car, I finally pluck up the courage to ask about Neighbor. Jerking my head in the direction of the other house, I ask, "Do you know who lives there?"

"Jake? Yeah. He's lived up here his whole life. Always been a nice boy."

"Is he… a hermit?" I awkwardly ask.

Grateful Bob barks out a laugh. "He keeps somewhat to himself, but no. He owns Wilcox Nursery and had to go raise some trees to bring back for his new field. The last batch he got delivered was diseased, so he went himself to make sure they'd be alright this time. It's been a bit now, so I expect he'll be back soon."

Once I realized the nursery was for plants and not children, picking up trees made more sense.

A yellow sticky note on Mom's fridge flashes in my mind – with a "J" and a phone number. Is "J" for "Jake"?

Engaging in my ongoing war with the house has kept me on my toes. I find a new "quirk" every day. The drawer under the oven won't open unless I kick it on the right side first. The bench swing on the back patio gives sizable splinters. The railing by the stairs out front now wobbles from how many times I've fallen into it because of the trick step. And I've blown more fuses than I can admit to anybody I respect. It's literally mortifying. "Charming house" indeed, Mom.

As the days pass, I start noticing changes around the house, and they're not ordinary things. It seems like the house is… healing? One day, as I walk to my car, I notice my one, sad bundle of firewood no longer sits alone in the wood storage rack. The iron structure has been filled and is covered with a dark green tarp.

I peek around my house to eye Jake's warily, but it's as silent as ever. As Grateful Bob predicted, though, I do think he's back from his trip. I know I've heard his car late at night and early in the morning — before the sun has risen — but I haven't seen a shadow of him or a light on in the home. I even try knocking again, but there is still no answer. The blackout curtains on those front windows were certainly closed by somebody. I think he might be actively avoiding me and decide to give him his space.

A few days later, I come home from the pharmacy to find my lawn has been mowed. Either that or Bambi had come by with a hundred of his closest friends and done the fastest eating I'd ever seen. The next week, I'm climbing the front steps and mistakenly put my foot on the bad part of the wood, but it doesn't flip up. It's solid. So is the banister I'm clutching out of habit.

Other than (presumably) Jake's midnight arrivals and sunrise departures, I never hear a sound or see anybody around my house, and the fact that I can be so oblivious makes me a little nervous. Does New Hampshire come supplied with handyman wood nymphs in addition to raccoons, deer, and four billion mosquitos? At least, it seems like my visitor is benevolent.

I feel guilty that somebody else has been taking care of my house and finally resolve to investigate Mom's boat and the shed beside it to take inventory of that situation. I haven't resorted to calling Grateful Bob for help with the boat — yet. I don't want to take advantage of his kindness and be a nuisance. I can at least check things out on my own first.

I put the boat keys in my pocket and head down the stairs toward the lake and over to the dock. The boat is happily bobbing in the water to the right of the dock and a sizable, enclosed shed is half on land and half over the water to the left. I unlatch the shed door, pull it open, and peer inside.

I instantly feel like there's a stray hair on my face and swat at my cheek, trying to brush it away. Then, I feel a tickle on my forearm. Another on my neck. And another… and another.

I fling myself backward and crash heavily into the door and it makes an angry cracking sound under my weight. I'm not sure what sound comes out of my mouth, or if it's even words. It's possible I've just invented some brand-new swear words. I dance around, flailing my arms and pulling at my clothes, trying to remove the spiders that were upset by my disruption of their home.

With my heart pounding and hands shaking, I heave the door closed. It hangs crooked since my fall snapped it off the top hinge but fixing it will be a problem for another day, assuming I don't decide just to burn the whole thing down. There were a *lot* of spiders.

I bend at the waist with my hands on my hips for a few minutes, catching my breath before warily peering over at the boat. It's a bit dirty from dust that got turned into mud from rain and then dried, but it doesn't seem to have succumbed to the spider overlords yet.

I head down the dock and put one foot on the boat before I begin untying its rope from around a solid post. Maybe a gentle drive around the lake and the wind in my hair is what I need to feel calm again. It takes some persuading to get the rope to let go after remaining tied for so long, but it eventually gives. I'm holding it in my hand as my legs begin to steadily drift apart from one another. I throw myself onto the dock, choosing the sturdier of my two feet to favor before I do the splits or end up in the lake. I hastily loop the rope several times around the post.

You win today, dock. I retreat back to the house, sweaty and with a few years shaved off my life.

I should have just called Grateful Bob.

CHAPTER 5

Jake

What on earth is this girl *doing*? I stand at my kitchen sink, looking out the window that faces the lake and watching my new neighbor jerk and flail across her yard. Her yelps drew me to the back of my house, and I half expected to find her on fire from the sounds she was making.

When I got home two weeks ago, she was just *there*. I guess I knew somebody had to buy Rain's house eventually, but I was hoping it would take longer to sell than it did. I'd really hoped it would just stay empty. Rain was a good neighbor, but I like my privacy. More importantly, I like the quiet. This new woman doesn't seem to know the meaning of the word.

I probably should have introduced myself by now, but I've been avoiding the human-shaped tornado. I make sure I leave for the nursery before any sane human would be awake and stay out as late as I can working or with Eli just to minimize the chance that I bump into her. I'm rarely home, but when I am, it's easy enough to keep to myself until I see her car drive away.

I can practically hear Rain's voice in my head, scolding me for being rude and un-neighborly. She had said the same thing to my face when I hadn't welcomed Rain herself five years ago.

In my defense, I didn't know Rain had come to stay. The house next to mine had spent a few years as a rental property, and I was used to different groups of inconsiderate vacationers stomping through one after the next. If I were lucky, this new person would also be temporary, but I wasn't holding my breath. People didn't usually come to vacation at lake houses when the weather was getting colder. Chances are, she bought the place.

She's finally stopped her shrieking and abandoned the shed. Even from here, I can see the door is barely hanging on. I swear she's determined to completely destroy Rain's house.

I take an involuntary step toward my back door when I see my new neighbor approach Rain's boat. I'm fiercely protective of the lake and have a sinking suspicion (pun intended) that this woman does not know how to handle a boat. After watching her nearly fall into the lake and flee back to her house, I release the doorknob I didn't even realize I had grasped. She had yanked the boat around, banging it aggressively into the dock when she pulled it back in.

I drag my hand down my face and groan. She's a menace.

My alarm is set for 5:30 a.m., but a low rhythmic thudding sound wakes me up before it has time to sound. I check the clock and see it's just after five. The sound continues. My body must have already been waking up for the sound to have stirred me. It's like somebody is very slowly hammering underwater.

I throw back the covers and roll out of bed, going to the window to see if anything is amiss. The upstairs bedroom window looks out over the lake, and everything seems fine at first glance, but the noise is coming from this direction. I force open the window and get hit with a blast of brisk air. It feels like a real New England fall, now.

Hearing the thud more clearly with the window open, I spot Rain's boat lazily bumping against the dock every few seconds after drifting a couple of feet out into the lake, slowly unwinding more of the rope with each pull.

You've got to be kidding me. She can't even tie a knot?

I heave the window closed with more force than is necessary and swap my pajama pants for thick sweatpants. I throw on a hoodie and my hat before grabbing some socks, trudging downstairs, and yanking on my boots.

My footfalls are heavy as I stomp down the steps to the lake and the back porch door slams shut behind me. I'm not nearly as quiet as I should be, considering the hour, but I'm getting real tired of picking up after my new neighbor. For half a second, I consider just leaving for the nursery and letting the boat drift out onto the lake, but I remember the joy on Rain's face when she'd come back from a drive on the water and dismiss the thought. I'm keeping that house standing and that boat safe for her, even if it kills me. Her home deserves better. Rain deserves better.

Once on the dock, I grab the extended rope as the boat drifts to the end of its lead before beginning its sway back toward the dock and slowly tow the boat back in, pulling it snug against the wood. I carefully loop the rope around the post, tucking it so each loop holds the end of the rope beneath it. Confident the little boat won't be taking any solo adventures today, I head back to my house but stop when I see the shed door barely hanging on.

I stop and look to the heavens.

This is for you, Rain.

Pivoting back to the door, I gingerly try to open it. The top hinge screws were ripped right out of the old wood on the door. The whole thing should really be replaced, but I can do a patch job for now. I spot a toolbox just inside the door and swipe at some spiderwebs to get to it. I find a screwdriver inside, unscrew the other hinges, and lay the door flat beside me.

It's just barely starting to get light out, so I'm grateful there's a flashlight in the toolbox. I quickly spot some wooden stakes that Rain previously used to support her tomato plants and decide she wouldn't mind if I repurposed part of one to fix the door. I pry off a few splintered pieces from one end and jam them into the striped screw holes on the door.

I heave the door back up and begin reattaching it to the hinges in the frame, using slightly longer screws for the damaged hinge, so they can grip the new wood pieces as well as wood further into the door. I swing it back and forth a few times and am satisfied that it will hold for now.

As I'm putting back the toolbox, I spot a broom propped in the corner. Hunching to reach it, I begin cleaning out more spider-webs, sending their inhabitants scurrying out of the shed. Find another home, fellas. This place is a *mess*. As I swipe around, the end of the broom hits a box on an overhead shelf that I hadn't seen in the dark. It shifts and tumbles onto my shoulder, making me swear loudly before I shove it roughly back on the shelf and resume my tidying.

Why am I doing this, again?

I'm still bent over inside the shed when I hear a shout from behind me a few minutes later.

"Hey!"

I close my eyes for a moment, hoping I've imagined the furious voice, but knowing I haven't. I let my head fall forward and take a deep breath. This is *really* not how I wanted to start today.

I guess my days of avoiding my new neighbor are over.

CHAPTER 6

Alice

By this point, I'm used to nature sounds waking me up with the sun, but the crashing and banging I hear this morning definitely isn't naturally occurring, unless a moose is running around.

That isn't a thing that actually happens, right?

A laugh huffs out of me at my own joke before I remember there's a very real something making noise somewhere on my property.

I reluctantly roll out of bed, letting gravity help me up. While I'm figuring out which way is up, there's a particularly loud thud, followed by a low voice grunting an angry curse.

Oh shit – it *is* a person – but it thankfully doesn't sound like they're inside… yet. My heartbeat skyrockets as an image of my undiscovered, decaying body flashes in my mind. I really need to make friends out here and avoid *that* bleak future. I look around my room quickly before remembering that I plugged my phone into the charger by the couch while I was watching a movie last night. I forgot to grab it before coming to bed.

I crouch down as if that will help and sneak over to the window that looks out back. I peek around the curtains, but an overgrown branch blocks most of my view of my yard. I make a mental note to get that trimmed and tiptoe down the stairs. I scamper to the kitchen, grabbing my cell on the way. I punch in 9-1-1 but don't dial yet. I don't want to call if there's no emergency.

I snatch up the iron skillet sitting on the stove a-la-Rapunzel and follow the sounds to the back of the house and toward the lake. This is for sure a terrible idea, but I shift the kitchen window curtain aside just barely and peek outside.

I see the boat gently rocking side-to-side in the water and the unmistakable figure of a man in the shed beside the dock. This man has to be the worst trespasser ever because he's on his way to waking up the entire lake, animal and human alike. Un-fucking-believable.

Rational thought isn't on the menu this morning because I'm out the door and shouting at this stranger before I can think better of it. My feet are bare, and I'm in my pajamas, but at least the pan is still in my hand. So is my phone, but I haven't dialed the police yet. I *really, really* don't want to make trouble if there isn't any, and I've made it this far in life handling things on my own.

"Hey!" I unintelligently holler at him.

He doesn't react.

"Hey, ASSHOLE!" I shout even louder.

Slowly, the hunched figure backs out of the shed toward me, and he turns his head to look over his shoulder. I'm met with the most disinterested expression I've ever seen. Apologies for interrupting your vandalism, sir.

"This is private property," I say stupidly.

"I know," he says in a gruff voice as he turns completely and stands to his full height.

He's wearing dark sweatpants and a charcoal hoodie that stretches around his biceps as he crosses his arms. He has a baseball cap on, so I can't see his whole face. It's kind of a cozy outfit for a looter. I realize he's massive and lose some of my steam. If he's a criminal, I'm for sure going to die.

"So, you-you need to leave."

Way to go, Alice. Very authoritative. I'm about to hit "call" on my phone when he looks up, and I can see his face.

He doesn't look evil. He looks… bored? Inconvenienced? He huffs a sigh, and his slouched shoulders are definitively non-threatening. Since coming to Wilcox Grove, I've been existing on vibes, and the vibes tell me he's ok.

"I'm done. So, you can get back to…" He glances at the pan clutched in my fist. "Breakfast." He turns toward the neighboring house. Is this… Jake?

"You're done? Done with what?" I prickle at being brushed off so easily by the Brawny man.

He spins back to me, clearly irritated.

"You've been treating this place like shit. If you're going to have a boat, learn about boats. This place is home for some people, not some cute place for you to traipse through and destroy. And stop leaving your garage door open!" Not only does he completely ignore my question, but now he's scolding me like I'm a child.

"*Excuse me?*" I literally cannot find other words to combat the audacity of this man. But I also hadn't even realized I'd been leaving the garage door open.

"You're excused," he grunts and starts walking away toward the house next to mine. Great. This *is* Neighbor Jake. And Neighbor Jake is a jerk.

"What the hell is your problem?" I start marching after him, riled up all over again.

"The lady who lived here cared about this place. You should, too," he barks so coldly that I stop short and take a step back like he's slapped me.

Does this giant think he knows more about my mom than I

do? The *balls* he's got to have. My mouth opens, but I have no words that match the incredulousness I feel.

My pause gives him enough time for his long legs to carry him across his yard and patio and to his back door. He wrenches it open, goes in, and it slams shut before I can say another word.

After a quick glance back to the dock to make sure he didn't untie my boat just to spite me, I decide to go after him. YOLO, right? Grateful Bob said Jake's a good boy, so what could go wrong? Since he took it upon himself to trespass on my property, I have no qualms about doing the same to him, and I barge right into his home.

Just like in my house, the door leads to the kitchen, and Oscar the Grouch is at the sink washing his hands. I'll admit I'm disappointed that he doesn't jump when I charge in, not even a little.

"I don't know where you get off speaking to me that way, but it doesn't work for me." I'm no longer shouting, but I can still feel my anger vibrating under my skin. "That 'lady' was my mother, and you have no right to assume anything about how I feel about that house. I'm doing my *fucking* best, ok?"

He stops moving, and the water runs over his still hands. He blinks with realization.

"You're Dumbo," he says quietly, looking at me and using the nickname my mom had called me for as long as I can remember. She said it was payback for how many times I made her play the Disney movie when I was a baby. Some days, it was all that would keep me from shrieking.

Hearing the name takes all the wind out of my sails. My throat suddenly feels sandpaper dry.

"It's Alice." My voice comes out as barely a whisper, one distinctly scratchy and hoarse.

Jake looks confused and personally offended by my name.

"Ace? Your real name is Ace?"

And the spell is broken with his ridiculous question. Why on earth would my name be Ace? And if it was, who is he to make fun of that?

"No. My name is Alice," I say deadpan.

"Jake." He waves me off, like my name is of no consequence anyway, splattering droplets of water across his countertop. That seems to alert him to the fact that his hands are in water. He turns off the faucet and dries his hands on a towel hanging from one of the cabinet knobs.

"I helped your mom with the place after she bought it, but you might even be more clueless than she was. I was making sure it didn't fall apart."

"Did you ever think to speak to me before running all over my property?"

He just shrugs as if the thought literally never crossed his mind. "Tie up your boat properly and this could have all been avoided."

I bite my tongue before I lash out at him for blaming me for his rummaging this morning and tell myself to be the bigger person. "I take it the lawn and the firewood and the step up front were your doing, too?" The thought that I had helpful wood nymphs had been fun while it lasted.

He blinks at me but says nothing. It's clear he helped and isn't about to discuss it. My manners finally kick in, and I decide to make nice. After all, he has been helping me, and he apparently helped Mom, too. I'd like for him not to hate me if we're going to be living side by side.

"We got off on the wrong foot this morning. I want to thank you for helping me… and my mom. Can I cook —"

"No," he says, cutting me off before I can offer an olive branch, and he's immediately prickly again. The barrier around this guy must be as icy as the Wall in the North. "Have a good day."

"Look. I swear I'm not usually this insane. I thought you were breaking into the shed or maybe going to murder me. I'd really like to thank you for your help."

"And now you have." He moves around me to push open his back door as he repeats, "Have a good day."

"You, too," I say somewhat sarcastically as I leave, surrendering in this battle. I've been dismissed, and Neighbor Jake is most certainly a jerk.

CHAPTER 7

Jake

I shake my head as I watch Alice walk across our yards and back to her house. She looks over her shoulder at me when she gets to her back porch, and I step inside and close my door. She is the last thing I need disrupting my life right now. It was easy to dismiss her when she was a nameless woman playing small-town-country-girl, but her being Rain's daughter is a complication I didn't expect.

Now that I know who she comes from, the similarities are unmistakable. Alice's brown hair has the same untamed wave that Rain would complain about when the wind would whip hers around out on the lake. More than that, Alice's expression was a spitting image of her mother's ferocity when she charged into my kitchen. Their differences are just as stark, though. Alice is taller than her mother and proud. Her blue-gray eyes felt like they pierced right through me in a way her mother's warm brown ones never did. Where Rain was a motherly friend who regularly reminded me of Mrs. Landingham from *The West Wing*, Alice is a challenge who immediately makes my blood boil.

Rain loved that girl more than life itself, always gushing with pride over her strength, kindness, and intelligence. With all the stories Rain told me about Alice, it's like I already know my neighbor, and I feel a pang of guilt for being such an ass toward her. Rain really would be disappointed in me, but it's for the best. I don't need another project or another person to look after, and Alice will certainly leave in time. A woman with that much city in her will never be satisfied in Wilcox Grove. Our little town will bore her stiff.

I set the coffee maker to brew a pot and head upstairs. I shower before getting dressed – again – for my day. I don't need to be at the nursery today, but I've got too much anxious energy to sit at home, and I need to put some space between me and Alice. Meeting her has reminded me of the stories Rain told me, and I briefly wonder if the furious woman I saw today is just impersonating the kind and giving girl Rain called "Dumbo." Alice seems like fire compared to the docile girl Rain described.

I fill a travel mug with coffee and head out. At least there's no longer a need to sneak in and out of my own house. I tell myself again that I just need some space, but I don't feel any better when I pull into the nursery lot fifteen minutes later. Usually, these expansive fields center me.

My friend Eli and I bought the land and the business from Frank, the prior owner, six years ago, using most of the life insurance money from my parents. Legally, my brother is a partial owner, too, but he hasn't been very interested in farming. I worked here full-time for five years before that and as a summer job in high school. When Frank announced he wanted to retire, I asked Eli, with his accounting and management knowledge, to be my partner. I've known Eli my whole life, but I still don't think he realizes exactly how badly I needed him to say yes. He and this place saved me.

I throw my truck in park and haul myself out of it. The slam of the door echoes across the fields. In the spring and summer, we've got acres of flowers in every color you can imagine, but right now, the apple orchard and pumpkin patch are the stars of the show. I look out over the land and spot the new section of Christmas trees I just hauled back from Canada. I can't say why we've never offered them, but it felt like time to add them to our fields. I decide to check on them later and head inside for now.

Besides storage sheds and garages for equipment and temporary greenhouses we set up and take down as needed, the only building on the property has an office space that Eli and I share to the left of the door and a small store with pre-picked and pre-cut options for our less adventurous guests to the right. The store side is also connected to the one permanent greenhouse at the nursery, where the smaller plants and flowers live in pots before they're sold or transferred to a field.

Eli is already looking toward the front door when I come through it, likely having heard my truck pull up. We're not expecting any deliveries today, and nobody else would be around so early. He raises his eyebrows disapprovingly at the sight of me.

"I thought I told you to stay out of here today," he scolds.

I've spent most of every day at the nursery since I got back from picking up the Christmas trees. Eli knew I was avoiding my new neighbor, but eventually, he got sick of me making up projects to give myself reasons to stay at work longer and away from my house.

"I met her this morning," is the only explanation I give before taking off my coat and draping it over the back of my chair.

I flop into the seat and turn on my computer so I can pretend to busy myself with checking inventory reports that have already been checked. Almost all of the back-of-house work is Eli's domain while keeping the plants alive is my job. Of course I have help in the fields and greenhouse, and we have people who manage the store, but Eli is very protective of his spreadsheets. In the man's defense, his system is a well-oiled machine.

I hear him tapping away at his keyboard, and I shouldn't be surprised when a new window pops up asking for a password before I can get into the folder on our system that has our current quarter files. My gaze snaps to him, and I fix him with a glare when I see the amused smile on his lips.

"There's no way I'm letting you fuck with my spreadsheets just because your neighbor is a gorgon." He must have felt the intensity of my look because he spoke without even glancing away from his monitor.

I shove my chair back from the desk.

"She's not. And *that's* the problem," I basically growl at him.

At that, he does look my way.

"Oh, so you *like* her? That'd be something new."

He barely gets the words out around his laugh. The fiercer glare I shoot him only makes him laugh harder.

"No." The sound is more bark than word. Not wanting to continue this particular discussion, I throw my jacket back on before stomping outside and yanking the door shut behind me. I immediately feel like the petulant toddler I'm impersonating but continue out to the fields anyway. I'll apologize to Eli later for being short with him.

The day is crawling by as I desperately search for things to do — I check the sprinkler and drainage systems, straighten signs that give directions to those in the fields, and make sure the pumpkins aren't crowding one another and that there's enough space to walk between them without crushing anything.

I must eventually lose myself in the work because I'm surprised to notice how far the sun has moved across the sky when I hear Eli hollering for me. I shout an acknowledgment back before heading toward him. As I near the lot, I see him standing by the open driver's side door of his Jeep.

"Get in," he commands. "We're going out."

Eli looks ready to go in jeans, his standard quarter-zip

sweater, and very clean shoes. With his boyish face and blond hair, he could pass for a hometown football star. I look down at my dusty boots and dirty hands, ready to protest and feeling particularly feral-looking next to him, but he cuts me off.

"I'm not your date, and you don't need to look cute. You *do* need to get out of your own head, though. So, get in the car." Eli has always been a good friend to me, one of the only ones I have, and he'll bully me into what I need, especially when I don't want it.

I get in the car.

The short drive to The Corner Post bar is silent but not awkward. I think we're both knowingly holding the conversation until we're comfortably seated and armed with a mountain of food. I stop at the bathroom to wash my hands while Eli takes a spot at the bar. As I reach him, Penny sets down two glasses of water and lets us know she already put in an order of mozzarella sticks. I guess we're creatures of habit and gluttons for fried cheese. It's a weakness, and I am not ashamed. Once she's brought back the two beers we order and we've each taken a long pull from our glasses, Eli turns toward me.

"So, what the hell is going on with you?" Eli has always been a straight shooter, so his words are sometimes harsh, even though he has a heart the size of Montana.

"She's Rain's daughter," I huff out, like it explains everything.

Thankfully, Eli knows me, so it at least explains some. He knew Rain and I looked after one another for the five years she lived in Wilcox Grove and that I took news of her death hard. We didn't talk much after she moved to Boston, but she'd check in on me from time to time. After not hearing from her in a while or getting a response to my call, I searched her name online and learned about her passing.

It felt like getting hit with a baseball bat. I thought I'd have more time. I thought I'd be able to say goodbye.

His whistle is low. "I didn't realize Rain intended to keep the place after she moved out. What's her daughter, uh —"

He looks to me assistance.

"Alice," I fill in.

"Alice. What's Alice doing up here? Is she going to sell?"

"I have no clue. Our *conversation* this morning wasn't a long one." I shrug.

"What did you do?" For my best friend, he's suddenly very accusatory.

"Why do you assume I did anything?" I snap defensively. I really am a prickly bastard these days.

"Because I know you." Eli is unfazed by my mood swings. I don't deserve his friendship.

"I, uh… well, I yelled at her." I'm a bit sheepish, feeling another wave of guilt as I replay my behavior in my head.

"How neighborly." Eli's voice is dripping with sarcasm. He shakes his head and then shoves me hard in the arm, and I have to grab the edge of the bar top to keep from tipping sideways. "What the hell is wrong with you?"

"I didn't know she was Rain's daughter at the time! I thought she was just some city girl here to trash the place."

I can feel Eli rolling his eyes. "Then, what's she like?"

I put my elbows on the bar and drop my forehead into my palms. "She's like Rain, but wild." I purposefully don't describe what she looks like, having spent a large part of today trying to forget her long legs and thin pajamas.

"So, what's the issue? You got along with Rain just fine."

"They're also very different. I never had it out with Rain like I did with Alice today. She came out swinging — not literally, but I wouldn't put it past her. Rain needed my help and asked for it. I don't think Alice thinks she needs anything from anybody. I don't need to try to be her friend. I don't *want* to be her friend. I need stability in my life." I turn my head in my hands and peer at Eli, and I see his exasperated eye roll this time.

"Dude, you're an idiot. Literally nothing you said sounds like a bad thing, and what tells you she's not stable?"

"Besides you, people don't stick around in my life. They never have. But it's fine, and I'm fine with how things are. She'll have her fill of Wilcox Grove soon enough and go back to Boston, so there's no point."

"You've had some shitty hands dealt to you, but that doesn't mean they're all going to be like that. You can't already be resigned to becoming an old curmudgeon. We are not nearly old enough for that yet. I was joking before, but I think you might *liiiike her*." Eli sing-songs the last two words, clearly trying to lighten the mood.

Honestly, it helps a little. He's wrong, but his optimism is nice, nonetheless.

Penny comes by and places a steaming pile of mozzarella sticks on the bar between us. Those *definitely* improve my day, as does the burger I have after. After Eli and I dig in, he doesn't bring up Alice again. I expect he's hoping I'll consider his advice, but I don't see any circumstance where being Alice McDermott's friend would end well for me.

CHAPTER 8

Alice

What a rude, pompous ASS! I've cycled through a few emotions since being evicted from Jake's and have gotten back to angry. I pace around my kitchen, mentally reliving the last several minutes with him. I feel so small after being told to go home, like he sent me to my room. But I haven't done anything wrong! He might have a point about home upkeep, but I've never owned a home before, certainly not one in the middle of *nowhere*, or had my own yard. I'm figuring it out as I go. I think I'm doing wonderfully, all things considered. Jake just needs to cool it and mind his own business.

I'm still fuming when the note on the fridge catches my eye again. J and a phone number.

Mom had a cell phone like almost everybody else these days and no reason to save a phone number on a piece of paper. She also didn't leave any other numbers around for me unless there was an explanation. I still have the phone, but going through her messages feels like an invasion of privacy, and it's a line I'm not willing to cross. She'd never have stood for Jake's attitude, so it's hard to imagine her letting him help.

I wish she were here to talk to. The thought sends a hard pang of loneliness through me.

I'm still trying to figure out how I want to deal with Jake when there's a knock at the front door. It's only been a couple of minutes since our showdown, and it's an ungodly hour in the morning, so I figure it's him back for round two. I march to the front of the house and yank the door open.

"You'd better be here to apolo—" The word dies on my lips when I see Piper standing before me with a small duffel bag at her feet. A squeal bursts from me as I launch myself at her, flinging my arms around her neck and knocking the wind out of her as she tries to say what sounds like "Surprise!"

I met Piper at the start of my sophomore year of college when I was working at the front desk of her freshman dorm building. We clicked almost instantly, and now it's hard to remember what my life was like before she was in it. We lived together for the next four years before she moved to New Jersey to get her Master's in Library Science from Rutgers. Thankfully, she came back to Boston two years later when she was done.

Now, she's standing before me, looking a little rumpled but still frickin' stunning. Piper is tall and slender with light brown skin and a head of the most gorgeous chocolate curls, though they're currently popping out of a messy bun on the top of her head. She probably could have been a model if she wanted to, but she prefers to use her height to reach books on the top shelf. I grab her bag and pull her inside, setting it down next to the couch. "What are you *doing* here?!"

"I wanted to come sooner, and I can only stay for two days, but it's been way too long since I've seen you. So I just got on a bus and came up. I wanted as much time as I could, so I took the early one. I hope that's ok?"

"Don't be ridiculous." I hug her again. "My home is always your home, no matter where it is."

I lead her back to the kitchen and start taking things out to make breakfast. Bacon is popping on the stove when I hear Jake's truck pulling away.

I must make a face because Piper slides up next to me and asks, "And what was *that*?"

"That was a truck. I'm sure you've heard one before."

"Don't be a wise ass. You know exactly what I meant."

I huff but stay fully focused on my frying pan. "*That* was Jake, my new neighbor. He's got the personality of a bear that's been poked in the eye with a stick. He's basically the size of one, too. Oh, and he *hates* me."

Piper barks a laugh. "That's not possible. You're un-hateable."

"Not to this guy. Trust me. I'm something foul stuck to his shoe."

"Well, screw him. It sounds like he sucks." Piper is the most loyal person I've ever met, my ride-or-die.

"That's how I want to feel, trust me. But I think he was friends with Mom. At the very least, he makes it seem like they were friendly. So, it *bugs* me. She was always a great judge of character, and there's no way she'd befriend a troll."

"Just because your mom got along with somebody, it doesn't mean you have to. It's not like you're dishonoring her by being your own person. She'd yell at you for doing anything less."

Piper makes good points that my brain accepts, but my heart still feels uneasy about Jake disliking me so strongly. I'm a people-pleaser and this feels wrong, even though I'm still ticked at him for being so unreasonable. I go back to breakfast prep, trying to shove Neighbor Jake out of my mind.

Having seemingly stuck with her "he sucks" conclusion about Jake, Piper changes the subject to somebody I want to think about even less than Señor Grump.

"Now that I'm here, you've *got* to give me more on what

happened with Reid. Because if you want to talk about trolls, *that man is a troll.*"

I laugh with her and shrug. I have years of reasons to end things with Reid, and I regret having ignored them all for so long. Whatever I was waiting for from him was never going to happen.

"I'm sorry it's not more exciting, but there isn't really more to say," I downplay.

It's an outright lie. I've never told Piper about how Reid belittled me, the way he kept me under his thumb year after year. It was mortifying, and there was always this little voice in the back of my head telling me that Reid was right. She knew he was a workaholic, and I felt neglected, so I leaned into that part of the story to avoid lying outright.

"He just did more of what he always did and put work before me. I realized I wasn't even that disappointed because I'd come to expect it of him. It was my job to be Reid's silent woman."

I bite out that last part and realize I've begun beating our eggs more vigorously than they need. I can hear the volume of my voice increasing, but it's like my rant is a runaway train now.

"I kind of got used to never being first on his list of priorities. It was dumb, but I did. At some point, though, he moved me to dead last. My needs and feelings only mattered to him when it was convenient, and it took way too long for me to figure that out. He just kept *taking* from me every single day. And then he made me feel *guilty* about asking to be seen as a damn person!"

In spite of my efforts to avoid that day, my mind drifts to our last fight, and equal parts rage and shame rise in me.

"I don't know who I was with him," I say.

I feel myself about to start angry crying when Piper slides her arms around me from behind, pinning my biceps to my torso and stopping my hands from mutilating our eggs. She takes the bowl from my hands and sets it on the counter before squeezing me.

"You are worth so much more than he ever realized, and I am *so* proud of you for leaving."

Her words are steady and clear even though her face is squished into my hair. I sink against her, and we stay like that silently until a loud crackle from the pan captures our attention. Thankfully, we both like our bacon extra crispy.

Piper reaches around me to turn off the stove before spinning me and wiping her hands on my wet cheeks.

"Fuck Reid, and may he rot in hell," she says definitively.

She directs me to set the table on the back porch while she quickly cooks our scrambled eggs before plating them with the bacon and some toast. Wrapped up in blankets and with a small space heater blowing on us, we're comfortable, and no view can beat the lake.

After we eat, I give her a tour of the little house and take her things to the second bedroom upstairs. While she showers, I look up scenic drives so we can do some top-notch leaf-peeping like the basic bitches we are at heart.

Once Piper's dressed, we're off, taking winding roads that head vaguely north. I crank the heat so we can keep the windows down and smell the wet leaves and nearby real-wood fireplaces burning. The trees around us are glowing with color, showing off like a bunch of hams while we prattle on.

"His name is Bernard, and it's not going well so far. He showed up out of nowhere, even though we have plenty of experienced librarians who are more than qualified to take on the director role, and he's unilaterally changing everything without soliciting any of our opinions or taking into account any of our feedback. His word is law, and the law is stupid."

The library Piper works at hired somebody new, and he's making everybody miserable. She's been telling me about the everyday struggles libraries face, like nonstop budget cuts and the need to defend their worth every single day, and it sounds like Bernard is only making things more painful.

"Once you're back in Boston, want to come with me to key his car?" she asks hopefully.

"Oh, for sure," I answer, and hope she can't tell that the enthusiasm in my voice is faked. I'd love to key Bernard's car, but I'm not exactly looking forward to being back in Boston.

She sighs dramatically, and I give her a sympathetic look. We approach a sign listing upcoming towns.

"Are you getting hungry?" I jerk my head toward the sign and take the opportunity to change the subject.

When we stop for lunch at a cute diner in a random town, she shows me pictures of the squirrels in the Boston Common, basically spherical as they pack on weight for the winter. They've always been one of my favorite parts of the city.

We wander in and out of shops in a large strip mall before catching a mid-afternoon movie, sitting in the far back of the nearly empty theater so our constant giggling and whispered commentary won't disturb anybody.

With her by my side, I feel safe and like I don't have a trouble in the world.

Since it's getting late, and the sun sets around five, we begin the winding drive back to my house. I tell her about how things have been going for me since I came to Wilcox Grove.

"Is it possible Mom's house is out to get me?" I ask, quite seriously.

"Honestly, it might be," Piper laughs, thoroughly amused by the various trials I've faced in the past couple of weeks.

"I'll have to figure out how to get the upper hand because I doubt I'll be getting much more 'help' from Jake after this morning."

"Jake has helped you? You didn't mention that when you were calling him a bear this morning."

Her eyebrows are basically at her hairline, and I can tell her attention is piqued, so I try to squash it down immediately.

"He was helping the house, not me. I don't want to waste my time talking about him, anyway."

"Ok, then tell me about the other people in your life up here."

I tell her about Grateful Bob, and she makes me promise that we'll go see him before she has to leave. She looks aghast when I tell her I have nobody else to talk about.

"You've been up here for weeks and it sounds like you've barely left this house! You need to go out."

The twinkle in her eye makes me feel very nervous.

CHAPTER 9

Alice

Apparently, Piper meant "We're going out *tonight*." Since I don't have a set schedule, the day of the week honestly has little meaning to me, but it's Saturday, and Piper sees that as a sign that we should rectify my "hermit existence" immediately. Telling her that I don't even know where one would go out in a town like Wilcox Grove only makes things worse. According to Piper, it's another indication that my situation is dire.

We're back at my house making several homemade pizzas together because we're indecisive and there's no such thing as too much pizza. Piper is excitedly chattering on about how fun our night out will be.

"I met this guy on the bus, Scott, who will know where to go. He grew up here and came back for the weekend to see friends and family, and I'd bet anything he'd be down to go out."

Before the words "stranger danger" can leave my lips, she's already fired off a text to him.

"Piper! What are you doing? We can't go out with some random bus guy. What if he's dangerous?"

She laughs at my concern, always the more adventurous one

of the two of us. Sometimes, we would joke that she was my mother's daughter with how similar their approaches were to taking risks.

Piper violently wrestles with the drawer under the oven, trying to retrieve a cookie sheet for our pizzas, but the thing won't budge. I come up next to her and kick the right side of the drawer twice. On her next pull, it slides open with ease.

"Your house is possessed," she murmurs before getting back on topic. "Don't be silly!"

A ping from her phone interrupts her rebuttal. She quickly reads his reply. "Perfect! He said the Corner Post Bar is the place to go. *And* he said he can pick us up!"

"Pipe — no. I'll go out with you and your new serial killer friend, but I am *not* giving him my home address. I'll drive."

She huffs but agrees to the compromise. "*Fine*. But you'll see he's perfectly safe. He has kind eyes."

"I bet people said the same thing about Ted Bundy."

A couple of hours later, after eating our combined body weight in pizza and watching *Gossip Girl* reruns, I'm sitting on the floor next to the bed in the guest bedroom as Piper twists my hair around her flat iron, yanking my hair this way and that like it's not attached to me. By the time she's finished, I'm not sure it still *will* be on my head. She blew a fuse when she first plugged the tool in because she didn't heed my warning to turn off the hallway light first, and I wonder if she's taking out her frustration on my scalp.

Half an hour later, she announces I'm free to get up, and I'm relieved to find I'm not bald. Instead, she's tamed my hair into soft curls.

Piper is giddy with excitement over her accomplishment and proceeds to run into my room and throw every article of clothing I own on my bed in an attempt to find two outfits she deems satisfactory. I steer her away from any fancy dresses, sure that there's no place in this cute little town where those would be appropriate. She counters by vetoing all of my coziest sweats. After more lighthearted bickering, she settles on skinny jeans and a slinky top, and we compromise on black leggings and a backless sweater for me. When I warn her that we're going to freeze, she mumbles something about a whiskey blanket and waves me off.

As discussed, I drive, already knowing I won't drink much and preferring to have an easy exit strategy over praying the one Lyft driver in town is available when I want to bail. It's already past my 10:30 bedtime — don't judge me — when we pull away from my house. I pointedly don't look at Jake's place as we leave and certainly don't notice the lights on downstairs in his house. I guess he's done hiding from me.

There are several cars parked outside the Corner Post, but I find a spot in the bumpy gravel lot easily enough. As soon as we walk in, an excited voice hollers "Piper!" and a man who looks like he's in his mid-twenties comes bounding over. He's wearing jeans and a flannel over a t-shirt, and I'm grateful that we avoided the city club dresses when getting ready.

I'll admit, he *is* cute. He's taller than I am but a few inches shorter than Piper, with dark hair cropped close. With that grin on his face, his blue eyes sparkle, and they do look kind.

He wraps Piper in a hug like they're long-lost friends before turning to me.

"Hi! I'm Scott. You must be Alice." He wraps me in a similar embrace to the one he gave Piper. As we separate, I see his eyes keep darting back to Piper. "You look preat. I mean, pretty. And great." He flushes a dark red and scratches the back of his head.

Piper laughs kindly at his stumble. "You look preat, too, Scott."

He dramatically bows and extends an arm to direct us both to the bar, looking at Piper like she hung the moon when she walks past. His mouth pops open as he stares, and I fake a cough to hide my giggle. This guy has got it *bad* for my bestie, and I'm fairly certain she's oblivious. It's adorable. Piper deserves a nice boy who's completely enamored with her. It must have been one hell of a bus ride this morning for him to have fallen so hard, so fast.

Scott pulls himself together once we get to the bar. He's chatty and all smiles, making rapid-fire introductions of Penny, the bartender, and some of his other friends, immediately making us both feel included. He's friendly, seemingly well-liked, and strongly rooted in this little town.

Ok. *Maybe* he's not a serial killer after all.

Before I know it, I'm laughing so hard I'm snorting as Scott tells us about the time he tripped over his own skates and face-planted into the glass while trying to impress a girl during a junior hockey game. He really is a charming goofball, and I feel completely at ease, even as a newcomer. I'm also thrilled to see Piper having such a good time.

Almost all of Scott's friends have known one another since they were in diapers, but one woman, Hannah, didn't move here until adulthood. She's clever, bubbly, and exceedingly friendly. Her wife, Leslie, is one of the Wilcox Grove lifers. Together, they own the bakery-slash-bookstore in town. (Can we talk about how cool it is that my current town has a bakery-slash-bookstore?)

I like Hannah immediately and spend much of the night chatting with her. We sit with our heads bent together and she sneakily tells me little tidbits about the people around us.

The night flies by, and I haven't even realized how long we've been there until Penny announces that karaoke sign-ups are open for the last hour of the night. Piper is tugging my arm, begging me to duet a Spice Girls song with her, but I'd rather eat my napkin. I give Scott a look of endless gratitude when he offers to take my place, but I think the squeal and hug from a very tipsy Piper are all the thanks he needs. He lights up like a firework, and his cheeks flush dark red as she takes his hand and drags him between tables to the karaoke machine.

They sing their hearts out and are clinging to one another to try to stay upright on their walk back to us, hysterical laughter keeping them doubled over. Piper stumbles and bumps into a chair, causing the girl sitting there to spill beer on herself and yelp. Piper immediately apologizes, but in two seconds flat, the night goes from joyous to tense. A burly guy at the table jumps to his feet and gets right in Piper's face before Scott sweeps her behind him and out of harm's way.

"Sit down, Troy. It was an accident and she apologized." All the humor is gone from Scott's voice as he stares the other guy down, even though Scott is a full head shorter.

A sneer splits across Troy's face.

"Scotty come back to town, huh? You want to start something?"

Scott puts his hands up defensively.

"That is literally the opposite of what I want, Troy."

The exasperated tone in his voice tells me that this isn't the first time he's had to deal with Troy's idiocy.

"We're sorry, and we're just going to go," he continues.

Scott keeps Piper behind him but starts moving back toward us.

"Yeah, little orphan Scotty. Get on out of here. Nobody wants you. Even your parents offed themselves to get away from you!" Troy's booming voice echoes across a suddenly silent room. Scott seems unfazed, like the taunt isn't new, but I flinch at the uncalled-for dig.

"You're trash, Troy. Always have been, always will be." Then

Scott makes the mistake of rolling his eyes and looking away for just a second. Troy's fist crashes into the side of Scott's face and sends him to the floor. Piper shrieks and crouches beside Scott, who's already getting back up, fury clear on his face despite the angry red splotch on his cheek. Scott's friends and I also all jump to our feet, moving toward him and Piper.

The blonde that Piper bumped into finally pipes up in a shrill voice, "Take your slut of a girlfriend and get lost!"

I see red, but Piper gets to her first, ignoring all the traditional "girl fight" options and opting to deck the girl instead. Before I know what's happening, it's all-out mayhem at the Corner Post. Scott's friends are fighting Troy's friends, and Scott gets up just to tackle Troy right back down. I shove my way to Piper and convince myself to pull her off the blonde girl, even though I don't blame Piper for taking a swing… or two.

It feels like only seconds have passed, but suddenly, there's a shrill siren outside, and people are scattering. By the time two officers come inside, Troy and his posse have all jumped ship. Scott's crew is too honorable to bail on one another or leave Penny to deal with all of this, so they're all standing around, looking sheepish. I catch Hannah's eye, happy to see both she and Leslie look unharmed.

I turn and see the bartender with her arms crossed. She has a sympathetic expression as she looks at Scott.

"I'm sorry, Scotty. I had to call them."

"It's ok, Penny. I'm really sorry about all this." Scott rights a chair that was knocked over.

The police cross the room, and one approaches us, even though we're not looking to run, while the other goes to talk to Penny. She's adamant that "It's that Basel boy's fault."

We are all chagrined, even though the officers are kind. My heart is pounding. I've never gotten in the slightest bit of trouble, let alone participate in a bar brawl.

Am I going to jail?

Oh my God.

We're all going to get arrested.

I might be sick.

"That might be the case, but this still needs to be handled properly," the officer by Penny replies. He turns to look at our sad clump of people. "I'm sorry, but those of you involved will need to come in with us."

Everybody starts talking at once. Penny is offering to make a statement. Piper is asking if we can just give statements here. Scott's friends are all protesting, insisting this is Troy's and his gang's fault.

Scott's voice breaks through the rest, loud and clear above the cacophony. "It was just me. They fought me. Nobody else was involved."

The officer by us — his nametag says Andersen, and he looks like he could be close to my age — takes one look at Piper's disheveled appearance and the scratch on her temple and raises his eyebrows at Scott in disbelief. A few of Scott's friends straighten their shirts or run their hands through their hair to clean up. Most look conflicted about Scott trying to get them off but don't seem to know how to defend him without making it worse for everybody.

"She just got caught in the crossfire." Scott insists.

"Then she was involved and will need to come, too." Andersen shrugs like he's uncomfortable. I imagine everybody in this room, other than me and Piper, has known one another for as long as they've been in Wilcox Grove. Maybe their parents, or even grandparents, were friends before them. It's got to be awkward when everything is so tight-knit, and everybody has been in everybody else's business for generations.

Scott reluctantly relents. "Nobody else though. *Really.*" His sharp but quick glare at his friends stops anyone who has decided to speak up.

Andersen isn't convinced, so he looks to his partner, a slightly older man.

"If this really was just started by Basel, then you're both victims. We need statements to document the incident. You're not in trouble unless somebody files a complaint to the contrary," the senior officer says.

Oh. I guess it's too late to tell the whole story since Scott insisted nobody else participated from his group.

The older officer looks to Penny, but she shakes her head.

"Troy attacked Scott."

Penny has been fussing behind the bar and lifts two dish towels with a handful of ice in each.

"Please, take these."

The officer takes them and brings them to Scott and Piper, who gratefully take them, pressing the cool bundles to their faces.

Piper looks at me. "Go home. I'll see you b—"

"I'm going with you. I haven't had anything other than water in a couple of hours, so I can follow in my car." I look to Andersen. "If that's ok? She's my friend, and she doesn't live here."

The officer's reassurances help, but being taken to the police station in the middle of the night still feels like a big deal. My adrenaline levels must be through the roof.

Andersen looks critically at me, like he's just noticed he doesn't recognize me. "What's your name?"

"Alice McDermott."

I see a sad look that's becoming familiar flash in his eyes when I say my last name. He nods.

"You can come to the station, too. If you're driving, and everybody is more comfortable with you than in the back of the cruiser, you can all just follow us back. The rest of you — get on out of here. Just go *home*."

Hannah, tonight's designated driver, pulls out car keys, and the rest trail out of the bar after her, heads bowed. She squeezes my shoulder sympathetically as she passes by. It's an awkward silence as we hear car doors closing outside and the sound of tires pulling away.

After they've gone, Andersen puts a hand on Scott's shoulder and the other on Piper's. "Come along, then." He guides them to the door, and I follow, with the other officer behind me.

At the dire look on each of our faces, he smiles kindly.

"You're really not in trouble. This is a *good* thing, to record what happened and the parties at fault."

"It still doesn't feel good…" Scott voices what we all seem to be thinking with an apologetic look back over his shoulder at Penny.

The parking lot has emptied significantly, and I can see my car a bit away. Even from the door, I can tell it's sitting funny. I spot the flat tire almost instantly, especially with the red and blue flashing lights illuminating the whole area. I stop short.

"You've got to be *kidding* me." It comes out of me as a plea, even though I know the tire won't magically repair itself and pump back up. I look over my shoulder and see Andersen about to close his car door. I briefly consider trying the Lyft, but I don't want to keep the police waiting, assuming the driver is even on duty at this time. Scott, Piper, and I look at each other.

"Hang on!" I call out, and Andersen turns to look at me. "I'm so sorry. I have a flat. Can we go with you after all?" I explain when I get close.

"Do you want help just changing it?" he offers.

"It's late, and I'd rather just come back for it tomorrow. I know how to change it, but thank you."

He looks over the car at his partner, who shrugs, looking like he's ready for this night to be over.

"Alright, get in." Andersen opens the back door, and the three of us squeeze in.

I've always been a good girl, and I swear I'm living somebody else's life as I voluntarily slide into the back of the squad car. I'm grateful we're not getting arrested, but this is still a disaster. I drop my head back against the seat and close my eyes, like if I don't see myself in a police car, this whole night didn't happen.

The short ride to the police station along deserted roads highlights my new small-town living. The officers park and open our door. We get out, and Andersen holds the station door open for us as we file through. He directs all three of us to a bench, and I sigh with relief. I think I might have fallen apart if we were put in an interrogation room.

Do small-town police stations even *have* interrogation rooms?

Another officer who walks like he's in charge approaches us and distributes a clipboard to each of us. I realize that nobody has said a word since we got in the squad car and my throat suddenly feels scratchy. I'm not sure I've ever felt this uncomfortable before in my life. My people-pleasing self is in a complete spiral.

"Look," the officer sighs. "We just need you to each write up what happened as you remember it, and we can all get on with our nights. Penny told my guys she doesn't want anything from anybody except to ban Mr. Basel and his crew from her bar, so this is to dot the I's and cross our t's. Once you're done, you can call somebody to pick you up and go home."

"That's it?" I blurt. I think I was still doubtful that we really, *really* weren't in trouble.

"That's it, ma'am." He nods at me and looks at Scott and Piper before hollering over his shoulder at somebody. "Mike! Can we get some new ice over here?"

Mike — I guess that's Andersen's first name — brings two of

those ice packs you pop to activate and some paper towels for Scott and Piper and takes their damp towels.

"Thanks, Mike, Allen." Scott addressing Andersen and the senior officer by name confirms my suspicions about familiarity.

I try to make myself as inconspicuous as possible and begin to write. My statement feels silly since I describe most of the parties by their appearances or shirt colors, but I do my best and finish up quickly.

Scott collects our clipboards to return them to Mike, and I take my phone out of my pocket. I stare at the screen, knowing I only have phone numbers for three people in Wilcox Grove saved: Denise from the shelter where I donated most of Mom's things, Grateful Bob, and Jake from Mom's note on the fridge.

I don't know Denise well enough to ask her to pick me up from the police station after two a.m. I know without a doubt that Grateful Bob would come get me and Piper without hesitation and likely without asking any questions. I'm mortified by our situation, even though we didn't get in trouble, and it would feel like I let him down. Still, without another option, I pull up his contact and hit call. It rings until his voicemail recording starts playing. Damnit.

That only leaves Jake and calling him is a non-starter. I'm about to try my luck with Wilcox Grove's Lyft driver when Scott returns to our bench.

"I called my brother, and he's going to come get us all."

I hate the idea of being a burden, especially so late. "Scott, thank you so much, but we can't ask that of him. I can figure something out for me and Piper." I ignore Piper's desperate look, saying she just wants to get home as soon as possible.

Scott waves me off. "Don't worry about it. Piper mentioned you live on Barefoot Lake earlier tonight. We do, too, so it really isn't a problem. He'll be here in a few minutes."

I open my mouth to object again, but Scott puts his hand on

my shoulder. "Everything that happened tonight is because Troy hates me. Please, let me make sure you get home safely." Ok, ok. Scott is a nice boy after all.

"Thank you." We fall back into silence while we wait. There's really no appropriate small talk for a police station in the middle of the night. Even the few police officers are quiet. The only sounds in the room are the occasional shuffle of paper or click of keys until the bell by the door rings. I look up as the new arrival steps through the door.

"Scotty, what on earth have you—" His gruff voice cuts off as his eyes meet mine, and his expression freezes.

Wouldn't you know Scott is apparently Jake's little brother.

CHAPTER 10

Jake

Living alone and enjoying a quiet life, I've only ever been woken up in the middle of the night by a phone call once, and it was the one telling me my parents were gone. When I see Scott's name on my phone tonight at two in the morning, my chest clenches like my heart has stopped. I knew he came up today and was seeing friends. He was going to come here after going out. Thankfully, he knows me well, and when I answer with a strained "Scott?" the first words out of his mouth are "I'm ok."

Once I can breathe again, I'm out of bed and getting dressed. I didn't ask for details before the call ended because I wasn't sure enough blood had returned to my brain to process it anyway. I got the important part. He needs me. I'm on the road within five minutes of my phone ringing.

As I pull into the driveway for the police station parking lot, I'm still not sure how to handle this. At twenty-two, Scott is an adult, but I still feel like he's my responsibility. How did he end up at a police station in the middle of the night?

I throw my truck in park and jump out of the cab, eager to get inside and find out what the hell even happened. I'm at the glass doors in just a few steps and feel jittery with the need to get my eyes on Scott to confirm that he wasn't lying when he said he was ok.

Not wanting him to see how anxious I am, I decide to play it off and give him some grief on my way in. "Scotty, what on earth have you—"

Before I can even see Scott, Alice McDermott's eyes find mine, and everything in me stalls.

For the second time this very, very early morning, I feel like parts of my body simply stop functioning as my voice cuts off. She's the last person I expected to see when I walked through those doors. Thankfully, she looks tired but generally unharmed.

I only spare her that quick glance before my eyes dart to my brother right beside her, holding an ice pack over half of his face, and all my attention zeroes in on him.

I don't remember moving, but suddenly, I'm in front of him, and my hands are on his shoulders. "What happened?"

He lifts the ice pack, and while he's going to feel like ass for a few days, it's honestly not so bad. He played hockey in high school, so I've seen him looking worse. I breathe a sigh of relief.

"Troy was being Troy," he huffs like he has many times before.

That piece of shit excuse for a person has been and always will be a bully.

My eyes jump to the chief, who stands behind Scott. "Allen?"

"We'll handle them tomorrow. You're all free to go." He pats Scott's shoulder and turns to go back to his office.

After he's out of earshot, I lower my voice. "Scott, you've got to give me *something* more. What happened, and what is *she* doing here?" I jerk my head toward Alice and spot a young woman I don't recognize on a nearby bench. Maybe, she's a friend of Alice's?

Polite as ever, Scott speaks up to introduce the women,

gesturing to the seated one first. "Jake, these are my friends, Piper and —"

"Ace." I cut him off and finally turn back to my new neighbor.

Her eyebrows pull together as she levels me with a stare.

"It's Alice," she barks at me, and I fight back a smirk. This isn't a very humorous moment. I just amuse myself sometimes. And like last time, I ignore her correction.

"I shouldn't be surprised that a call to pick my brother up from a *police station* involves you." The words tumble out of my mouth before I can stop them, and I really don't know why I'm being such a jackass.

After talking with Eli at dinner, I intended to be nicer to Alice the next time I saw her. Granted, I didn't expect that next meeting to be in the middle of the night in a police station. And I sure as shit didn't expect her to look like *that*. I hate myself for noticing the way her white sweater sits off her shoulder and the way her pants hug her damn legs. I do not want anything from this woman, and even if I did, this is *not* the time.

The other woman, Piper, stands abruptly at Alice's side as if she were more than willing to provide backup if needed.

"Do you two know one another?" Scott asks.

I keep my eyes on Alice when I answer. "Scotty, *Ace* here is our new neighbor." I emphasize the nickname, deciding I like how much she seems to hate it.

Alice is staring me right back down, just as stubborn and fierce as she was yesterday morning, finding some unknown man rifling around her shed. I silently admit to myself that I like that, too. Silent admissions don't count anyway.

The tension is broken when a loud snort comes from Alice's friend, who quickly slaps a hand over her mouth like it'll undo the sound she just made.

"I'm sorry, I'm sorry!" She's presumably laughing at herself and her inability to keep a straight face. "You're not what I imagined when Alice talked about Neighbor Jake, and the fact that you're Scott's brother is just *too much*. Like, what are the chances?"

Alice spins toward her friend. "Piper!"

I look between the two women with my eyebrows raised. It's… interesting that Piper knows my name.

Has Alice been talking about me? What has she been saying?

Now, I do let myself smirk. Seeing Alice off-kilter is making this morning just the tiniest bit enjoyable. I bask in it for a moment before I remind myself for the umpteenth time that this is neither the time nor the place and clear my throat to focus the group. My eyes drift back to Scott.

"It's not their fault, I swear. Troy was talking shit. He came at me first. They were backing me up," he explains.

I feel an immediate rush of gratitude to the two women for standing up for Scotty when I wasn't there to do it myself. I look toward each of them and nod my thanks, not quite sure how to put it in words.

"Let's get out of here," I offer, jerking my head toward the door and turning. The three troublemakers follow me outside, but Alice stops when we're standing under the light by the door.

"You don't need to drive me and Piper back. I'll take care of us," she says.

I roll my eyes. Unless she's going to get back in a police car, I don't see how she's getting home. Does this woman have an innate need to argue with me?

"How do you plan on managing that without a car?"

"I can figure it out."

"At this hour, you have no other options. A Lyft won't come. Don't be stubborn. We share a driveway."

"No. I've got it. Really." Now she's pouting. I respect her pride, but this is ridiculous.

I groan and turn to face her head-on. "I'm tired, and I want to go home. Get in the truck, Ace." I point her in the direction of my parked truck.

She opens her mouth like she's going to keep arguing but snaps it back shut after surveying the glare on my face. She crosses her arms and follows my outstretched hand to my truck. I do *not* watch her go as she walks away from me, purposefully looking skyward in prayer instead. When I look back down, I see Scott and Piper exchange a look, and I'm grateful neither of them says anything as they hurry to the truck. This excursion needs to be over.

As I walk over, I hit the remote on my key fob to unlock the doors and watch Scott open the back passenger-side door of the cab and help Piper in. When Alice gets to him, he scoots around to open the front passenger door for her before she can go in the back seat with Piper.

"You can take shotgun. I'll sit with Piper." The guy just got out of a police station, but it seems like he's still going to shoot his shot with Alice's friend.

I can't see Alice's face since the car door blocks her, but I hear Scott's "Please?" clearly enough. She climbs in the front seat, and Scott is basically giddy as he closes her door and launches into the back seat with Piper, grinning like a doofus.

I try not to be frustrated with Scott for choosing to sit next to Piper, but it'll be much harder to ignore Alice with her beside me. I already caught a hint of her perfume when she walked by, and I can't imagine surviving the drive back with the annoyingly pleasant smell so close by. I say another prayer for strength before I climb in.

The drive home is tense and silent, aside from the twittering whispers between Piper and Scott behind me. I consider turning on the radio, but that would be admitting I'm uncomfortable, and I refuse to give any more evidence than I already have that Alice is getting under my skin. I stare straight ahead for the whole trip, only giving my right mirror the most minute glances and only when absolutely necessary.

The ride feels like it takes three times longer than usual, but I'm finally pulling into our shared space around Barefoot Lake. Even though the houses are side by side, I pull in front of Alice's first so she and Piper don't have to walk across the gravel lot in the dark. I don't see Alice's car tucked beside her house, where she's kept it every time she's home. I figured the police had brought her to the station, and she'd just hitched a ride with somebody to the bar earlier.

"Where's your car?" I blurt before I remember my mission to ignore Alice.

"Outside the bar with a flat. I'll get it tomorrow — today. Whatever," Alice says, finally sounding tired, quiet. As abrasive as her usual tone with me is, I certainly prefer it to this defeated-sounding version of her.

My manners choose now to show up.

"I'll take you to get it later." I *can't* not help her.

She looks at me quickly, obviously surprised, but I just put the truck in park and climb out before she can object like I know she will. Alice's eyes track me as I come around to her door and open it. Scott slides out of the back to help Piper down.

Alice is still staring at me, silent and unmoving. I go to reach across her to unhook the seatbelt, but she snaps out of whatever daze she's in and does it herself. I step back, and she slides down from the truck.

"It's ok. I'll take a Lyft back to the bar tomorrow for my car."

I roll my eyes and repeat myself.

"I'll take you to get it later."

"I—" she starts, but I cut her off.

"We can go at nine." I give her a pointed look, silently asking if she wants to go another few rounds of bickering. Despite being clearly exhausted, she looks ready to take me on.

"Just say yes, Ace," I plead. She blinks, looking confused, but her expression softens.

"Ok. Thank you. And —" She pauses but seems to reconsider. "And good night. You too, Scott."

My brother and Piper have just been watching us behave like the two most awkward teenagers on the planet. One look at Scott tells me I'll hear all about this once we get inside.

Great.

"Goodnight, Ace. Piper." I get back in my truck and immediately drive the handful of yards to park it in front of my garage. Scott can walk his smug ass home. I use the side door to the house to go inside and try to ignore the way the distinctly "Alice" smell lingered in the cab of the truck.

I hear Scott come in through the front a few minutes later. He meets me by the base of the staircase.

"You want to talk about what happened tonight?" I ask. He's been dealing with Troy for forever, and Scott has thick skin, but that bastard really knows where to poke for it to hurt.

"Only if you want to tell me more about what's going on with Neighbor Ace."

I glare at him. "Her name is Alice, and there's nothing going on."

"Oh yeah? Because I think you *liiiiiiiike* her."

"Go to bed, you criminal." I give him a hard but playful shove up the stairs and follow after him.

There's *nothing* going on.

CHAPTER 11

Jake

It took longer than I'd hoped to get back to sleep, so I'm a grumpy bastard when I get up for the day. It's a big change from my recently sunny personality, I know. Scott, on the other hand, is painfully chipper. His night ended in almost getting arrested, and he's sporting a nasty shiner today, but he doesn't seem to care.

"What are you smiling about?" I grumble as I make myself a bowl of cereal.

"Just thinking about Piper." He isn't even trying to downplay his giddiness.

"Of *course* you are." I roll my eyes. Scott has always felt his feelings in a big way.

"She's just so *alive*. She's funny and creative, and I swear she's read at least one book about everything."

I take a seat, and when I look at him across the kitchen table, I'm surprised I don't see cartoon hearts in his eyes. I'm not sure I've ever seen him so smitten, and he looks completely dopey after just one night with this woman.

"What, are you trying to sell me on her? I'm not sure she's my type," I joke because this is too damn funny. I chuckle to myself as I keep eating my cereal.

Scott's face falls, and a crease appears between his eyes. "No! You stay away from Piper. You have Alice."

I stop with the spoon halfway back to my bowl and point it at him.

"Hey. I do not have Alice. I do not *want* Alice."

Now it's his turn to laugh as he gets up and takes his bowl to the sink. "Sure. Keep telling yourself that." He sighs dreamily. "Maybe I'll see if Piper wants to go out on the lake today."

"Get your head on straight. You'd both be shivering too much to flirt," I scoff.

It's been getting steadily cooler each day, and the wind and spray on the lake would be miserable.

"I could keep her warm—"

I smack him upside his head before he can finish the thought.

He glares at me before glancing at the clock on the microwave. "Aren't you going to be late to rescue Alice?"

"She *doesn't* need rescuing," I huff under my breath. I can only imagine how she'd react if she heard him saying that.

I look over at the clock. Scott's right, and I need to head out. I finish my breakfast, drop my bowl in the sink, and grab my keys from the hook by the side door. Do I go knock on her door? Drive over there and pick her up? My dilemma is resolved when I hear a knock on the front door and spot Alice through the window.

Scott beats me there and flings the door wide.

"Alice!"

His voice booms far too loudly for the morning after a late night. Next thing I know, he's thrown his arms around Alice, and she's laughing. Scott's always been an affectionate guy but seeing him wrapped around Alice makes me feel something I do not care to analyze. Instead, I come up behind them and clamp a firm hand on Scott's shoulder. Pulling him back, I maneuver past him and then Alice on the staircase, which has never felt narrow before but suddenly feels far too small.

"Let's go, Ace," I grunt and stomp around the house to my truck. Would it have made more sense to just go out the side door?

Who's to say.

I hear Alice asking Scott about his eye, which has been progressively darkening all morning, and him casually brushing off her concerns, insisting he's fine. She appears around the corner of my house a minute later. I'm standing by the passenger side of the truck, holding her door open.

"Thanks," she mutters, as she hops in. It's hardly the greeting that Scott got, but at least she didn't tell me not to call her Ace.

The car ride starts just as silent and tense as it had earlier this morning. Alice stares at her hands in her lap and picks at her nails.

I can practically feel the "don't talk to me" vibe I'm emitting and remember my conversation with Eli yesterday. Alice really has done nothing to deserve me being such an ass. I take a deep breath.

"I'm sorry about your mom," I say. The words rush out of me on my exhale, like they need to escape before I lose the nerve to say them.

Alice looks at me, likely surprised that I spoke. I peek at her out of the corner of my eye when she doesn't respond. She's opening and closing her mouth like she doesn't know what to say.

Finally, she settles on, "Thank you. And thank you for looking out for her."

I shrug. "It was nothing. She looked out for me, too."

"That guy last night, uh, Troy? He said some stuff to Scott about your parents dying…" She trails off in a way that's not uncommon when people bring up dead parents. "Can I ask what happened?"

I rub my hand on the steering wheel as I think of how best to tell this story. It's been a little over a decade since they died, but it still hurts to talk about it. Their death was sudden and violent.

"They died in a freak accident when Scott was just a kid. They went to some old bed and breakfast for a weekend together while Scott was with a friend. There was a real nasty storm, and a tree fell on the building. It wasn't good."

I say it quickly and mechanically, disconnecting myself from the details as much as I can. I don't like to dwell on it. Instead, I focus on Scott.

"After that, I moved home, and it was just the two of us."

There's silence in the car long enough for me to glance over at Alice. She's looking at me with true sorrow in her eyes, and it doesn't seem like she knows what to say. I look out the windshield again and let the quiet settle around us.

"I'm sorry," she eventually says, barely above a whisper. There isn't pity in her voice. Instead, it's the honest sympathy of somebody who might understand my pain.

I only nod in response, knowing she'll see it. I can feel her eyes on me still. Once the dead parents conversation starts, there's only so much to say. I feel an itching need to say something else.

"What did Troy say?"

"Jake… I'm not sure it's worth repeating. I *know* it's not."

"Please, Ace?"

She looks down at her hands again. "He said they died to get away from Scott. Some people are truly evil."

I tighten my grip on the steering wheel so hard that the leather squeaks against my hands.

"That's an understatement. Thank you for being there for him."

This is an attack that Troy has used before, harping on the fact that they were on a trip without Scott. The comment makes no sense, but it's cruel and vicious anyway.

The remainder of the ride is quiet again, but it's not so tense anymore. When I get there, the Corner Post lot is empty other than Alice's car, so I take up two spots next to it, leaving enough room between the cars to deal with her flat.

Alice is unbuckled and has her door open before I've turned off the truck.

"Thanks for the ride!" she says, overly cheerful after our somber discussion earlier. "I've got it from here."

She's out of the cab and closes her door before I can answer. I roll my eyes, turn off the engine, and get out. I walk around the back of my truck as she opens the back hatch of her crossover.

She glances up at me when I come up next to her, looking defensive. She's already opened the hatch to access the spare and has a tire iron in her hand. I eye it warily. She wouldn't hit me with it… I don't think.

"I can handle this. Really." She says it like somebody who's been doubted too many times before.

I chuckle because I'd bet there are few things Alice *can't* handle. "I have no doubt that you can, but will you let me help you anyway?"

She looks in the car and back to me before shrugging. "I guess… if you want to?"

"I do." I hold out my hand for the tire iron.

"If you're sure…" She seems suspicious but hands the tool to me anyway.

I start loosening the lug nuts while she sets the emergency brake and wedges something against the opposite tire so the car won't roll once it's jacked up. She really does have this under control. I catch myself smiling. It's just changing a tire, but she can do it, and I kind of like that.

I also like that she's still letting me help her. She brings the jack over and bends to set it on the ground near me. My hand brushes hers as I take it, and she immediately hops to her feet, taking a step back. I try not to think too much into it.

I finish removing the flat tire, feeling Alice's watchful eyes from over my shoulder. I have no doubt she's making sure I don't fuck anything up. As I set it on the gravel, the flat rotates a bit and I spot the shiny nail head wedged in the tread.

I stand and brush off the knee of my pants.

"You got nailed," I announce, crouching down to keep a hand on the upright flat. A beat of absolute silence fills the space.

"I — *what?!* No, I didn't!"

I purposefully keep my head down, staring intently at the tire and pressing my lips together to keep from laughing. I know exactly what I said, and her flustered reaction is all I'd hoped it would be. She'd been so efficient and *stiff* all morning, and I was itching to get a rise out of her. I collect myself and roll the tire so the nail is clearly visible on top.

"You ran over a nail."

I look up at her with my best blank expression. Her cheeks are flushed, and her eyes are still a bit wide. I get the pleasure of seeing her expression morph into one that says she's *so* done with me. Her hand flashes out and she whips her fingers against my shoulder as if it's the most natural thing in the world for us to mess around with one another.

"You didn't have to word it like *that*!" She's admonishing me, but she's smiling, and her face glows. She really is a very pretty woman, and it's hard not to like her, just a little bit.

I know I didn't.

I don't say it out loud. I remember I shouldn't be flirting with her.

Instead, I stand and lift the tire, heaving it into the bed of my truck. "Tony can patch it up, no problem. I'll introduce you." I bend to pick up the tire iron, holding it out to her. "It's probably easiest if I just give you a ride over there so you don't have to put the spare on your car. We can just leave your car here for now."

She hesitates to take the tool from me but relents and wraps her fingers around it.

"I guess that makes sense." She looks ready to bolt, but she seems to acknowledge my suggestion really does make sense. She locks up the CRV and trudges back to my passenger side door, with me following behind her.

"It's only a few minutes from here." I feel the need to assure her, somehow, that it won't be so bad.

"Isn't everything 'only a few minutes' from anywhere in this town?" She hops into the truck and gets settled.

"You're not wrong," I admit, chuckling as I close her door. I circle the truck, get in, start it up, and back out. I refuse to have another silent drive, even if it's only for a few minutes.

"Did Rain teach you how to change your tire? She never indicated she was handy when we were fixing things in your house."

Alice nods. "Yeah. I guess she never wanted me to get stranded somewhere. As for the house stuff," Alice pauses and chuckles, seemingly getting lost in some memory. "She was like that with me, too. Once she knew I could fix something, she'd leave me to it. Usually, she'd make some joke about earning my keep, but I didn't mind. It was nice to feel useful."

I realize with a jolt that Rain had given me the same gift — the contentment that comes with feeling useful.

"You know, your mother was kind of a sly woman."

"Oh, I know."

I pull into Tony's lot and see him look up from under the hood of a sedan. I park and hop out but wait for Alice so we can approach the mechanic together.

Tony is a bit shorter than I am but built sturdy. He has salt-and-pepper hair and a thick beard. The stiff material of his work shirt and pants is spotted with grease and dirt, but his face has one of the kindest smiles I've ever known.

"Tony, this is Alice, Rain's daughter."

"Nice to meet you, Alice. I'm sorry about your mom." He wipes his hand on a red rag hanging from his pocket before reaching out to shake her hand.

"Thank you. I was hoping you could help me with a flat? I ran over a nail last night." She releases his hand and points her thumb over her shoulder back to my truck.

"We've got the tire in the back of Jake's truck."

"I'd be happy to." Tony follows us back to my truck and takes the tire away. He says we're welcome to wait in the office while he does the patch. We file inside and take the only two seats. Yet again, we fall into silence.

I look over at Alice while she stares, again, at her hands. It feels good to help her out after being such a dick at first, like I'm balancing the scales and repaying Rain for some of her kindness toward me.

Rain told me it was only her and her daughter, so I know Alice doesn't have more family, except maybe Piper, who looked as close to Alice as a sister would be. And while it's clear Piper would come out swinging for Alice — she did for Scotty after just meeting him, after all — I feel just a little bit protective of Alice, too. I want her to have another person in her corner.

It's a bad idea, and I blame Rain entirely for making me such a sucker. I didn't have trouble minding my own business before she blew into town.

Alice must feel me staring because she looks over at me, and then quickly back down. I look away, too.

This is a *bad idea*.

Maybe fifteen minutes later, Tony comes to retrieve us, letting Alice know the tire is all set and back in my truck. He refuses to let her pay him, and we're off.

I'm happy I'm able to help Alice, and things have been civil, but that's all this should be. I shouldn't be this interested in learning more about her. I shouldn't be focusing on the smell of her shampoo, perfume, whatever, filling my truck again. I search for a safe, boring topic as we head back to the Corner Post.

"What do you do for work?"

"I work in the English department at a university in the city, but I'm on leave for the semester. Usually, I work on curricula and coordination and teach a little."

"Impressive," I say honestly.

"I started as a teacher, but when someone in admin retired less than a year after I started, they asked me to help with organizing things, and it kind of stuck."

"Do you like it?"

"Sometimes." It sounds like a lie, and when I look over to see if she's joking, I find her looking sadly out the passenger window. "Other times, the bureaucratic bullshit makes me want to scream. I wish I taught more, like I used to, but so far, the good outweighs the bad, so I'm happy to keep at it. It also makes me feel, I don't know, accomplished? I wouldn't want to disappoint my mom. Having such an influential position in the department at such a young age is an honor. It's 'the dream,' you know?"

I'm grateful the drive is short, because I don't know what to say to that. The way she puts air quotes around "the dream" makes me wonder if it's *her* dream. I hope the hum I give is sufficient.

Once I've put the truck in park near her CRV, Alice launches out, but I'm surprised when she's waiting by the bed of the truck for me.

"Can you help me get the tire out?" The request is small, but it feels like a big deal that she asked instead of fighting to drag the tire out on her own.

"Happy to." I get it out and hold it on her car while she snugs the lug nuts. I release it but stand nearby while she finishes up. Her shoulder bumps my arm when she stands, but she doesn't leap back like she did when our hands touched earlier. I don't either.

I retrieve the wedge from the other side of her car as she loads the jack and tire iron away.

She looks up at me before nodding stiffly and getting in her car. She pulls out of the space while I head to my truck but waits for me to get in and exit the parking lot first.

I lead the way back home even though there's literally no reason since she knows where we're going. I still don't like the idea of just leaving her behind. It feels rude.

When we get back, I park in front of my garage but go around the house to the front door anyway. I look over and see that Alice did the same, even though I know she has a side door, too.

"Thanks again for your help today!" she hollers.

"Don't mention it."

She opens her mouth like she's going to say something else but closes it and gives me a quick nod before going inside.

I might be in trouble.

CHAPTER 12

Alice

I close my front door and lean back against the thick wood, suddenly feeling like I need something stable to ground me. Shutting my eyes and taking a few deep breaths, mentally berate myself for nearly attempting to invite Jake to a thank you dinner again. His adamant refusal of my last offer was just over twenty-four hours ago, and I don't need another rejection so soon.

I feel a gaze on me and peek through one eye. Seeing Piper's knowing and satisfied grin from the kitchen table, where she sits munching on cold pizza, I groan and thud my head against the door a few times. She bursts out laughing, easily identifying my inner turmoil after years of friendship.

"Soooooooooo, Neighbor Jake…" she prompts.

"No." I expect my attempt to shut down the conversation is likely useless, but I try, nonetheless.

"I'm just saying, he didn't seem very troll-like to me. But I *do* get the bear analogy. You could climb that man like a tree."

"Piper!" I flush at the thought.

"Come on. You have eyes. Don't act like you haven't already thought about it."

"I have *not*!"

I'm a liar.

Piper snorts when she laughs at me, but there's no need to verbally call me out. We both know I'm full of crap. I huff and try to change the subject again.

"Let's go for a walk around the lake. I have a missed call from Grateful Bob, so he's probably expecting an explanation for why I called him at two a.m."

"Great idea!" Piper hops up. "You can tell me all about your morning on the way."

Respectfully, Piper waits until we're a decent distance away from my house, and more importantly Jake's, before peppering me with questions about "Jake's rescue."

"It wasn't a rescue. It was a flat tire, but yes. He was… useful." I brush at a tickle on my arm that I pray isn't a mosquito.

"I don't think somebody who *hates* you would go out of their way to help like that. I think there could be something there!" Piper is giggly and clearly feeling romantic. I blame Scotty.

"Based on what?"

"He's gorgeous. You're gorgeous. It's simple!" She laughs again before getting a little more serious. "Plus, he came home to take care of Scott like that. There's some real good in him, and I think you deserve somebody who would look after you like that, too."

I look over at her questioningly. I hadn't told her what Jake had explained about his and Scotty's parents.

"I texted Scott to check in earlier. He explained what Troy was going on about. Scott told me Jake gave up everything to come home for him," Piper explains.

My chest squeezes for the brothers' pain. What Jake did for Scott when they were both so young is nothing short of amazing.

I let the thought roll around in my head for a while and swat at a sharp, stinging bug bite on my calf. Crap. I should have put on bug spray.

Reid was never protective or particularly helpful, if I'm being honest. I've always taken pride in being self-sufficient, having been taught how to work through any challenge by a mom who did the same as a single parent. I don't *need* to be taken care of, but I can admit it might be nice for somebody to want to do it.

"I just don't think that's going to be Jake. This morning was nicer, sure, but I doubt I'm making his Christmas card list."

Piper shrugged. "I dunno about that. Last night, I think he was smiling more than you saw. And considering the fact that he was picking us up from a police station in the middle of the night, it's a surprise that he smiled at all."

I can practically see Piper writing my love story with Jake in her mind.

"Pipe, you spend too much time lost in your romance novels."

"I spend the *perfect* amount of time with my books, thank you very much. This is a good story. Trust me."

"That's it, though. It's just a story." I sigh because briefly letting myself think about Jake that way is exciting. Another piercing bite on my leg snaps me back to reality. "Are you seriously not getting eaten alive by mosquitos right now?"

Piper shakes her head. "Nope! Just you."

"Life is *not* fair."

We hear a deep belly laugh as we pass through the opening in the trees that leads to Grateful Bob's house. I briefly worry we're interrupting a visit from guests as we walk toward the opening between his house and his neighbor's, but then I distinctly hear Scott's voice.

"I thought we were going to get arrested *for sure*." He's laughing again as Piper and I come around the side of the house and spot the two men on Grateful Bob's back patio. We're clearly interrupting Scott during his dramatic retelling of this morning. He cuts off when he sees us.

"Piper! Alice!"

Grateful Bob turns around in his chair and waves us over. "Ah yes. Some more delinquents of Wilcox Grove."

"Hi, Grateful Bob." I squeeze his outstretched hand with both of mine when we reach the men. "This is my friend, Piper."

Grateful Bob rises to shake her hand. "Pleasure to meet you, miss. Please, have a seat."

Scott immediately leaps to his feet.

"Take mine!" he exclaims. Grateful Bob looks at Scott with raised eyebrows before pointedly looking at the four other open chairs on the patio.

"Boy, sit down." Grateful Bob chuckles.

Piper and I take two of the empty chairs before she turns to Grateful Bob. I notice the cushions we're sitting on are all embroidered with a pattern of tiny loons.

"It's wonderful to meet you, Grateful Bob. Alice wouldn't tell me, though — why are you called Grateful Bob?"

"Ah, it's a fascinating tale. When I was young, I spent several years studying Tibetan Buddhism and the importance of the virtue of gratitude. I learned to express it in every aspect of my life, and the nickname just stuck." Grateful Bob clasps his hands together, closes his eyes, and bows his head, as if remembering a very peaceful past.

Scott snorts. "That's not what you told me! You said it was because of all the ladies who thanked *you* for the pleasure of your company!"

Grateful Bob pins Scott with a glare and smacks him upside the head with speed I wouldn't expect from the older man.

Scott jolts and grumbles something that sounds like "Twice in one day!"

"Excuse you! My past is one of virtue. I would *never*." Grateful Bob's mock outrage is enough to have us all in stitches.

We chat easily for a while about how nice Scott's friends are and how fun the night had been before its abrupt ending. At her request, Scott passes along Hannah's number to me with a plea for me to text her so we can meet up. I feel giddy at the thought of having made another Wilcox Grove friend.

Eventually, I get around to apologizing for calling Grateful Bob in the dead of night.

"At least you had Jakey come to the rescue," Grateful Bob says. "I still wish I could have been there for you all."

"Please don't worry about it. We were just fine." I place a hand on his forearm. "I can handle Jake's judgment."

"Nah, Jake didn't mind. I'm sure he doesn't think anything of it," Scott defends his brother.

I snort loudly. It's *very* dignified.

"Trust me, your brother is NOT my biggest fan. He —"

I cut off and look awkwardly at Scott. He immediately catches my eye.

"What?"

"Never mind."

"No! Go ahead."

"I feel weird talking about your brother in front of you!"

Scott scoffs. "Puh-lease. This is a safe space. I'm just one of the girls." His eyes dart over to Piper, wide with regret. "But not like that! Not that girls aren't great! I love girls! They're the best!"

The poor man takes a deep breath as the rest of us try not to laugh.

"I mean that I can keep my mouth shut," he finishes.

"Ok, ok. I just feel like Jake thinks I'm inept, or a moron, or both."

Probably both. I like it when the people near me are happy, and it bugs me that I've been such a disaster, especially around somebody that my mom thought was important.

"First, he schools me about how I was failing to take care of Mom's house, and then he has to pick us up in the middle of the night from a *police station*, and *then* he helps me with my tire. I feel like a walking disaster. Plus, he helped my mom when she lived here. I'm hardly thanking him for that."

"Jake doesn't do what he does for thanks, so you don't need to even the score or anything. He's just somebody who likes to help. Always has been." It's clear from the way that Scott talks about Jake that he adores his brother. "He upended his whole life for me, and never let me thank him for it because he's insisted there was never anything to thank him for."

I look down, feeling another sudden rush of affection for my burly neighbor. I keep getting glimpses of his kindness that are completely at odds with the growly beast in my shed yesterday morning, and I like them.

"It sounds like he's basically a fairy tale hero. Don't you think, *Ace*?" Piper raises and lowers her eyebrows so dramatically that she looks like she belongs in a comic strip.

"He's a very nice man," I grit out, willing her to knock it off. Scott and Grateful Bob politely ignore her shenanigans. I continue, "I know I don't need to 'even the score,' but I do want to thank him properly. You know, try to start with a clean slate after threatening him with a frying pan the first time we met."

Scott and Grateful Bob both bark out laughs.

"You *what?*" Scott wheezes, and I explain the story.

"I thought he was some kind of ruffian!"

That just has them laughing harder. Apparently, ruffians are few and far between around Barefoot Lake.

"Will you two knock it off and help me?" I plead. "I tried to offer to cook him dinner, and he basically kicked me out of his house. Is there something unobtrusive I can do to help him out and say thanks?"

The two men furrow their brows as they seriously consider my request. Scott speaks first.

"There's not really anything Jake wants. He's a simple guy."

"Hm… That's not true," Grateful Bob counters before turning to me. "Ever since he was little, that boy has wanted a golden retriever. You should get him a dog."

"That's right!" Scott says. "I remember him asking our parents for one all the time when he was in high school. He'd love a dog."

I sag in my seat. "Guys. 'Unobtrusive,' remember? I love dogs as much as the next person, but I want to make his life easier, and they're a ton of work. Do you have any other ideas?"

They think for another minute.

"It's boring, but you could clean his boat," Scott suggests with a shrug. "He'll have to take it out of the water soon to store it for the winter, and it should be cleaned before it goes into storage. It would be one less thing for him to do, and it's no more difficult than cleaning something like patio furniture."

I perk up. "I'm a *great* cleaner! I could totally do that!"

"If you're sure…" Scott seems dubious of somebody so excited about cleaning but probably just writes it off as me being a weirdo. "I can get him out of the house for a few hours this afternoon if it would help."

"That would be perfect, thank you." I feel good about this. Acts of Service is my giving love language, and it's satisfying to have found a way to help my enigmatic neighbor.

I sit on the couch scratching the dozens of mosquito bites peppering my legs while Piper paces near the front windows, waiting for Jake and Scott to leave.

"Are you sure you didn't get *any* mosquito bites? I swear I got bit like thirty times."

"I'm sure! They must just love you."

Piper laughs when I groan and flop back dramatically on the cushions. One of the nice things about living in the middle of Boston is that the city has few mosquitoes. There's just so much *nature* at Barefoot Lake. I can learn to share space with deer and raccoons, but I wouldn't shed a single tear if all of the mosquitos died. They're demons.

"Oh!" Piper darts to the door and presses her back flat against it, twisting to peer out of the window beside it when she hears Jake's truck start.

"Piper, he can't see you. Quit being a lunatic."

She shushes me and remains perfectly still until the sound of the truck fades away down the street. I roll my eyes.

"Let's go!" she barks like a drill sergeant before darting to the back door, where she shoves her feet in her shoes and scoops up a bucket of cleaning supplies. She opens the screen. "Come on! Go, go, go!"

"Yes, ma'am!" I snap to attention before grabbing an armful of rags from the counter and following her out the back door. She's very excited about our secret cleaning mission, and I'm grateful for both her help and nonsense. It makes the whole cleaning process go quicker and feel more fun.

Jake's boat is similar in size to Mom's and generally tidy, but it has some silt inside and outside, and the falling leaves have begun collecting in various corners. Grateful Bob loaned us his favorite cleaning solutions for the floors, seats, exterior, and various doo-dads in the boat and gave us a quick lesson on what to use where. As long as we keep the boat turned off and don't mess with any buttons or levers, the job basically just requires elbow grease.

Piper sets us up with music from her phone so our cleaning party can also be part dance party, and we get to work dusting, wiping, and shining every single surface. It takes a couple of hours, but that boat looks beautiful when we're done, and I'm incredibly proud of the results. Piper and I stand side by side on the dock, admiring the boat that now literally shines.

"Now he'll for sure fall in love with you," Piper laughs.

"Girl, don't make me push you in this lake. It's cold, but I'll do it." I knock my shoulder against hers.

"I was just saying he'll appreciate it!!" Piper holds up her hands in surrender. "I want to go shower before we head out. Are we all done down here?"

"You go on in. I'm just going to hose down the side again, and then I'll meet you inside."

Piper scoops up the bucket of supplies and sodden rags and goes back to my house. I pick up the hose nozzle from the deck and carefully spray down the side of the boat, making sure not to splash water inside. As I maneuver around the post on the dock where the boat is tied, I notice the careful looping of the rope, so each ring secures the prior one. I turn off the hose and wind it back into a neat coil like I found it.

I go back to the rope tying up the boat, remembering Jake's admonishment from yesterday morning. Was it really only yesterday? The way he tied his boat doesn't look complicated, and I bet I can figure it out by reverse engineering it. It'll be one less lake house thing for me to be incompetent at.

Very carefully, I unwind one loop of the rope and redo it the exact same way. I've always learned by repetition, so I repeat the process again and again before undoing two loops and redoing those. It's *not* a complicated tie or a fancy sailor's knot, but I make sure each of my loops is as neat and tight as Jake's were. I continue the process over and over until it's second nature to loop the rope over and snug it up. I unwind the whole thing, ready to time myself this time because I'm a freak.

I'm startled when my phone buzzes aggressively in my pocket, and the rope falls from my hands.

Crap. It's probably Piper wondering what's taking me so long.

I pull the device out and freeze when I see Reid's name lit up on the screen. I haven't heard from him in weeks. The phone sits flat on my palm as I let it ring out. I didn't expect to have contact with him ever again, and it had been a peaceful existence. Even after my phone sends him to voicemail, I remain frozen, staring at the now-dark screen.

I feel small and stupid, loud and obnoxious — all the things he told me I was.

Just seeing his name causes a wave of nausea to wash over me. I'm disgusted by him and by myself for staying with him so long.

I shake my head and tell myself again that he was wrong.

"Alice! You coming?" Piper's shout from my back patio pulls me out of my stupor.

I adamantly remind myself that Reid's behavior is *not* my fault.

I am free. I am strong.

"Sorry!" I jog back up to the house so I can drive Piper to the bus station.

CHAPTER 13

Jake

For the second night in a row, I'm woken up from a dead sleep by my phone noisily rattling around on my night-stand. I bolt upright before remembering Scott is safely sleeping in his room right across the hall. I have to blink a few times to clearly see the bright screen. It's four in the morning, and the call is from Grateful Bob.

Shit – did something happen?

"Hello?"

"Goooooood morning, Jake," he practically sings the greeting, and I can immediately tell this isn't bad news. I sigh heavily and wonder how many years of my life I've lost from panic. "How are you doing this fine day?"

"Grateful Bob, it's four a.m. That hardly counts as day." I'm still trying to sort out why he's calling me so early. "Is everything ok?"

"Oh yes, yes. Just fine."

I'm tempted to hang up on him, but he continues.

"It's just that there's this boat knocking against my dock, and I know I pulled mine out of the water a week ago. You don't happen to be missing one, do you?"

"Missing a boat? I don't — hang on." I flip back the covers and swing my legs over the side of the bed. Pushing back the curtains on my back window, I look out at the lake. It's dark, but I can still clearly see my dock and the empty lake beside it where my boat should be.

I drag a hand down my face. Can I not catch a damn break? I groan in frustration and try to figure out what on earth could have happened. I keep that boat secured at *all* times and nobody else—

Scott must have taken Piper out, completely disregarding my advice.

"I'm going to murder Scott."

"That seems a bit drastic, don't you think? The boat looks fine. It just went out for a midnight float." Grateful Bob is laughing now.

I'm glad one of us finds this amusing. Scott has grown up around water and boats, but the kid can still be *so careless*.

"I'm sorry, Grateful Bob. We'll come collect it now. Thanks for the call."

"Never a dull day, boy. Never a dull day." Grateful Bob snickers again before hanging up.

I grab a pillow off my bed on my way across the hall. I fling open Scott's door, letting it hit the wall behind.

"Wazzamatter?!" Scott yelps as he sits up, a second before I smack him in the face with my launched pillow.

"Just got a call from Grateful Bob, letting me know our boat is at *his dock*. Were you fucking around with the boat again? With Piper?" I realize my hands are on my hips and drop my arms to my sides before I turn into our father.

"What are you talking about? I haven't gone anywhere near the —" Scott cuts off so suddenly that I'm immediately suspicious. He looks at me wide-eyed like he's just realized something.

"Out with it. What happened?"

"Nothing! Like you said, I was messing with the boat. I wanted to impress Piper. I must not have tied it up properly. I'm sorry." Scott has to be the worst liar on the planet.

"Bullshit. You want to try again?"

"Nope! It was me. I'm sorry."

I'm not buying it, but we don't have time to fight right now.

"Fine. If you're not going to fess up, you're going to come with me to get it. Let's go."

A few minutes later, Scott and I are in sweats and on our way to Grateful Bob's. Thankfully, the walk isn't long because it is *cold* out in the low forties. The days are breezy, and the trees are gorgeous, but when the sun's down, there's little warmth left these days.

I try to figure out what game Scott is playing, but he won't budge, insisting he was showing off for Piper. It just makes no sense. The guy barely shuts up about her. There's no way he'd have been able to keep from detailing the entire encounter to me as soon as I saw him. Something is up.

"Howdy, boys!" Grateful Bob greets us as we come through the trees and up to his house. He's chipper as ever, despite the early morning wake-up.

I elbow Scott hard in the side. If he's taking the blame for this, he needs to apologize to Grateful Bob.

"I'm sorry for the disruption, Grateful Bob. *I'm* careless, and *I* didn't tie up the boat properly yesterday," he says each word forcefully, with his eyebrows basically touching his hairline.

Grateful Bob chuckles. "It's alright boy. I know *you* didn't mean it."

Ok, so Grateful Bob is in on whatever's going on here.

"You both know I'm going to find out eventually, right?"

"No clue what you're talking about, Jake. I'm just going to go back to bed." Grateful Bob gives us a quick salute before heading back inside.

I nudge Scott ahead of me, down the side of Grateful Bob's house and to the back. Sure enough, our boat is hanging out at the dock like a dog that came to visit the neighbors. Grateful Bob must have tied it down when he found it because it's secured. I inspect as much of it as I can and am relieved to see what Grateful Bob had already said — it seems just fine. We're lucky.

Scott steps on board first and puts the key in the ignition. I climb in after him and take a seat.

"If you did this, you can drive us back. Let's make sure you haven't forgotten anything."

Scott dramatically rolls his eyes but doesn't protest. I lean back and prop my hands behind my head. He starts the engine and collects the rope into the boat, tucking it neatly to the side. A few lights flick on, and I sit back up, looking around.

Everything is where it should be, but something is *different*. My eyes trail along the floor of the boat, bow to stern. It was significantly dirtier the last time I saw it. I whip around and jab a finger at my brother.

"Scott, what happened to my boat?"

"It got loose and went to Grateful Bob's house for a visit." Scott's voice is monotone like he thinks I wanted him to recite his mistakes like some kind of lesson.

We pull away from the dock and start heading home slowly so we make as little noise as possible.

"No, that's not what I mean. It's clean. Like, really clean."

"I don't know about that. Maybe?" Scott stares straight ahead over the front of the boat and away from me like he's trying to act casual, but he's being the least casual person I've ever seen.

"Scott, it's literally spotless. Did you do this?"

He hesitates like he's having some kind of internal dilemma.

"No. Don't be mad. It was Alice and probably Piper, too. Alice wanted to thank you for helping her and her mom, and she asked for ways to do something nice without bothering you. This is what Grateful Bob and I came up with. She was so excited, and I'm sure she didn't mean to let the boat loose. It *had* to have been an accident. And they did a *really* good job on the boat. Even you said so." I'm not sure he breathes once while getting that out.

I groan for what feels like the thousandth time in the past few days and press the heels of my palms into my eyes. Alice is going to be the literal death of me.

"It's fine, but I'm teaching her how to tie up a boat *today*."

Scott sighs with relief, and I immediately feel guilty. I don't want Scott, or anyone really, to ever worry about how I'm going to react, especially when he's just trying to help a friend and Alice is just trying to do something nice.

We're quiet the rest of the short ride home.

Scott skillfully parks the boat at our dock, getting close on the first try. I watch like a hawk, but he perfectly ties the boat. He steps back on board and turns off the lights. I finally get up and move toward the back of the boat to get off.

"It's fine, Scott. Really."

"Yeah?"

"Yeah."

I stand with one foot on the dock and the other on the boat, waiting for him to collect the keys and get off. As he's coming back toward me, his foot catches on his baggy pants, and he pitches forward. Instinctually, I lunge for him, going to grab the back of his hoodie, but he catches himself and stands up quickly, knocking into me.

Next thing I know, there's nothing between me and some very cold lake water.

CHAPTER 14

Alice

I jolt awake abruptly, feeling alert and anxious. I stay still and silent for a moment, trying to figure out what pulled me out of sleep. The house is quiet, but it must have been *something*. I sit up when a loud banging echoes around the room. I'm on my feet, and I find the clock on my dresser. It isn't even five yet, but there's a very angry somebody at my door. I snatch up my phone, about to call the police, when a voice follows the pounding.

"ACE!!"

Oh shit!

I hurry out of my room and down the stairs as quickly as I can, sliding across the wooden floor in my socks and grabbing the doorknob to stop myself. I fling open the door.

"Jake! What's —" The number of times this man has left me speechless is abnormally high for having known him only two days, but this time it's really not my fault. How is somebody supposed to react when their neighbor is standing outside their home before sunrise looking like a drowned cat, right down to the irritated expression?

"Um… Jake? Why are you all wet? And why are you here?"

"Well, Ace, it's a hilarious story. Did you know that my boat went for a little joyride by itself last night? Most boats tend to stay put, but I guess mine is just friendly. Wanted to hang out with Grateful Bob. Usually, I put a stop to that kind of behavior by tying it up, but somehow it got out. You wouldn't have any idea how that could have happened, would you?"

Both of my hands steadily creep up to cover my mouth as he tells his story. The *rope*. I pull my hands away.

"Oh my god, Jake. I'm *so* sorry!"

Embarrassment fills my entire body, and my heart drops into my stomach, thudding with the realization of what I did and what it caused.

"But wait, there's more!" he says like a game show host. "After I went to get it back, in the freezing cold, with Scott, who tried to take the blame for this little getaway stunt, the klutz basically shoulder checks me into the water. It's certainly one way to make sure I'm wide awake, but I'll admit, it's not my favorite."

Despite my guilt, a laugh bursts out of me. I snap my mouth shut at his quick glare. "I'm sorry!" I'm a little frantic, still in shock that I was such an idiot. I start rambling.

"I was being so careful, I swear. But then Reid called me, and I was *not* expecting to hear from him again. Then Piper needed me to take her to the bus station, and I didn't want her to be late. If she missed her bus, she'd have missed work, and she has this awful new boss who I know wouldn't have given her any slack. I'm so, so sorry."

Jake smacks his hands against the door frame and leans in, keeping fierce eye contact.

"You can't keep *not tying up boats*! It's irresponsible, but it's also dangerous! Somebody could have gotten hurt, or there could have been some serious damage to the boat or somebody else's property!"

For a few seconds, the only sounds between us are the steady drips of lake water falling from Jake onto the wooden steps and his heavy breathing.

I make an enormous mistake when I let my eyes follow a drop of water from his hair straight down to the porch and see his sweats are basically plastered to him, and his chest is heaving. He's such a *large* man, and Piper's comment about me climbing him like a tree flashes in my mind. I look back at his face as quickly as I can, but I can already feel the heat rushing to my cheeks.

"I'm *sorry*."

My voice cracks, and his expression softens the tiniest amount.

He lifts his left hand and runs it through his hair.

Lord, help me.

He looks down at himself for a second before coming back at me with that intense eye contact.

"I fell in the *lake*."

Another laugh forces its way out of me, no matter how hard I try to hold it back. I look down, ashamed, and try to compose myself when I hear a deep laugh. I glance up to see Jake pressing a fist to his forehead, smiling.

"I *fell* in the *fucking lake*."

Next thing I know, we're both in stitches, gasping for air. I open the door further and step back into it, holding my side.

"Come in, please. I'll get you a towel."

Jake squeezes out the sides of his sweatshirt and water splashes around him. He steps forward but tries to make himself as small as possible on the mat just inside the door.

I hurry upstairs and come back with two large, fluffy towels and a fleece blanket. I hold the towels out to him, but he peels off his sweatshirt instead of taking them, and I freeze. His t-shirt sticks to the sweatshirt at first, lifting up until Jake peels it back down. I expect I resemble a fish, openly ogling my neighbor.

Every inch of him looks perfectly… firm. What does he do at that nursery? Bench press tree trunks?

I think I forget to breathe for a second.

He finally takes a towel from my hand and begins squeezing water out of his clothes with it as best he can. When he turns to the side, I get my first look at a tattoo covering the upper half of his left arm. It's our lake with tree-covered hills on the opposite bank, tattooed in all black. Above it is a gorgeous night sky with a full moon and stars that look like they could twinkle at any moment.

It's this moment when I notice Jake has stopped moving and is observing me. I shake my head quickly.

"Sorry, I was just admiring your tattoo. It's beautiful."

Was that weird to say? It feels weird. Does he think *I'm* weird?

What am I saying? Of course he does.

It could have been worse. I could have said *he's* beautiful. But that would *definitely* have been weird.

"Thanks." Jake resumes his drying, dropping the first towel on the ground and setting the wet sweatshirt on top of it before taking the second towel. "Do you have any?"

I shake my head. "No, but I've always wanted one. I've just never been able to decide on something I like enough to have on me forever."

He balls up the second towel and places it in the pile on the floor.

"Here." I hold out the blanket, gesturing to the table. "Let me at least make you a cup of coffee."

He nods and toes off his shoes before peeling off his socks and setting them beside my line of shoes. He follows me into the kitchen, arranging the blanket around him so he doesn't get anything else wet. It would make more sense for him to go back to his house, shower, and change into dry clothes, but for some reason, he's choosing to sit bundled up at my kitchen table. I like how it feels to have him in my space, so I don't point out that it's illogical for him to have accepted my invitation to come inside.

I start brewing coffee and lean back on the counter, looking at him. I might be permanently blushing from here on out, but I can't stop *looking* at him, even when he's just sitting there.

The house isn't particularly big, and neither is the furniture Mom filled it with, so it's doing an excellent job of accentuating Jake's sheer size. The blanket is wrapped over his shoulders, so I can't continue my perusal of his torso, but his arms are propped on the table and even they look... solid. All of him is just so sturdy.

Also, contrary to nearly every other time I've seen him, Jake's face is relaxed. It takes me a second to figure out why he looks different. Then, I notice his brow isn't furrowed. He's usually so serious and seeing him at least somewhat relaxed is like breaking the surface after holding your breath underwater as long as you can. He's... well, he's beautiful.

He must feel my gaze because he looks up at me.

"Ace, who's Reid?" The question comes out of nowhere.

My heartbeat ticks up.

"Why do you know that name? Did somebody contact you?" I can see the slippery slope to panic and resist sliding down it.

"No?" Jake's clearly confused by my reaction, and the furrow in his brow is right back where I'm used to seeing it. "You said it when you were rambling outside."

I hadn't realized I'd let the name slip. I feel some relief knowing Reid hasn't tried to hunt me down up here, but just the sound of his name from somebody in my "new life" is enough to maintain a feeling of anxiousness. I wanted Reid to stay securely in my "old life."

"He's a troll," I say simply, remembering the comment from Piper and finding it to be a very apt description.

Jake raises his eyebrows but stays silent, waiting for more.

"He's a mistake, one I don't want to waste any more time on. He's... he's not a nice guy." I shake my head like I'm trying to clear an Etch A Sketch and delete Reid from my brain.

Jake opens his mouth like he's going to say something, but I'm saved from having to explain further by the coffee maker bubbling and hissing as it spits the last of the water into the pot. I quickly turn my back to Jake before he can get out whatever he's planning on saying.

"How do you take it?" I ask as I retrieve two mugs that are more like bowls, and pour a healthy amount of coffee into each, leaving some room in both. I set them on the table and slide one toward Jake.

"Just cream. No sugar." He seems to have taken the hint that the Reid conversation is over, but his brow is still all bunched up like he's displeased.

I retrieve half and half and vanilla creamer from my fridge and pass him the smaller of the two bottles. He tips just a splash into his mug and then watches, horrified, as I sit across from him and pour vanilla creamer into mine, stopping just shy of exceeding the coffee quantity with creamer.

He's still staring, looking alarmed.

"Can I help you?" I call him out on his expression.

"Does that even taste like coffee anymore?" He sounds like I've dishonored the mug of bean water in front of me.

"Nope," I laugh. "That's the point."

"Like mother, like daughter." The corner of his lips quirk up as he continues to stare at my abomination of a morning beverage. Mom also preferred a bit of coffee with her creamer.

"'You really were her friend." I say it softly, mostly to myself, before I realize it could come across as an insult and quickly backpedal. "I'm not saying it's unbelievable that you could be her friend. I can very easily picture you helping her and her mothering you. I'm just surprised because we told each other *every-thing*, and she didn't tell me about you."

"I think she didn't want to burden you as things got harder for her." He looks into his mug as he speaks. "She talked about you *a lot* and how she didn't want to pull you away from your life. I think she also mentioned the 'troll,' though not by name or title. She thought he'd be upset if she distracted you from him."

"He almost certainly would have," I admit. When I saw how much Mom had deteriorated by the time I finally convinced her to move in with me, I knew that she'd been hiding how bad it was, but it hurts nonetheless to realize that she felt like she couldn't be honest with me.

"She was so proud of you." He laughs when I give him a disbelieving look. I think he's just trying to make me feel better.

"I mean it. She wouldn't shut up about her Dumbo. She told me it was just the two of you, but what was it like growing up with such an… energetic mom?"

I chuckle at his choice of adjective. Rain certainly was energetic, seemingly able to run on zero sleep.

"Honestly, she was my best friend. She told me when I was young that I came about as a result of a fling and that my dad wasn't an evil person, but he also wasn't around." I tell him the story I've told anytime somebody asks about my father. The lie slides off my tongue easily, even if it leaves a sour taste in its wake. "After that, I rarely thought much about him because Mom filled both positions in my life and did everything she could to make sure I never felt like my family was lacking." I smile to myself, shoving my dishonesty to the far corners of my mind and focusing on my mom's rambunctious enthusiasm when I was growing up. It's nice to reminisce about her and share the incredible person she was for me.

Jake gives me a nod to continue.

"She worked a lot, but she'd still sit with me after she got home while I did my homework. She was still a parent, but she let me make and learn from my own mistakes. She was straight with me about adult subjects — our financial situation, dating, whatever. It was easy to talk to her, even when I was confessing something I'd fucked up. She was firm, but fair. Even my bratty teenager phase didn't last long because it made so little sense with how she treated me."

I stop for a sip of "coffee" because I realize I've been prattling on for a bit now. Jake hasn't made me feel like I'm boring him, though. His eye contact has been intense, attentive.

"You can always talk to me about her if you want to. I don't mind. Actually, it's nice. I only knew her for a few years, but she was a good friend. Sure, she was well-liked around here, but it's different to talk about her to somebody who knew her so well," Jake says kindly. Either he's really intuitive, or his encouragement is just an uncanny coincidence.

"I feel like you know more about her life up here than I do, though," I'm ashamed to say it. "I should have visited, Reid be damned. Whenever we spoke, she focused on me, my life, struggles, job, and triumphs. She would say Wilcox Grove was 'just what she'd hoped it would be.'"

I should have paid more attention, asked more about her life here, done *something* more.

Jake doesn't seem to judge.

"What do you want to know?"

"Anything. Everything?"

Jake takes a drink of his coffee, and stares into the cup for a moment before speaking.

"She shook things up when she came into town. We really don't have a frequently changing population in Wilcox Grove. People can still be fairly judgmental sometimes, so an unmarried woman of a certain age inserting herself into everything turned heads. She would just start talking to people in stores or around town, introducing herself and inviting people to whatever she could think of. She started a bunch of different meetups like book clubs or craft corners. And she would have people over for barbecues, sunrise yoga out back, or anything else she could think of. I swear she added a few years to a lot of lives up here."

I can picture Mom doing every one of the things he's describing. When she first bought the lake house, she was barely showing symptoms of her sickness and was determined to do things that brought her joy. It makes me happy to hear that she was happy in Wilcox Grove and that she was surrounded by people who appreciated her light.

"We met when she started yelling at me one day — again, I see the family resemblance." Jake pauses, and I purposefully look anywhere but at him, pretending I have no clue what he's talking about. He lets out a low, amused sound. I have to ask.

"What did you do to make her yell at you?"

"Why do you assume it was something *I* did?"

"Well, it was your fault when *we* met, so…"

Jake rolls his eyes at me.

"She berated me for being unneighborly," Jake admits, and I snort into my coffee, amused that Mom got the same warm treatment I had.

Jake sighs but otherwise ignores my reaction and continues.

"Before I could decide if I even wanted to apologize to my new lunatic neighbor, she told me I'd be having dinner with her, and then I'd be helping her hang that swing on your back porch. That was that. She'd share her opinions and her cooking, and I'd fix things for her. She didn't give me a choice in our friendship, but it felt…" Jake presses his fingers into the back of his neck and clears his throat. "It felt nice to have a parent figure to talk to. She made it easy to feel comfortable around her."

Jake makes it easy to feel comfortable around him, too. I'm

feeling a little dreamy and contemplating the consequences of just blurting that out when Jake surprises me.

"I'm sorry, by the way."

"Huh?" I'm so eloquent.

"I'm sorry. For being an ass the last few days."

I blink stupidly back at him. I was not expecting an apology from Jake since I basically turned his life upside down these past few days. I try to brush it off.

"What? No. You weren't. You…"

I stop when Jake looks at me, completely unamused. He kind of looks like the emoji with the horizontal line for a mouth. I should get an award for not laughing.

"Ok, yeah. You were. *Why* were you?"

"I think I'm mad at your mom for leaving." The rawness of his admission shocks me even more than his apology. I can practically feel his pain, and it reminds me of my own. "And now I feel like an even bigger ass for saying that to somebody who just lost their *mom*." He groans and folds forward until his forehead thuds against the tabletop.

I push back my chair and walk around the table to stand beside him. I put my hand on his shoulder, feeling the heat of him even through the blanket and his cold, wet shirt. The man is still a furnace even though he took a swan dive into a freezing lake before sunrise.

"It's ok, Jake. Sometimes, I'm mad at her for leaving, too."

He picks his head up off the table to look at me and when he sits up straight, I realize how close we are. Since he's such a giant, even seated, we're not *too* far from eye level, and I'm not a short girl.

"First, I thought you were just some vapid city girl here to bring down the neighborhood. Once I figured out who you *really were*, I think I projected some of that resentment on you. I figured you'd be leaving soon, too, and it didn't matter anyway."

He's vulnerable in a way I never would have expected so soon after meeting him, especially not with how cold he's been most of our time together. I immediately warm to him even more.

Grieving is hard. It's exhausting.

I give him the only stability I can offer.

"For now, I'm sticking around."

Thoughts of responsibilities waiting for me in Boston ping around in my head, but I lock them in a box for now.

He nods and takes another swig of coffee, draining the mug. He stands, and I step back to give him space. He folds the blanket over the back of my chair. His shirt is still plastered to his body.

Do _not_ check him out, Alice.

"Thanks for the coffee and" He vaguely waves his hand toward the table like our conversation is something corporeal sitting atop the surface. "everything. Talking."

We walk to my front door. Jake collects his discarded clothing, shoving his bare feet into his wet boots.

"Anytime. And I'm sorry again about your boat."

Jake shrugs. "I guess the universe felt like I needed one more swim in the lake this season."

CHAPTER 15

Jake

I've felt lighter since I left Alice's house after the I-fell-in-a-lake incident. I tell myself it's because it feels good not to have a toxic dislike for the person living beside me and not because I might *like* her, but there's no need to focus on that for too long. Just like there's no need to focus on the tension I felt when she stood beside me with her hand on me that morning.

It was nothing. We'd just bonded over shared pain, nothing more. *Nothing.*

I now know she's not here to destroy the town and bring down property values, so we can just be cordial neighbors.

It's been impossible not to notice her, though. Since my brain figured out I was done being a complete tool to Alice, it started taking a *lot* of notice. It's like I'm attuned to her, and her mere presence raises the hairs on the back of my neck. When that happens, I can't help but look. And then I can't pull myself away.

One day, I see Grateful Bob come by with his truck to help Alice pull her boat out of the lake for the winter, presumably taking it to storage. I'd brought mine to the marina the day it made its escape attempt and wanted to offer to pull Alice's out, too, but she wasn't home when I knocked. I regret not offering when I'd seen her home another time. I pointedly don't ask myself why.

I watch Grateful Bob show her how to drain the fluids for winter from my window before realizing I'm being a creep and go back to minding my own business. Grateful Bob is a kind man, and I know he was happy to teach her, but I still wish she had asked me for help.

I try to shake it off and go about my business. Fall is busy at the nursery with the pumpkin patch and apple orchard. Plus, I'm putting a lot of time into the new Christmas trees to make sure I didn't drive all the way to Canada for them just to let them die. I have visions of a sprawling field filled with hearty trees for families to bring back home. I need to stay focused, or something will slip.

Even though I tell myself to focus on me, my attention still goes to *her*. Every time I leave my house or drive into our little clearing, my eyes dart to her house. Will she be outside? Is her car parked beside the house? Does something look like it's about to fall apart and crush her?

Most of the time, the house is quiet, but sometimes I do see her, and I see changes around her property.

Alice has been working hard at taking better care of her new home, raking leaves, picking weeds, and constantly cleaning something. She smiles and waves when she's outside and spots me inevitably staring. My frustration with her is gone, as is the punch of sadness when she reminds me of Rain. Stubborn as an ox, I refuse to acknowledge the new feeling her attention stirs in me.

I remind myself that we've clocked no more than a few hours together and that I know very little about her. Reasoning doesn't get me far, though, because I feel drawn to her, nonetheless. I *want* to spend time with her. I *want* to get to know her.

Instead, I do my best to give her space and not find anything else to admire about her.

It's not going well.

CHAPTER 16

Alice

It feels like Jake and I have reached some kind of truce. We're not about to have any more heart-to-hearts, but I think we'll maintain the peace. To help with that, I try my absolute hardest to stay out of his way, politely waving when I see him but minding my business. Ten out of ten times, I get a quick head nod in return before he turns away.

For a while, I became a homebody, trying to figure out all it takes to care for my home. Once, I slipped away to the outskirts of Boston for a couple of hours to connect with part of my old life. With the several-hour-long round-trip drive, I surrendered my day to the task and snuck back into Wilcox Grove without seeming to have raised any alarms.

Grateful Bob came by to visit and help me winterize my boat. In return, I gave him a small crocheted stuffed loon I made. Even with all the house projects, I've got a *lot* of time on my hands these days.

Since this is the first time in my life when I haven't had school or work to keep me busy, I've been, well, vibing. After yet another morning of cooking, cleaning, crocheting, screaming at something broken in the house, and reading in my library squashy chair, I decide it's time to push myself to try new things.

I also need to get out of this house before I decide the "charm" isn't worth it and burn the place to the ground.

This was Mom's haven. I would never.

(But I bet she'd forgive me if I did.)

Since arson is off the table for now, I try to think of something else to do. For a city girl, "new things" probably means spending a lot of time outdoors. I'm just not sure what to do. Should I wander around and look at plants? That feels like a surefire way to get poison ivy.

Since I'm completely out of ideas after that extensive (read "five-second long") brainstorming session, I grab a bottle of pink wine and my phone and head to my back porch swing to video call Piper.

As the phone rings, I convince myself that since I'm outside, it's a step in the right direction. I start lazily swinging back and forth. I notice there are no longer any splinters stabbing me and silently thank Jake for sanding the swing down.

Luckily, Piper's home and answers my call quickly before I can dwell on my neighbor any longer.

Once the video connects, I'm met with chaos on the screen. Between the flashes of light and bits of Piper, I realize she's shoving her arm through a sleeve while still holding the phone. A moment later, the image centers on her face, and her mouth splits into a grin.

"Hiya!" she basically shouts the greeting at me.

"Did I catch you at a bad time?" I ask as the background behind Piper moves.

I can tell she's taking me through her apartment to the bathroom. She props the phone on her counter and starts running her fingers through her hair. I unscrew the top from the wine and take a swig straight from the bottle.

"It's all good! I'm just multitasking. I need to leave for work in like ten minutes. What's up?"

"Nothing in particular. I'm just enjoying the great outdoors."

Piper glances away from the mirror and down to her phone screen.

"Babe, it looks like you're enjoying your great backyard. I'm not sure that counts." She laughs as she says it, and I know it's all in good fun, but I groan anyway.

"I don't know what to do. I feel so boring." I know I sound whiny, dragging out the last word, but I also know I'm safe to be as dramatic and ridiculous as I want with Piper. Anything goes between the two of us.

"You could start by seeing other people," she suggests, her fingers twisting in her hair as she makes a tight French braid. "You know, *not* drinking wine straight from the bottle alone at one p.m. on a Wednesday?"

I gasp in mock outrage at the judgment and clutch the bottle to my chest like I'm comforting it. At least, I *thought* this was a safe space.

"Alright, alright. Enough with that." Piper laughs again, and I laugh with her. "You know that I don't have any issues with drinking wine straight from the bottle. It's just more fun if you do it with a friend."

"Yeah, that's why I called you."

Piper finishes her hair and picks the phone back up, giving me her undivided attention.

"You know I'm always here for you, but I can't be *there*, and you need to stop hiding in that house. I'm a little worried about you."

Her concern is heartwarming, even though she called me a hermit.

"I'm ok, I promise. I'm not withering away or anything," I try to reassure her. I really have been dealing ok enough with losing

Mom and the sudden move. And ditching Reid has been fantastic.

Piper scrutinizes me for a moment with a withering glare. When I don't crack, she relents.

"I trust you but do me a favor. Go do something in that weird little town. Anything. It'll make me feel better about being all the way down here while you're all the way up there."

We're on the move again in her apartment. I hear the jingle of her keys and know she's got to go, but won't hang up until she's satisfied I'm alright.

"Ok! I'll text Hannah and see if she wants to hang out."

"Perfect! Tell her and Leslie I say hi!"

I can tell Piper is by her door.

"I will. And thank you, Piper. For giving me a little kick."

"I love you, Alice. Now I've got to go. Your swinging is making me motion sick."

She laughs again when I flip her off, and we both hang up.

I screw the cap back onto my wine bottle and pull up Hannah's number.

ME

Hi! It's Alice. Scott passed along your number, and I'm so sorry it took me a bit to reach out. It's possible I failed friend-making in kindergarten. Would you maybe want to do something tomorrow?

She answers right away.

HANNAH

I'm so happy you texted! I was worried the whole police incident scared you off. I'm at the bakery tomorrow. Why don't you come by to taste-test some new fall pastries?

ME

Seriously?? A thousand times yes! That sounds incredible. Thank you!

HANNAH

Yay! I can't wait!

Well, that was easy. I go to reopen my wine for a celebratory drink, to congratulate myself for friending so well, when I feel a pinch on my ankle. I squash the mosquito with my hand but decide that's plenty of the outdoors for today.

As I head back inside, I hear Jake's back door opening. Looking over, I see him stepping outside with a mug in his hands. His head turns toward me, so I smile and wave. I'm already half inside, eager to give him privacy, but I swear he smiles this time when he nods.

The next morning, I'm finally ready to admit that Piper's demand to go out when she was here was good for me, even though it ended in a police station. It got me to meet Hannah and Leslie, who are just as kind as I remember, and the pastries they've crafted are to *die* for. I shove another bite of apple Danish into my mouth and sink into my chair, cozying up to a hanging vine beside me.

Barefoot Bake is the bakery half of the bakery-slash-bookstore that the couple owns and the most charming place I've ever seen. Everything is dark wood and mismatched. There are plush vintage chairs and an enormous glass case on both sides of the repurposed wood counter space. Small plants sit in all different kinds of pottery on nearly every flat surface, and the air smells like a mix of coffee beans and vanilla.

The wall to the right of the door has an enormous archway connecting the bakery space to the adjacent bookstore, Literary Lake, a place that is similarly mismatched in a way that just seems to fit. The store has new and used books and a rotation of other trinkets and surprises, many of which are handmade.

The names of both places are cheesy as hell, and I'm obsessed.

Hannah and Leslie are perfectly mismatched, too. Hannah's pixie-cut hair is dark, but there's a shock of white above one ear where flour has settled in the pretty waves. She wears a cropped tank with little flowers on it under her overall dress, her arms left bare so nothing will get in her way while she's baking, and I can see a little croissant tattooed on her triceps whenever she turns to get yet another delight for me to try.

Hannah is cottagecore personified, with a love of baking, painting, and flower pressing. She even has freckles across her cheeks and nose. She's sweet, organized, and efficient.

Meanwhile, I don't think Leslie has ever met an athletic activity she didn't like, no matter how dangerous. She's run marathons, completed those intense obstacle courses that involve jumping over fire and had a phase where she considered becoming a professional diver. When she tells me about her summer plans to try "extreme bungee jumping," (isn't regular bungee jumping extreme enough?) I swear I see the color drain out of Hannah's face.

Leslie is tall, toned, and could kick my ass with one hand tied behind her back. She has straight blonde hair, but it's currently twisted up in a large bun so it stays out of her way. I don't think she's remained still for five consecutive seconds since I showed up this morning.

"So," Leslie starts. "How can I bribe you to join the Wilcox Grove flag football team?"

I snort a laugh and nearly choke on my Danish. I'm not sure

I'd even be disappointed if that's how I went. The flaky crust is worth it. I furiously shake my head before gulping my iced chai latte.

"You don't want to do that. If you want me to help your team, put me on the *other* team. I'd destroy them from within without even trying."

Leslie and Hannah laugh, and I'm not sure if they realize I'm not joking. I'm *that* bad.

"That's alright," Hannah says, but Leslie pouts. Hannah ignores her and continues. "Are you equally opposed to *watching* football? That's my role, and I swear it's fun. You sit, trash talk, and eat snacks."

"Wouldn't you know, I'm great at all of those things!"

It's incredibly easy to be Hannah and Leslie's friend, and I find myself thanking Piper again. When she's right, she's right.

That's how I find myself sitting on hard metal bleachers at seven in the morning the following Saturday. The air is damp and cold, so I gratefully accept the paper cup of hot coffee from Hannah. At least the chill should keep the mosquitoes at bay. If not, the industrial sized bottle of bug repellant in my purse will certainly help.

When Hannah huddles by my side, I half wonder if she invited me just to have somebody with whom to share body heat, but as the game gets underway, I realize the invitation was for my own benefit.

Grateful Bob is the announcer for the game, his voice projected from a speaker propped on the bench a row down from him, but I'm not sure he possesses the requisite amount of knowledge for the job. He regularly blurts nonsense, making up yardage distances and talking about home runs. He's also already howled "goaaaaaaaaaaaaaal" twice for our team's two touchdowns and sings along with the music between plays.

As a result, he regularly argues with the refs, which causes the

Wilcox Grove team to come to his defense. Then, the other team shouts about delaying the game, which riles up the crowd to the point where I swear our little field is as noisy as a sold-out NFL stadium. At least we're just as dedicated.

Before I know it, I'm joining right in, booing and shouting along with my Wilcox Grove compatriots, most of whom I've seen somewhere around town, but many of whose names I do not yet know. It doesn't matter, though. When I shouted for the ref to lay off Grateful Bob, they accepted me as an ally without question, with our announcer shouting along with them.

I realize suddenly that it's very likely Grateful Bob is making trouble for his own amusement.

When the roar of *YEAH!* Comes from behind me, I turn to see my new people. I *don't* look for a grumpy lumberjack. But if I did, he wouldn't be there.

Things carry on easily after that. I spend a decent amount of time at Barefoot Bake, reading, crafting, taste-testing, or helping to water the eighty-four potted plants throughout the bakery and bookstore. I go to softball games and pick flowers with Hannah for her to press. I keep looking for the Brawny man, and I keep smiling.

One afternoon, Jake and I end up on our back patios at the same time again. When we catch sight of one another, I smile and wave. He nods at me.

I take a deep breath to steel myself. Now that I have a place in this town, I've been working up to talking to Jake again. I feel steady enough like I can be his friend without accidentally burning down his house or sending his brother to jail or something.

"How's Scott doing?" I shout over before I can talk myself out of it.

I haven't heard from Jake's brother since his visit. Even though I know he's fine and his eye has fully healed from his chats with Piper, I still plan on using him as a plot device in my friendship with Jake. Thanks, Scotty.

Jake seems to start, and he's too far away for me to be sure, but I think he rolls his eyes before trudging over to my yard. He stops at the edge of my patio and surveys me on my swing.

"You know you could have come over like a civilized person if you wanted to chat instead of disturbing the peace, right?" he scolds me, and I wonder if I made a mistake opening my mouth.

Then Jake smirks, and the world stops turning. The movement completely transforms his face, making him look playful, younger. And damn, he is fucking handsome.

I must stare dumbly at him for longer than is socially acceptable before remembering he asked me a question.

"Of course, but where's the fun in that?" I try to match his teasing energy and smile.

I see him swallow hard, watching his throat move.

"Scott's fine. Nothing can damage his hard head."

We talk about nothing of consequence for a few more minutes. Gun to my head, I couldn't tell you a word of what we discussed because I'm too busy drinking him in.

I'm done staying away.

CHAPTER 17

Jake

My mission to maintain my distance from Alice is challenged when she shows up at the nursery without warning late one morning a few days after our backyard chat. She sweeps into the office on a gust of autumn wind with bright eyes and flushed cheeks from the chill that had descended on Wilcox Grove. In spite of the blustery day and the mess of leaves that has basically coated the whole town, sneaking into everything, everywhere, she seems happy.

She quickly chats with one of my sales associates, Tim. People talk a lot in a small town, so I know Alice has been integrating into Wilcox Grove. She seems comfortable talking to Tim, and I wonder if they know one another already. I wonder who else has gotten to know her while I've been as welcoming as a porcupine.

I watch a huge smile spread across her face as she follows Tim's pointed finger and turns toward me. My chest squeezes when I realize that seeing me can make her look like that.

"Hi, Neighbor!"

Her bright voice causes Eli to look up, too. He's also smiling now, but his is much more Cheshire Cat than Alice's. He's deeply engrained in the gossip mill of Wilcox Grove and often supplies me with tidbits about her that he's heard. Through him, I learned that Alice and Hannah are basically joined at the hip.

Thankfully, Alice is fully focused on me and doesn't seem to notice Eli is even there. I preen a little under her gaze, standing from behind my desk as she approaches me.

"Ace. What brings you here?" I silently will my heart rate to calm the fuck down.

"I just figured it was time to come see where you work. Plus, it's October. I *need* pumpkins. Could you help a girl out?"

She looks up at me hopefully, and I nervously clear my throat. I want to say I'd do anything to help her but stop myself.

She pauses at my hesitation, and her face falls. "I can also figure it out myself. I don't want to be a burden."

"No," I say, more aggressively than I intended, eager to remove the sadness from her voice. I never want to be responsible for crushing that spirit. "Sorry— I mean— let me take you out to our patch personally."

She lights up again, just as quickly as she'd deflated a moment ago, and I sigh with relief. I hold out my arm to guide her toward the door, praying I'm about to escape successfully without Eli embarrassing me.

No dice.

Eli nearly dives over his desk in an attempt to get to us before we get to the door, tripping over a box of mulch samples and making enough noise to wake the dead. Alice, unsurprisingly, turns back to see what the commotion is, and Eli pops up like a spring daisy beside us.

"Hi! I'm Eli." He shoves his hand toward Alice, who giggles but takes it.

"It's nice to meet you, Eli. I'm Alice, Jake's neighbor."

"Oh, *are you*? I've heard *so much* about you."

I want to punch Eli in the throat.

"You *have*?" Her head swivels back to me, a grin back on her face, but this one matches Eli's mischievous one. She thinks I'm the one who's been talking to him about her. And I have, a little. But not nearly as much as the rest of this nosy town's population.

Great.

The last thing I need is Eli telling Alice *anything* that I've said about her. Since that first dinner with Eli, he's asked for "neighbor updates" every time I've seen him. I've kept my answers as short and fact-based as possible, but this man can twist "She's taking better care of the house" into a proclamation of love.

How?

Don't ask me.

"We need to go, Ace, or there won't be any pumpkins left." I put my hands on her shoulders and spin her toward the door, giving her a gentle push. She leans back hard against my hands to try and stop her forward progression, but we still shuffle toward the door.

"I can't wait to have a looooong talk with you sometime, Eli!" she calls back over the shoulder, and I can hear Eli cackling until the front door closes behind us.

Once we're outside, Alice stops resisting me, but I keep my hands on her shoulders, guiding her to the pumpkin patch, where dozens of pumpkins sit in happy rows, without a single person perusing them.

"'There won't be any pumpkins left,' huh? It's almost like you didn't want me and Eli chatting. What, worried we'd gang up on you?" Alice lazily walks toward the patch, correctly guessing I didn't want her and Eli talking and, inevitably, somehow conspiring against me.

My lie is obvious, but I couldn't care less. I'm just now realizing this is my first time initiating contact with Alice, and I can't focus on anything but the feel of her in my hands, even through her thick sweater.

She looks over her shoulder at me when I don't answer. I'm more affected by my proximity to her than expected. I'm not sure I trust my command of the English language, so I keep my mouth shut.

"You haven't been talking about me, have you?" she asks.

I find myself smiling in spite of her cheek. As we reach the pumpkin patch, I reluctantly release her shoulders and stand beside her. I swallow and hope my voice will sound normal.

"I'm just looking out for your pumpkins, Ace."

It slips out before I can stop myself.

Alice immediately snorts and slaps her hand over her mouth, elbowing me hard in the side with her other arm. It's becoming too easy to tease her, and I'm not a teasing guy. Taking responsibility for Scott when I was so young made me a serious person, always overthinking what I did or said before I did or said it, constantly hoping that I wouldn't do or say something stupid and fuck him up for life. Alice makes it too easy to just *be*.

"Ok, wise guy. Show me where you keep the good pumpkins. The prize-winning, top-of-the-line Maseratis of pumpkins. I want to make a good impression on Halloween, and I can't have sad, wimpy pumpkins on my porch."

This girl is nuts.

"You won't find any crappy-ass pumpkins here. Might I suggest choosing an assortment of sizes so they can complement one another as well as your home?"

I sound so stuffy, and I have no clue where it's coming from. I guess I want to impress her… with our *pumpkin supply*? Her insanity must be contagious.

"Show me the way, good sir!"

Her laugh carries across the fields, loud and unrestrained.

When the sound tapers off, she adds, "You know, this is my

first time having a porch of my own to decorate? Mom and I always had apartments, then I lived in dorms, and then back to apartments. I want to deck the whole place out, front and back, even if you and I are the only people who will see the ones out back."

"Actually, most people will come to the back of your house because it's easiest to go house-to-house by walking along the lake. You've got the right idea decorating both sides. But, if this is your first time, you should know pumpkins could attract wildlife, so be careful if you leave them outside, especially when it's dark and they start to decay."

"I figured, but I can't *not* have pumpkins. I'm sure it'll be ok."

Her voice has softened, and I can tell she's picturing what she wants her home to look like on Halloween. She looks wistful and authentically happy, and I find myself staring until I trip over a vine and nearly go face-first into a pumpkin the size of my head. Thankfully for my ego, I catch myself.

"Obviously, that one was determined to be picked," Alice says, looking back at the gourd that tried to take me out and completely overlooking my lack of grace.

I can feel my face and neck heat up with embarrassment, but I appreciate her trying to let that one slide. I feel like tripping over my own crop in my own field might get my farmer card revoked or something, and I wouldn't want to lose the nursery so shamefully.

"First pick of the day is a violent one." I bend down to pick up the pumpkin, my new enemy, and make sure my foot didn't damage it. Alice beams at me. We spend a while going up and down the rows of pumpkins, picking a variety of colors and sizes. Periodically, I haul them to one of the wheelbarrows we keep stationed near the patch to help people move their selections more easily.

We fall into a comfortable silence, and her lazy perusal gives me a very reasonable excuse to soak her in. Her hair whips around her, lifting and tangling, but she doesn't seem to mind. I'm reminded of the first time I saw her storming down from her house like a hurricane. She might be from Boston, but there's some wild in her for sure. I like it.

I might like *her*.

Shit.

Once she's selected twelve "perfect" pumpkins, she proclaims she's got enough for a first run, and we head back inside to ring her up. I park the wheelbarrow outside the door and carry a couple of the pumpkins inside. As soon as I follow Alice over the threshold, I immediately shoot Eli a deadly glare. He's halfway out of his chair, eager to cause trouble, but he huffs and sits back down when he sees my expression.

"Hey, Tim. You can take your lunch. I've got this." I move around the counter to take the kid's spot by the computer.

Tim looks a little confused, probably wondering why I'm ringing this woman up, but he also always kind of looks a little confused. I'm fairly certain he's been stoned for several shifts, but he does work hard, and he's a nice kid, so I haven't called him out on it.

"I feel like I'm getting VIP service, here. Grateful Bob told me you own this place, so this can't be normal," Alice comments as I weigh the pumpkins and enter her order into the computer.

Seeing the process, Alice steps outside and returns with two more pumpkins, handing them to me.

"Eli and I own the nursery together," I gently correct. "But, uh, we're both hands-on. So it's really not abnormal. I'm happy to help."

I'm grateful Alice can't see Eli's face from the shop side of the building. His expression would surely give away that I'm full of shit.

Since we hired a full staff, I've only helped haul pumpkins

and worked the register once. That was because half the town and half our employees had the flu. She doesn't need to know that, though.

We continue with our little assembly line until all of the pumpkins have been rung up.

"Well, thank you. I had fun. You'll have to let me know what you think of my decorations when you get home later." Her comment is innocent enough but hearing her say "home" as if it's a place we share short-circuits my brain.

"Hmm," is the noncommittal non-human response I deem appropriate to give. "I— uh, here." I turn the credit card keypad toward her to show the total. I applied a very heavy discount, but she doesn't need to know that, either.

We take a few trips to load the pumpkins into the back of her car.

"Thank you again, Jake," she says once we're finished. She's fiddling with her car keys and absentmindedly walking me back to the door to the offices and greenhouse. "I'll see you around?"

"You're very welcome." I've thankfully regained the ability to use words as I open the door and step inside. "I'll see you later."

Before she heads out, she squeezes by me to poke her head into the office space and conspiratorially says, "Bye, Eli! We'll have to set up our chat another day!"

"Just say when and where," Eli says and then cackles some more. He should consider a career change to being a damn clown.

I point aggressively at Eli.

"You, shut up." I turn to Alice and usher her toward the door. "And you, quit causing trouble."

Her laughter follows her all the way to her car. I only close the door after she pulls away. I look down at the mess of debris I let in, but it really doesn't bother me.

"You've got it bad, man," Eli says

I don't disagree.

I don't disagree.

CHAPTER 18

Jake

It's after eleven when I finally get home, much later than I'd intended. The wind had only gotten worse at the nursery as the day progressed, basically giving us a thunderstorm without the rain. Eli and I spent most of the late afternoon driving thick stakes into the ground around some of the younger trees and tying the fragile ones to the added support. We even dug up and re-potted some of the smaller plants to move them inside the greenhouse, having to rearrange a lot to make room. Even though Tim stayed late to help, it took hours. We did all that we could, so now we just wait and hope most of them make it.

I park in front of my garage and walk around to the front of my house so I can see next door. I am disappointed but not surprised when I see all the lights are out.

Was I going to use her decoration-viewing invitation as an excuse to see her again today?

No.

Maybe.

Yes.

It's for the best that I couldn't. I may have admitted to

possibly liking her, but I'm still convinced pursuing her is a bad idea. She'll leave, and it all will have been for nothing.

Nonetheless, a smile creeps onto my face when I see faint outlines of the pumpkins near her steps.

I suddenly think of the furniture we both have out back and hope it wasn't thrown around during the storm. With enough wind, a chair can cause a lot of damage.

I quietly hurry between our homes toward the lake to see what kind of damage the day did to our patio furniture. At least I know the boats aren't getting beat up. I come to a sudden stop when I clear the side of my house and see my table set on its side, with the tabletop angled against the back of the house and the chairs stacked and laid down. I look over at Alice's patio and can see enough in the moonlight to know hers are similarly secured from toppling or flying around. I smile.

Alice took care of both of our homes.

I'm relieved when I wake up the next morning to a text from Eli saying that things at the nursery are better than we'd expected and almost everything made it. I'm supposed to be off today, so we'll reevaluate what should be re-planted in the fields once both of us are there together. I slept in, but it's still before noon, and I don't have much on the agenda, so I'm not in a hurry to get anywhere. I put on some sweatpants and head downstairs.

I consider stopping by Alice's place to thank her for taking care of the patio furniture but decide against it. A visit specifically for that is a bad idea. I can just thank her next time I see her.

I'm making coffee and grabbing some toast when I hear tires crunching outside but convince myself to stop being so intrusive in Alice's life. I mentally give myself a pat on the back for not seeing who came to visit.

Minding my own business isn't something that should need praise, though. I drag a hand down my face. I used to find it easy to keep to myself. Now, I'm like one of those nosy old lady neighbors that sitcoms love to make fun of.

I sit on my couch and turn on the TV but raised voices outside draw my attention to the window, and I immediately turn it back off. I hear a distinct male voice shouting angrily, and I rush to the window. A shiny sports car is parked diagonally across the gravel.

Alice stands behind the car, facing me. The alarm in her expression is clear as a man towers over her, screaming so aggressively that the back of his neck has turned deep red.

"You think you can just *leave*?! *Humiliate* me like that? You think you can do better?"

I can hear every word clearly, even from inside. I shove my feet in my boots and fly out the door in seconds. I stop on my top step.

"Ace!" I call, keeping my voice calm. "Everything ok?"

Her gaze jerks to me, and the other person spins around. This guy has to have the most punchable face I've ever seen. He's tall, but lanky, with way too much gel in his hair. It's convenient he's wearing a suit since I might use that tie to strangle him.

"We're fine. This has nothing to do with you," he spits at me, his face twisted in an ugly rage. He turns back to Alice, disregarding me. Alice keeps looking at me over his shoulder, even as he starts to whisper-yell at her.

I'm about to reiterate that I had asked "Ace" if everything was ok, when I see him roughly grab her left wrist, and yank, uncrossing her arms. Alice pulls back and shoves him with her other hand, but he holds strong.

"Reid, let GO of me." Alice's voice is clear and firm. "I mean it. We're *over* and you need to *leave*."

I'm down the steps and running to them before I realize what I'm doing.

As I come around his car, I see him shoving a ring onto her left hand, ignoring her protests.

"You've made your point. Stop this temper tantrum and come back home. *Now*." His hiss is low and furious.

Alice flinches and casts her gaze down.

I grab the hand he has on Alice's arm and easily peel back his fingers from their death grip. Once his hand is off of her, I shoulder-check him, and he falls back against his car. I step between him and Alice, facing her.

I gently take the hand that had just been commandeered, spotting the hideous diamond on her finger and the red mark on her wrist. I stoop to look into her eyes as she continues to stare at the ground.

"What the fuck is your problem?!" I hear behind me.

I ignore him.

"Ace, are you ok?"

She nods, but tears glitter at the corners of her eyes. She looks at her hand, and I follow her gaze to the ring.

"I want him to go." Her voice cracks when she speaks, barely above a whisper. She tries to take off the ring, but her hands are shaking. I carefully slip it from her finger and squeeze it in my fist.

"Go inside," I tell her, just as softly. She looks up at me but doesn't move.

Reid puts his hand on my bicep and yanks, presumably in an attempt to turn me around, but I shake him off.

"Go," I repeat. She nods and starts backing away, her fingers slipping from mine.

"You need to back off, *asshole*. She's my *fiancée* and—" Reid puts his hands on me again. I let him turn me this time.

I mentally will him to hit first. My prayers are quickly answered.

The heels of both of his hands connect with my chest as he shoves me.

"You need to back off before I make you."

His threat is laughable, literally. I chuckle, and he pulls back his arm to hit me.

I don't hesitate, swinging until my fist, with the ring still inside, connects with his nose. He falls against his car again, this time grabbing at his face where blood has already begun to gush.

I hear a squeak from behind me and turn to see Alice near her door with her hands over her mouth and her eyes wide in shock. She catches my gaze for a moment before scurrying up her steps and inside, the door slamming shut behind her.

I'm immediately afraid that I crossed a line when I punched Reid, maybe frightening her, but Reid pulls my attention back to him.

"You motherfucker! You broke my nose!!"

I know I didn't. There was no telltale crunch. The guy just has a nose of glass. As he shrieks at me, I feel like I might not have hit him hard enough since he can still speak, and the sound is grating. Maybe I *should* have broken his nose.

I grab the front of his suit and resist the urge to pull on that stupid tie when I heave him upright, and I lean in close.

"Lose her number. Lose this address. She made it clear that she wants you gone, so go."

Again, I keep my voice low and calm, but I let the hatred I feel for this scum drip from every word. The fear in his eyes says he thinks I might kill him.

"Fine!" he sputters from beneath his hands. "Give me the ring and I'll go."

I'm about to drop it on the ground when he adds, "You can keep the bitch. I've already used her, anyway."

I heave Reid up and throw him back into his car, enjoying the satisfying sound of him smacking into the metal. I run toward the lake between my house and Alice's until I'm close enough to launch the ring into the water. Watching it drop under the surface with a satisfying "plink," I turn back toward Reid, who is slumped against his car, mouth hanging open. Blood drips from his chin onto his fancy suit.

I come back up the incline with long strides. Reid fumbles with the car door behind him, seemingly afraid to tear his gaze away from me until it's open. He's in his seat when my hand reaches out and grabs the door he's trying to close. I bend low to look at him.

"I never want to see you near her again. Do you understand?" It's a rhetorical question. I stand up and slam the door. He starts his car and hits the gas, his tires spinning for a second before they gain purchase, and the car lurches away.

I look toward Alice's house and see the curtain beside her front door shift.

There's a small step ladder beside the patio and lights hanging from the home. She must have been decorating when Reid showed up.

I wait, but Alice doesn't come back outside. I look down at the blood on my hands and drag myself back to my house to take a breath before I try to talk to Alice.

So much for keeping my distance.

Fuck.

CHAPTER 19

Alice

I slide down the wall next to the door and land with an ungraceful thump on the ground. I look down at my left hand and see my finger and wrist are red. I think back to the grip Reid had on my forearm like my bones were being ground against one another, and I'm disgusted. I move my wrist and fingers gingerly, and I'm grateful that, while a little sore, things seem to move the way they're supposed to.

I feel a wave of shame over having let such a brute into my life and for having put up with him for so long.

I still can't believe Reid came all the way up here, expecting to haul me back to Boston. Actually, he expected that I'd go willingly and maybe even thank him for going through all that trouble to find me. I don't even know how he got the address. It must have been written on something I left behind. This was more effort than I remember him ever putting into our relationship while it still existed.

I cover my face with my hands. Jake came to my rescue. He *just* accepted that I wasn't here to "bring down the neighborhood," and now my presence invited *that* fiasco right outside of his home.

I'm humiliated.

I'm also a little jealous that he's the one who got to punch Reid in the face. I hope he didn't hurt himself on Reid's hard head. I can't help the deranged laugh that bursts from me. The shot of ill-timed glee over Reid getting what he deserves dissipates as quickly as it arrives.

Jake and I had been doing so well, I think. Yesterday was a *really* good day, and now I feel like I've ruined it all. I want to thank him for what he just did, but he went straight back to his house as soon as Reid left. I doubt he wants to see me.

I heave myself off the floor and walk the few steps over to my couch, pulling an oversized blanket off the back and cocooning myself in it. As the shock of Reid's visit starts to wear off, my tears start again. Reid took so much from me, and now it's like he might have taken the peace I feel at Barefoot Lake, too. I mourn the joy I fear I've lost until I cry myself to sleep.

I wake some unknown amount of hours later to knocking on the door. Based on how frantic the tapping sounds, I expect I slept through at least the first attempt to get my attention. I jolt upright when the events of this morning come back to me.

Did Reid come back?

"Ace?" My stomach flips when I hear Jake's voice edged with worry, calling through the door. "Ace? Are you in there?"

I launch myself off the couch and stumble when my legs get caught in the blanket I'd been wrapped in. I'm at the door in seconds and pull it open. Based on the glowing golden-hour light outside, I clearly slept at least several hours.

"Ace." Jake's breath leaves him in a rush, and his shoulders visibly lower once he has eyes on me. "You scared me. Are you ok?"

He steps forward, and I back up so he can come inside. I close the door behind him. He scans me from head to toe, but his eyes linger on my left wrist, where Reid had held me. Thankfully the red splotch faded away.

Jake's words finally process in my muddled brain.

I *scared* him?

"Jake, I'm *so, so* sorry. I feel like I'm always apologizing to you, but I really do mean it. I had no clue he was going to come here and cause such a scene—"

I stop when Jake's hands land on my biceps.

"You cannot blame yourself for the choices made by a bad person," he says the words slowly and clearly, like he's trying to make them sink in. "Are you ok?"

I shrug noncommittally and avoid Jake's eyes.

"Ace…?" he urges. "What was that out there?"

For the first time, I don't feel the urge to hide what Reid was like. Even though my friendship with Jake is new and tenuous at best, I *want* to tell him what happened. He saw what Reid was like and chose to defend me. He came back. New friend or not, I trust him.

I look over my shoulder at the couch. Jake takes the hint, releasing me and going to sit down. I follow and sit beside him. I twist my fingers in my lap and look at them rather than Jake, but I start talking about what it was like with Reid.

"He was really good to me when we first met. He acted like I was his whole world, and he wanted to give me everything my heart desired. But things changed when he started working."

I tell Jake everything. I tell him how Reid excluded me from his work life and regularly left me behind for corporate commitments, even the ones that were optional. It got to the point where I'd be surprised if plans with me *weren't* delayed or canceled. I talk about Reid's mind games, and how he'd twist my concerns until I agreed that it was in my head or my fault or something I should really be grateful for.

Jake stays silent while I go on and on. A couple of times, I glance up at him, and find his eyes on me and his expression blank, but his hands are fisted tightly together between his knees.

I even tell him about the nastier parts — how Reid would take every chance he could to tell me how lucky I was to be with someone like him, someone smart, attractive, and successful. That he put up with my loud mouth and annoying friends like nobody else would. I kept giving more and more to try to be worthy. I made myself small, pliant, and quiet.

It was awful.

Then, I get to our last fight before I left.

"Mom always said funerals were expensive and depressing and that she didn't want one. Instead, she wanted her ashes spread in the ocean, and a celebration of life wake so her friends could say goodbye together. I took her ashes to the ocean myself and organized something for the people she knew in Boston. I was a mess, and I'm so sorry I didn't think to invite people from Wilcox Grove. I didn't realize the life she had up here."

I pause, but Jake waves me off, forgiving my oversight on behalf of the whole town, and urging me to keep going with the gesture.

"Reid never showed. He promised he'd be there, but something came up at work. He said he'd be late, and then later, and later... and then he said he'd just see me at home. He didn't even leave work early to meet me. He strolled in that night like it was just a regular day. He even poured himself a drink before saying hi to me.

"He got angry when I said I was upset. He said it wasn't a real funeral, and I was being a drama queen. I'd never been more furious with him, and the sheer disrespect he had for my mom kind of opened my eyes to the terrible man he'd become — or maybe always was. All of our old issues, the way he tore me down constantly, everything came out of my mouth, and I couldn't stop it. I'm not sure I wanted to.

"Something in him kind of snapped. He said the nastiest things about me." I swallow and force myself to keep going before I chicken out again. Hot tears well in my eyes. "He said I was worthless, and Mom was a lunatic. He said it was good she died so she could stop dragging us down."

Jake starts next to me, and I look up at him again. His eyes are pure fury, but they soften when they meet mine.

"What happened next?" he asks gently.

"I was shocked. I told him to get out. I think he might have even surprised himself because he just left, unlike today. By morning, he still hadn't come back. I tried to call so I could tell him I was done, but he sent me to voicemail. So, I left his ring and a note explaining that it was over on his nightstand and shoved the key to the apartment under the door after I locked up. I took whatever would fit in my car and came here."

A heavy silence fills the room for at least a full minute after I finish speaking.

"I should have punched him harder," Jake finally says.

"I…" I don't know how to answer. I look up at him. "Is your hand ok?"

I remember the surprisingly loud sound of Jake's fist connecting with Reid's face. It was startling.

"Are you seriously asking about my *hand* right now?" Jake looks incredulous.

I shrug again.

"Yes?"

He sighs and composes his face into something more neutral.

"You're worth a thousand of him."

"I wish I could see how terrible he was sooner. I'm so sorry to involve you."

"Don't worry about me. I'm not sorry for hitting him, but I didn't mean to frighten you. That's why it took me so long to come by. When you didn't answer my call or text, I wasn't sure if you'd want to see me. I must have started to come over here a dozen times before finally making it." He moves to stand, maybe to move away, but I reach for him, just touching his fingertips with mine.

"I'm sorry. I must have slept through my phone buzzing. I wasn't frightened," I say softly because loud noises suddenly seem out of place, and this conversation feels important.

But it's true. Jake doesn't frighten me.

"You were my knight in shining armor. Thank you."

Jake is looking at our touching hands, and a flush rises above the collar of his shirt. He rubs the back of his neck, which is his nervous habit, I've noticed.

"It was nothing. I did what anybody would do if they saw somebody hurting somebody else. That jackass should try picking on somebody his own size." Now Jake is looking anywhere *but* at me. He drops my hand. "It wasn't a big deal."

A wave of frustration hits me, and I stand. I walk around to the back of the couch to put something between us.

"Why do you always do that?"

Jake looks legitimately confused.

"Do what?"

"Downplay when you do something good? You did it when you talked about taking care of Scott and helping my mom and every time you've helped me since I got here. I think you're so damn scared of anybody knowing you care that you try to convince even yourself that you don't."

I realize the irony of raising my voice at somebody right after thanking them for saving me, but I can't help it.

"It *was* a big deal. To me. It was a *huge* deal for you to defend me like that. So, do you care, Jake? Or is it all in my head?"

"I *care*." Jake's on his feet now, too. I think his voice was louder than he intended because he lowers it as he continues, prowling toward me. "Sometimes, you drive me crazy, but I fucking *care* about you."

His eyes are on fire, lighting up every nerve ending in my body. I must lose control over myself because I'm suddenly launching myself at him, standing on my toes, with a hand around the back of his neck to pull him down toward me and the other on his chest, and I'm kissing him.

His body is as solid as I'd thought it would be. All of him is warm, and his lips are soft on mine. He angles his head slightly to the side, and I spring back.

I clap my hands over the lower half of my face, speaking through my fingers.

"Oh my god. Jake, I can't believe I did that. I'm—"

CHAPTER 20

Jake

The second Alice's lips touch mine, I completely lose my ability to think. All I can do is feel. One of her hands is searing into the skin behind my neck, and the other must feel the erratic beat of my heart leaping around my chest like a bucking bull. She smells like cinnamon apples, and I could drown in that scent. Her lips are warm and soft and *demanding* and — fuck, if I wouldn't give her anything in this moment.

But that's all it is, a moment.

Before I can give her anything, she's gone. At some point, I must have closed my eyes because I have to open them to see the panic shining in Alice's.

I barely hear her apology because I neither need nor want it. For that second, I had *her*, and I'm not ready to give her up yet.

I take one large step toward her, gently taking one of her wrists in each of my hands, pulling them away from her face, and lowering her arms. I release her so I can slide one hand into her hair and put the other on her lower back to haul her against me.

My kiss is not apologetic, and it is not hesitant. I pour every ounce of want I've had for her since I laid eyes on her into that kiss. My fingers tangle in her hair, and a part of my brain notes how soft the strands are before I squeeze my fingers and angle her head back for better access. Alice makes a soft, content sound low in her throat, and I know it's mine. I press into her further, claiming, needing… *more.*

Alice's fingers find my belt loops, and she pulls, hard. She shifts back, taking me with her until she bumps into the back of her couch. Thank God this woman is tall because all she has to do to sit is lift slightly on her toes. I wrap my arm further around her waist, tighten my grip, and lift until she's more settled and I can stand between her parted thighs.

Alice yanks on my belt loops again, making sure there isn't a breath of space between us, and my hand falls to her ass. I silently thank the universe for whoever invented elastic leggings when my fingers press into her soft skin, and the heat of her drives me insane. Her thighs tighten around my hips, and she hooks her ankles together behind me. The movement presses my hardening erection against her, and I have to swallow my groan. Her hands slide up my sides and under my shirt. She squeezes, dragging her nails against my back, right above the waistband of my pants.

I bite her bottom lip in response, and a breathy sound rushes out of her.

"Jake," she breathes against my lips, a prayer, and I can't stop the grin spreading across my face.

I lean my forehead against hers, both of us breathing heavily.

"Jake," she repeats, still gasping for air.

Something in my brain tells me not to get carried away. Alice deserves more than a hormone-fueled fuck seconds after we admit there's more between us than neighborly concern.

I lean back and look down at her, even as her hooked feet behind me keep me close to her. Her hands are still against my skin under my shirt, and she begins lazily sliding her fingers back and forth. I'm not sure she even notices she's doing it, but goosebumps rise down my arms. I can't help but shiver.

I untangle my fingers from her hair and reluctantly slide my hand from her ass and up her arm until I'm cupping her face in my hands with my thumbs along her jaw.

"I— I don't—" she stumbles, trying to figure out what to say. Her eyes dart around my face. I'm not sure what she sees there or what she's looking for, but she's still smiling, so I'm not too concerned. It's almost like she's embarrassed about being so pleased.

"It's ok, Ace," I say, rescuing her. "It's been a very long day, and I should go."

Her face falls slightly, but I know it's the right — the responsible — choice. I'd happily lose myself in this woman immediately, but I don't want to fuck things up, and she's had an emotional rollercoaster of a day. I should also probably sort out what's happening in my head, too.

"But I'll come back in the morning, and you can show me what you did with all those pumpkins, ok?"

I look around the room and for the first time, notice orange twinkle lights above the television, and almost an entire wall full of paper bats, even going so far as to spread across part of the ceiling. The more I look around, the more bits of Halloween and fall I see in the colors of the blankets, throw pillows shaped like ghosts and pumpkins, and the little fake autumn leaves scattered on every flat surface.

Her lips quirk again, and I hope she understands that this is *not* a rejection. I could just as easily see her decorations on my way home. But I don't want to. I want to come back and see *her* again.

"Then I guess I'll finish setting up outside, too."

I kiss her lightly on her forehead before reaching behind me to unhook her ankles and forcing myself to take a step back. Her fingers slide against me as I separate from her, and it's delicious torture.

She's still smiling at me, a little dopey, matching how I feel. I try to discreetly adjust my sweats to hide the raging erection just having her mouth on mine caused, but she catches the movement easily. I see the pride on her face over how she affected me and shake my head.

"Good night, Ace."

"Good night, Jake."

The cool air outside is a slap on my skin. I feel like I'm on *fire*. Denial and distance clearly didn't stack up against the want I have for Alice. The crisp air clears some of the fog from my head, and I briefly worry if I've made a huge mistake opening this door with Alice. Then, her smile flashes in my mind, and I shove those thoughts away. I'm on cloud nine, and nothing can bring me down.

As I step away, the glow of twinkle lights around her door flickers on. I look over my shoulder and see Alice coming down the front stairs, arms filled presumably with more decorations for her yard.

When I get back to my house, I call Mark's Pizza in town and order two pies with everything on them, one for me and one to be delivered to Alice's house. It seems like a melted cheese kind of night.

It takes me a while to fall asleep, but when I finally do, I dream of Alice and what could have happened on the back of that couch if I had stayed. My morning shower is ice cold.

I feel like an anxious teenager as I flit around my kitchen at the crack of dawn, full of nervous energy. I want to see Alice as soon as possible, but it's still way too early, and I don't want to disturb her or seem needy. I try to pass the time, but I'm too jittery to eat and there's nothing to clean. Even the inside of my microwave is spotless.

I finally decide to take out some of my own Halloween decorations from the garage, remnants of mine and Scott's childhoods. Alice had been so excited about decorating her place, and it got me kind of excited about decorating mine.

Next thing I know, I'm in my driveway surrounded by open boxes, with decorations from various holidays spilled everywhere, and I swear a string of orange lights is trying to strangle me. I may be a clean freak, but I'm not organized. I'm tying a skeleton to the outside of my staircase in an attempt to get him to stand up when I hear Alice's door open and close. I whip around so quickly that my abandoned knot pulls free, and the skeleton's skull smacks against my own.

Smooth.

I rub the sore spot as my eyes find Alice coming toward me. She laughs at my lack of coordination, and she's stunning. She's in an oversized burnt orange sweater, boots, and another pair of those goddamn black leggings, so she looks like a walking Halloween decoration herself. It takes me a second to figure out what she's carrying, but when I recognize it as a couple of slices of Mark's everything pizza on a plate, I grin.

"Breakfast?" Alice says, holding out the plate when she reaches me.

"That's for you, Ace."

"One each, then?" She takes one slice off the plate and nudges the other toward me again. I have half a pizza in my fridge right now, but I can't turn down her generosity a second time, so I accept the offer. I'm surprised when it's warm. I figured she'd be a cold-pizza-for-breakfast kind of girl.

"Sorry I didn't bring enough for your friend." She gestures to the skeleton crumpled on the ground behind me. "If I had, maybe he wouldn't have assaulted you."

"So, my potential concussion is your fault?"

"Oh, you'll be fine. You've got a hard head." We both polish off the pizza and she sets the plate on my bottom step. "I'll help before you hurt yourself."

After we finish with the skeleton, she wordlessly wraps the banister with lights I'd left coiled on the porch.

As we work, I eagerly wait for her to bring up last night, but she just keeps going from project to project, only speaking to ask if I'd mind if she started playing music from her phone. I guess the silence bothers her as much as it bothers me.

The music doesn't help.

I thought her coming over this morning was a good sign, like she didn't want to wait for me to come knock on *her* door again, but now I'm not so sure.

Does she regret the kiss? Is that why she's not saying anything? I settle in for a full internal spiraling session.

I feel like I should say something, but I want to follow her lead, and it feels a lot like she wants to pretend like the kiss never happened. The nervous energy I woke up with transforms into plain old nervousness, and I feel like the longer I go without speaking, the worse it gets.

We hammer gravestones into the lawn, secure wooden bats hanging off the roof, and prop plastic jack-o-lanterns up on the sides of my steps. We even move around to the back of the house and deck out the back patio. All without talking. It's horrible.

I can't take the quiet anymore. It's so uncomfortable that I feel like I want to crawl out of my own skin. I'm working to pluck up the courage to ask if she'd like to have dinner with me when she slaps her hands on her thighs.

"There! Now it looks almost as good as my house!" Her excitement is fake, and the loud statement bounces awkwardly around in the uncomfortable yard.

I look over at her house, finally taking in her decorations. It feels like defeat after I went out of my way not to look last night and all morning so she could give me the grand tour. I'd pictured her smile while she explained each piece, not this terrible plastered-on grin. Since I've seen the real thing, this fake joy is just painful.

The space is cozy, with far more pumpkins than the small yard needs, but also spooky, with fake webbing stretching around both banisters leading up to her door. Several witches are around the yard, some around a cauldron, two more playing a board game, and another that looks like it face-planted into her home while flying on a broomstick. She also strung purple and orange twinkle lights wherever she could reach. It was clearly a labor of love.

"I'm happy to take second place. Yours looks fantastic." The compliment feels like sand in my mouth. This is not how the morning was supposed to go.

"Thank you!"

She's so chipper that I find myself wishing for the awkward silence again. Thankfully — miserably — it returns. We just stare at one another. I take a deep breath.

"I was wonder—"

"Well, I'd better get going!"

We speak at the same time.

More awkward silence.

"Thanks for your help," I say.

"You're very welcome." She collects her plate. "Um… bye."

She basically flees back to her house.

CHAPTER 21

Alice

The last few days have been torture. I thought the first weekend after meeting Jake was painful, with his brutish attitude and my long list of unfortunate screwups, but the last seventy-two hours have been so much worse. Losing Jake's warmth after getting the tiniest taste made the days feel colder and the nights darker.

After he gave me the most mind-scrambling kiss of my life, we had one of the most awkward mornings. I can hardly think about the "decorating incident" without cringing. Even my best playlist didn't help hide the blaring silence between us. I haven't seen Jake since I fled his front lawn, and I'm afraid he's gone back to coming and going when he knows he can avoid me.

If he regretted kissing me, why wouldn't he just say so? Are we still children who just avoid things until they go away? I don't want to be, but I couldn't bring myself to just ask, afraid a blatant rejection would hurt even more.

I've avoided Hannah for the past few days, too. She's very perceptive, and I was afraid she'd see something on my face that screamed, "I kissed Jake!" and ask about it. I was, and still am, too mortified about the kiss and subsequent rejection to hash it out, but after going full tilt into Wilcox Grove life, the solo life has felt particularly lonely.

I try to put Jake out of my mind and relish in the excitement of Halloween day. For no reason in particular, it's one of my favorite holidays. I've always decorated the inside of my home with whatever I could find, but having a whole house and yard to decorate this year triggered a new rush of endorphins. I've been baking my feelings away, so the whole house also smells like pumpkin bread.

I'm stocked with about twelve thousand pounds of candy and tiny plastic toys, eager to send kids back to their homes fully loaded for a year's worth of sugar rushes. This *will* be a good day, whether Jake is immature or not.

Suddenly, I know exactly how to vastly improve my day. I wrap up one of my loaves of pumpkin bread and head out to go visit Grateful Bob. He's so relaxed and ridiculous that I feel confident he won't notice if something is off with me.

I head through my yard and down to the lake to take the unofficial pathway that cuts along the shore, meant for just the lake's residents. It'll have a lot of traffic tonight as families use it for the easiest access to the lake houses for trick-or-treating.

As I walk around the lake, I feel like I must be living in a fantasy world. Since I'm bundled up in the squashiest sweater ever, fleece-lined leggings, and a wool beanie with a fluffy pom pom on top, the chill in the air is refreshing. Leaves of the most vibrant reds, oranges, and yellows line the dirt path beneath my feet as more fall around me. I can smell the fires people have lit in their homes. The world feels peaceful and quiet like this place is protected from the daily nastiness that's out there.

My mind jumps back to Jake. I was elated when he kissed me the other night. After he had been running hot and cold since we met, he'd finally given a clear signal that he was interested, and *all* of me had responded to it. It was easy and natural to surrender to him. I *wanted* him to take whatever he wanted from me. The way his touch lit me up made a fully-clothed kiss feel like so much more.

Jake's departure after had felt a bit like ice water being dumped on my head, but I wasn't terribly surprised. Jake is Mr. Responsibility, and immediately letting me take him to my bedroom wouldn't exactly have been responsible, even if I'm certain it would have been fun. After he left, I found myself replaying our few minutes together over and over in my head. If I closed my eyes, I could still feel his lips smiling against my own. My toes curled at the thought of how they would feel elsewhere on my body.

I was giddy even before I got my surprise pizza delivery, which warmed all of me in a completely different way. It had been a while since somebody had taken care of me. I think that made the complete shutdown the next morning that much more heartbreaking.

When I get to Grateful Bob's house a few minutes later, I shove Jake back out of my mind. I spot Grateful Bob on his back porch as I start walking up the steps that lead from the path to his house and happily return his wave. He heads inside before I reach him, coming out with a steaming cup of coffee. He holds it out to me as I settle into my usual chair beside him and set the bag with the bread on the table. The mug has a loon on the side above the words "We're all a little loony."

I happily accept the cup and take a long drink, noting he added my usual half-cup of creamer. Grateful Bob and I have had several coffee chats since I came to Wilcox Grove. The man is one of the biggest gossips I've ever met, and he's an effective one, too. Because nobody would suspect him, they're eager to tell him *everything*, and since he's lived here so long, he knows *everybody*.

"Is this pumpkin spice?" I raise my eyebrows in surprise.

"Damn straight." Grateful Bob grins. "I'd say it's an old man's guilty pleasure, but I don't feel the slightest bit guilty. This shit is delicious."

I laugh easily with Grateful Bob. He's right. The brew is spectacular. Grateful Bob spots the new package on his table.

"What did you bring for me, today?" he asks.

Historically, I've always brought some treat when I see Grateful Bob. The first few times, he insisted it wasn't necessary, but stopped resisting after I came by with a pan of buffalo chicken tater tot casserole that the two of us absolutely destroyed.

"Ta-dah!" I open the bag with a flourish. "Pumpkin bread." I retrieve the Tupperware and offer it to Grateful Bob. He takes a piece and consumes a quarter of it in one bite.

"Mmm!" He makes a satisfied sound around the bite and holds up the "ok" sign to show his approval. After he washes it down, he pins me with a look that I immediately dislike. I feel busted.

"What...?" I quickly run through what I could possibly be blamed for and come up with nothing. "Whatever it is, it wasn't me. I swear."

His expression softens, and he smiles kindly.

"No trouble here," he assures me. "I'm just on to you. Your cooking matches your mood. Pasta is when you're feeling cozy. Spicy food is when you're bored. And baking... baking is when you're in your head. You going to tell me what's eating you up inside?"

He takes another bite of the bread like he didn't just call me out on my shit. My mouth falls open in what I tell myself is well-faked offense. It's possible I was completely wrong about Grateful Bob's level of attention to detail.

"I'm not in my h—"

"You are. I'm old enough to have seen it all, and your acting needs work." I guess it wasn't that well-faked at all. The man is a mind reader.

Rude.

He could have lied at least a little bit.

"It's…" I huff. I don't want to admit I'm this bothered by a *boy*. I look over at Grateful Bob, but he's just munching on his pumpkin bread, patiently waiting for me to come around. I don't want to seem petty, and I certainly don't want to get into details. I think I'd die of embarrassment and briefly wonder if this is what it would feel like to talk to a father.

"It's Jake. I thought we were… getting somewhere… but the next time I saw him, it was the most awkward encounter of my life, and I really don't think that's an exaggeration."

"Ah." That's all Grateful Bob says for a bit, and I wonder if that's the end of the conversation, but he eventually takes a deep breath and continues. "Jake got dealt a tough hand early in life — both he and Scott did. What those two boys became as a result is real special, but let's not pretend that losing their parents so young and Jake becoming a guardian when he was still just a kid himself didn't change them."

I sit back in my chair. I already know about how Jake stepped up for Scott. Of course it changed him. It would have changed anybody.

Grateful Bob continues.

"It's almost like they went in opposite directions. Scott gives love freely, never wanting to miss out on a single minute of happiness because he knows how quickly it can end. Jake hardly gives love at all.

"After their parents died, Jake came straight home from college. I heard the lawyers kept offering to send Scott to some other distant relative they dug up, but Jake wouldn't hear of it. He kept in touch with his friends for a while and tried to take classes nearby, but it was hard, and he ended up working at that nursery instead. He was suddenly in a completely different stage of his life from everybody he knew. He was a parent at twenty to a twelve-year-old. One by one, except for Eli, his friends just kind of drifted away. Relationships are also hard when you're putting somebody else first, second, and third, but that's what Jake did for Scott."

I twist my hands around my mug, the warmth from the steaming cup suddenly feeling muted. I think my heart is breaking in my chest.

"Jake just kept going. He became ok because he *had* to be ok for Scott. I'm not sure Jake let anybody really in until your mom moved up here, and she had to fight for it. I think she saw him as the boy he never got to be, and, eventually, he trusted her. When she left, unfair as it is, I think he felt like another person abandoned him. He's guarded and might always be."

My eyes burn with unshed tears. I hadn't really thought about how incredibly lonely it must have been for Jake after he moved back home for Scott. My chest hurts at the thought of him having to figure out how to parent his brother while letting everything he was familiar with slip away. I look up and blink rapidly to keep from crying.

"Well, I feel like the biggest asshole ever," I admit.

"Hey." Grateful Bob's voice is firm, and his hand falls on top of mine on the chair's armrest. I look over at him and see his serious expression. "None of that. There might be a reason for Jake's issues, but that doesn't mean that you need to put up with a lack of communication or less respect than you deserve. He's a grown man now, and if he wants a special girl, he needs to figure out how to earn her regardless of life's challenges. I told you his story to help you both, not to give him an excuse to keep you at arm's length. Never forget your worth."

I flip my hand over and squeeze Grateful Bob's. I think his kids were very lucky to have him. And now I am, too.

Grateful Bob and I gab about lighter topics and have lunch together before I head back home. When he tries to bring up my job in Boston, I clumsily change the subject. I've been hiding from Boston and my impending return in the spring. The realization of how much time has passed since I left sends a pang of guilt through me. I need to plan a visit down soon.

For now, I want to continue that escapism by carving a few of the pumpkins into jack-o-lanterns so I can fill them with tea lights after dark. Sadly, those will have to get trashed, recycled, or mulched — wherever pumpkins go to die — tomorrow to avoid attracting animals, but I think the effect tonight will be worth it.

Once I'm home, I line up some of my favorite pumpkins on a newspaper-covered table and dive in.

Scooping pumpkin guts — and cutting out different expressions — takes a few hours, but I have so much fun creating different faces. I have minimal artistic talent, so they're all a bit wonky, but I think it gives them character. Plus, now I've got a few pounds of fresh pumpkin seeds roasting in my oven.

I spend most of the afternoon eagerly awaiting the first knock on the back door, but I still jump when it finally comes, leaping from the couch and clumsily sliding on the floor in my tights. After carving my pumpkins, I finally changed into my costume. To match the coven of witch decorations surrounding my house, I'm in sheer black glitter tights, a bodysuit with puffy sleeves, a black mini skirt with a jagged bottom edge, a long velvet cloak, and a pointed witch's hat. I slip on black pumps to complete the look at the last minute.

I open the back door to a chorus of "TRICK-OR-TREAT" and just about *melt* at the adorable children before me. I load them up and watch as they scurry down my steps and back to their parents waiting on the shoreline path.

I'm about to close the door when I notice another group of kids coming across my yard from Jake's house. I look over and see Jake poking out of his back door. In a red flannel shirt with the sleeves rolled up and dark jeans, I think he's *seriously* dressed up as the Brawny man. He catches me looking and leans out further. He even has a roll of paper towels in his hand. I can't help but chuckle — it's a *great* costume for him with his dark hair and natural scruff.

Stiffly, Jake raises the hand holding the paper towels and jerkily waves at me. I wave back, hopefully less awkwardly, but I doubt it.

So glad to see things aren't weird between us anymore! I cringe at the interaction.

The next several hours repeat the process dozens of times, and I mean the *whole* process. Kids arrive, I nearly burst with how cute it all is, I hand out fists full of candy or toys, and every single time I catch Jake's eye, we repeat the same *painful* wave. By the time the trick-or-treaters stop trickling by, I'm basically jumping out of my skin with how uncomfortable those waves have been.

Like, *seriously*?!

Finally, I flick off my string lights and step outside to collect my carved pumpkins so I can store them indoors before I get rid of them tomorrow. After I blow out the last candle from the jack-o-lanterns, I look over and see Jake, shutting down his yard. So help me god if he—

He waves.

I can't take it anymore. I pile my armful of pumpkins on a patio chair and stomp across the gap between our houses with a flashback to our first meeting playing in my mind. He stops working when he sees me coming and stands to await my arrival.

"Look, I get it. You've got commitment issues, or maybe

you're just not that interested. It's fine, really. I'm a big girl, and I can handle the rejection. But this?" I gesture between us and do an over-animated wave with my face screwed up. "*This, I cannot handle*. But I *like* you. You're good, even when you're surly, and I can't *stand* the awkwardness. So please, *please*, I beg you, just make it *stop*."

I'm breathing hard when I finish my plea. He can accept my friendship, or he can cut me off completely. Either would be better than perpetual weirdness. He blinks at me a few times.

"Have you eaten?"

That wasn't one of the responses I'd prepared myself for.

"What?"

I frown as my brain processes his question.

"Food. Have you had food? Besides inhaling Halloween candy, I mean."

Busted.

"Um… no? Not since lunch."

He hesitantly smiles.

"Would you like to have a late dinner with me?"

"I— I—" I stutter, still reeling from the change in attitude and unexpected invitation. "Yeah. I'd like that."

Now he's fully grinning.

"I have a feeling our wires got crossed the other day, so to avoid another case of miscommunication, this is a date."

CHAPTER 22

Alice

Instead of a table, Jake has a large custom-made kitchen island with two bar stools along one side. Another two stools are pushed against the wall, waiting to be needed. I'm currently inhabiting one seat at the island, stationed across from where Jake has piled a mess of ingredients and tools on the butcher block top.

I'm impressed… and kind of confused. I think Jake has been quietly humming while he collects whatever he needs, and I'm still not sure what he meant when he said our wires got crossed, or why he's so chipper, but I love that he called this a date.

"You eat everything, right?" He quickly peeks over his shoulder to check in with me while he's preheating the oven. I nod. He comes back to stand across from me and holds my gaze.

"Excellent," he says.

His eyes sweep down the part of me he can see above the countertop, and he licks his lips. I'm immediately very aware of the fact that I'm still in a little sparkly witch's costume and slide the tall hat from my head. The corners of Jake's lips quirk up in the shyest smile.

Jake has collected two bell peppers, two gigantic tomatoes, an even larger eggplant, ground beef, a bunch of spices, and everything for a salad. He picks up one of the tomatoes, which suddenly looks small in his hand. This man really is massive. He carefully slices the top off the tomato, keeping the disc intact, before scooping out the seeds and guts from the base.

Now that Jake has set down his roll of paper towels, his costume looks like it could be an everyday outfit. Knowing what I do about Jake so far, I expect it likely is. The flannel suits him, and his rolled-up sleeves suit me. I'm so mesmerized watching his hands work, seeing the muscles in his forearms tense and release with each precise movement, that I'm startled when Jake speaks.

"I'm sorry," Jake's voice is clear over the quiet thud of his knife against a cutting board while he chops the scooped bits and starts on a pepper.

"You're… sorry?"

"You were right before. It's been awful since the other day, and if I'm understanding now, there was no reason for it."

He pauses and looks up from his work to catch my gaze again. I roll my lips together to keep from interrupting him.

"You were also right — and wrong — about me. I've got issues, but they aren't commitment-based, and this *definitely* isn't a case of not being interested. I honestly tried to stay away from you. At first, it was because I thought you were a menace, but then it was because I realized how much you *weren't*, and it was difficult for me to admit how much you affected me. It meant it would hurt that much more if things went sideways. Convincing myself to take the risk was hard, but once I did, committing to trying something with you wasn't difficult at all."

I gasp at his admission, and he pauses again, his hands stilling this time, too. He makes eye contact now, and I'm frozen in place by the intensity of his gaze.

"I like you, Ace. In fact, I think you're magnificent."

"You do?" My voice is quiet, but Jake's grin spreads wide when he nods. "Then why did you shut me out when we were decorating your house?"

"I didn't want to make assumptions, and I was waiting for you to bring up the kiss."

My mouth pops open in disbelief. Is it possible it was really that simple?

"But *I* was waiting for *you* to bring up the kiss."

Jake nods again. "I figured that out when you were putting me in my place on my back patio earlier."

"So, this was all completely avoidable?"

"Yup," Jake pops the "p" and chuckles at the lunacy of what we did entirely to ourselves. "I'm not looking to repeat something like that, so I've decided to just be blatantly clear. I'm following your lead here, but I like you and want to spend time with you."

He's the one being vulnerable, but I'm the one blushing.

Communication is kind of sexy.

"I'm on board with that."

"Good." His shaky breath is the only noticeable sign that he's nervous, and I find it endearing.

"Can I help with dinner?" I reach for the head of lettuce, but he lightly swats my fingers.

"Absolutely not. I'm taking care of you tonight."

This time, Jake's flush matches my own.

"Here." He wipes his hands on a towel and retrieves a bottle of red wine and a wine key. "If you *must* help, you can open the wine and then hold your glass so you keep your mitts off the food prep." His smile has morphed into a smirk, and I decide I like playful Jake.

He stares at me pointedly until I begin my assigned task. Only when I'm twisting the corkscrew into the cork does he turn to retrieve two wine glasses. And only after I've taken a sizable gulp from my glass does he go back to work.

He moves around the kitchen like he could complete this dance with his eyes closed. His hands work efficiently hollowing out the other tomato and pepper and the eggplant, which he cuts in half due to its height. He cooks the stuffing stovetop before filling everything and popping them in the oven. I'm back to being entranced, watching how his body moves so easily, an impressive feat for somebody his size.

Briefly, I tear my eyes away from him to survey the space around me. The house's general layout is the same as mine, but where I inherited a chaotic hodgepodge style from my mom, this space exudes calming warmth. Other than the overhead kitchen light, the space has gentle glowing lamps, presumably connected to dimmer switches and turned low.

The inside of Jake's home matches the outside world around us, with furniture in various browns, grays, greens, and tans, with splashes of blue for the lake and the sky. The door to the room beside the kitchen, a library in my house, is closed, and I wonder how he's decided to use it, but then my eyes fall on the stairs. I quickly turn back to my wine when my mind reminds me that his bedroom is just a handful of steps away.

Down, girl!

I take another gigantic gulp from my glass.

Jake sets two bowls of salad down and claims the stool next to me, turning to face me until his knee presses into the side of my thigh. He reaches out and tucks my hair behind my ear, running his thumb along my jaw as he draws his hand back.

"Bon appétit," he says.

Every ounce of awkwardness is gone, and a warm heat fills me. I could claim it's from the wine, but it's all Jake. Still, we end up talking way too late.

Whether it's that knee against my leg, Jake's hand on mine, or his shoulder brushing my skin, we never stop touching. It's the best torture. I don't know how I make it through the rest of our evening without jumping his bones, but I deserve an award for my restraint.

Everything Jake made is delicious, but when he leaves me across my threshold with a too-short kiss and a firm squeeze of his hand on my hip, I find myself wishing he was on the menu instead.

CHAPTER 23

Jake

I'm standing in the fields at the nursery the next morning, but my mind is miles away, picturing the way Alice looked last night, sitting in my home as a glittering little witch. There was nothing outwardly promiscuous about her costume, but her stockings had these seams up the back of each leg and my fingers itched to trace them right under the hem of her skirt.

Last night was about getting to know one another on purpose, rather than just through random snippets of our pasts, gossip, or inconsistent attempts at friendship — my fault for pushing her away and avoiding her for so long. I just wanted to enjoy her presence in my space, something I haven't shared with anybody other than Scott in a long time. Still, I couldn't help but touch her. She's like a magnet, and I wasn't resisting very hard.

I battle between wanting to take things slow, knowing she just got out of a disaster of a relationship with city boy, and wanting to be as near her as possible. I have already wasted enough time trying to keep my distance. She must have some kind of life waiting for her back in Boston, and if she intends to return to it at some point, I want to make the most of the time I do have with her. I keep thinking back to what Eli said the first time he and I discussed Alice. I don't *have* to be so cynical about other people. With Alice, I'm going to try not to be.

When a hand lands on my shoulder, I nearly jump out of my skin. I spin around to find Eli staring at me wide-eyed, hands raised in surrender.

"You ok, man? I yelled your name like six times." Eli looks legitimately concerned.

"Yeah, sorry. I'm good." I shake my head.

I really hadn't heard him yell a thing. Alice has taken over my every waking thought. Her laugh, her glowing eyes, her wit... those damn stockings.

"Oh, I can see that," Eli says through a laugh. I look back at him and see his expression has softened.

"What on earth are you talking about?"

"It's all over your face, brother. You've finally admitted you like Alice, haven't you?"

I immediately fix my face into its usual stony expression, not having noticed it was any different. I don't dignify his prying with an answer.

"Was there something you actually needed?"

"Nothing important. Anything you'd like to share about neighbor girl?"

I shoot him a glare, but he's not deterred.

"Come on. There's no way nothing's happened."

"You're as bad of a gossip as Grateful Bob."

"How dare you," he says. "I just want to know for me, to look out for my best friend."

He's laying it on thick.

"I'm fine. So, I'm still not talking about it."

"I just want to help."

"With your years of relationship experience?" I ask sarcastically.

Eli is one of the best guys I know, always has been. But he's not a relationship guy. There's nothing wrong with that. He's happy and always upfront with the women he's with, but nothing ever lasts more than a few days. Tourist season is his Christmas.

"Use me for what *not* to do, then."

"Fine," I huff. "But if I hear any of this around town, I'm burying you in the fields, and nobody will ever find you."

Eli motions like he's zipping his lips closed, and I roll my eyes.

"Alice and I… *talked*. And we're trying things out." There. That should be sufficient. I start walking back toward the offices.

"That's *it*?! You've got to give me more." Eli catches up to me easily and gives me a friendly shoulder bump.

I keep my lips sealed, hoping he'll tire himself out and give up.

"You've been dancing around her for *weeks*, stomping all over this town like it dishonored your ancestors. Today, you've basically got roses coming out of your ass, and you're really going to act like this is no big deal?"

"Yes."

"Don't do this, Jake. Let me be your friend and share in your excitement. It's ok to fucking feel something."

I huff a sigh. I want to keep this thing, whatever it is, with Alice safe, but I'm not being fair to Eli. He'd never do anything to hurt me or put my joy at risk.

"It was a good talk," I offer, trying to figure out how to open up without oversharing something private.

I can tell by Eli's expression that he's not satisfied. He looks annoyed. Then, he smirks.

"I'm sure it was. But you've described her like she's a damn hurricane. I bet she's a real wild one in be—"

Eli cuts off when I pivot and plant myself in his pathway, one finger held up in front of his face.

"You really don't want to finish that train of thought. You will treat her with respect," I snarl. Eli and I rarely disagree, and it's even more uncommon for us to fight, but I'm ready to throw down if he keeps going.

"Ha!" Eli shouts, triumphant. "I knew it!"

He's grinning, and I'm confused.

I lean back, giving Eli some breathing room, and cross my arms.

"And what exactly do you think you've proven? That you're a pig?"

"What? No. I just wanted you to express something, to admit that this matters. That *she* matters to you."

"Yes. Fine — she matters! What's your point?"

"I'm just happy for you, man."

I turn and walk away from him, still not seeing why he's so elated. Again, he matches my stride.

"I *am* sorry about what I said about her. I really was just trying to get a rise out of you, so you'd open up a tiny bit."

I look at him sideways before giving him a swift smack upside the head.

He laughs.

"As an apology, I'll keep an eye on things for the rest of today. Why don't you go see your girl?"

I curtly nod and peel off to head to my car, already digging my keys out of my pocket.

"You're still an ass," I say loudly enough for him to hear.

"I know, and you love me anyway!" he calls back.

He's right. I do.

At home, I throw my truck in park and stop by the garage to grab my toolbox before I jog over to Alice's house. As I pulled in, I saw her car parked beside her house, so she should be home. The walk to her door would take less than a minute at a normal speed, but I can't help going a little faster to see her a few seconds sooner.

I take the few stairs to her door and knock. I feel myself buzzing with unspent energy at the thought of being around her again and resist the urge to bounce on the balls of my feet. I'm a grown-ass man and need to act like it.

The curtain beside the door shifts, and I see Alice's face peek through. The delighted look that spreads across her face has my stomach twisting in knots.

I did that, and I feel damn lucky for it.

The door opens a second later, and I feel a wave of contentment wash over me.

"Hi." Her greeting is breathy but warm. Two letters, but they sound perfect from her.

"Hi." And I'm back to feeling like a schoolboy presented with the opportunity to talk to the pretty girl.

Alice catches sight of the toolbox in my hand.

"What do we have here?"

"I'm hoping I can help turn the tides in what I assume has been an ongoing battle with this demon of a house."

Her eyebrows lift in surprised amusement, but she steps aside for me to pass.

"Then, by all means, come on in!"

She watches me as I pass her, and I can't help but look over my shoulder to keep my eyes on her another second longer. Once she shuts the door, I take off my shoes and set them beside hers under the bench behind the door. It's a little thing, but I like seeing them side by side.

I move further into the house and pull a rag from my back pocket. I unfold it and set my toolbox on it on the table before flipping open the lid. Grabbing a screwdriver and a mallet, I kneel on the floor beside the oven. I give the right side of the warming drawer a swift hit with the side of my fist and slide it open.

"How'd you know?"

I look up and see Alice with her hip leaning against the countertop, arms and ankles crossed, eyes trained on me.

"This house has been like a hydra for as long as I can remember. Fix one thing and two more suddenly decide to stop working. This drawer has been playing the game for *years*. Rain never thought taking the drawer apart to fix it properly was worthwhile. So, it would eventually fall back out of alignment no matter how many times I smacked it. It'd have been a better investment to just get a new oven ages ago, but as long as it keeps fighting, so will I." I laugh because my nemesis is an oven drawer. "It's the principle of the thing, and now I'm going to rip it apart and straighten the track properly."

"Honorable even when it comes to an oven. You're a strange man, Jake…"

She pauses, and I look up at her. Her brow is furrowed.

"Wait, how do I not know your last name?"

"You know, it's been a long time since there was something about me that somebody in this town *didn't* know. This is kind of nice." I work on disconnecting the drawer from the track it attempts to slide on so I can whack the pieces straight again.

"You know, I could always ask literally anybody and find out. Or I could just snoop through your mail."

"You could, but there's no need." I glance up at her again. "I have no desire to keep things from you. It's Preston."

"Jake Preston." She smiles sweetly like she's enjoying the feel of my name on her lips. I immediately decide that I do, too. I remember her saying it like a prayer when we kissed the other night and wonder how it would be to hear her scream it.

Get a hold of yourself, Jake.

I sharply turn my focus back to the oven drawer. Now that

I've detached the drawer completely, I lean forward to peer into the cavern below the oven and evaluate the janky drawer track within. It's dusty, and the air is stale. I concentrate on how entirely unsexy an oven is to keep my thoughts from drifting to Alice and my desire to pull my name and other sounds from her.

"What's the verdict, doc?" Alice's voice is playful, exuding simple happiness. It makes me want to play, too. To let go just a little bit.

"Definitely a demon." I shift the mallet into my left hand and employ some expert percussive maintenance to persuade the track back into a straight line. "But I think we can handle it."

"Can I help?" Alice goes to push off the counter, but I give a casual wave over my shoulder.

"This one should be good… for now." I reassemble the drawer and stand, brushing off my knees and moving to stand in front of her. "Next?"

"You're going to regret offering your services," she says with a devilish grin. She pulls her phone out of the back pocket of her jeans and opens the notes app to one labeled "The House's Charm." The list of bullet points on her screen is amusingly long.

We begin to work our way through the list, one by one: something in the ice maker rattles, the lock on the study window is extremely sticky, and the water pressure in the downstairs sink is abysmal.

I try my hardest to stay focused on each project, but it's nearly impossible with Alice so close. She's curious and interested, and I feel her everywhere – when she leans over me to point at whatever I'm fixing while she asks a question, when her squeal of delight fills the room after we triumph over the house, when she places a casual hand on my forearm, lighting up my nerve endings like Fourth of July fireworks.

Every part of her is energetic, making every part of me feel alive. She's eager to help, to learn, and to *praise*. When Alice focuses on you, she gives you her all, and I'm flying high as the object of that attention. I keep my hands busy to help resist the urge to wrap them around her waist and haul her against me so I can worship her the way she deserves. I want her, but more than that, I want to wait until she's ready for that. Being in her presence is enough, even if I'm a walking live wire.

After I reinforce the wobbly banister, Alice looks up the stairs and pulls her bottom lip between her teeth. I raise my eyebrows to encourage her to identify the next project.

"The sliding closet door won't stay on its tracks." She pauses for just a moment. "… in my bedroom."

She immediately blushes, and I feel a spark of hope that I'm not the only one here who is maybe struggling to keep control tethered. I step aside and hold out my arm to direct her up the stairs.

"After you."

Picking up the toolbox that has moved around the house with us, I go after her. I realize my mistake the second I turn. She's a few steps ahead of me, and her ass is nearly at eye level.

As I follow her upstairs, I think of the feel of her in my hands. I force myself to look down and start mentally reciting the states in alphabetical order.

I can't get past Connecticut.

We get to the second floor, and the hallway feels narrower than it ever has in my house, even though the two layouts are identical. She reaches into the doorway of the master bedroom and flicks the light switch on the wall.

I step forward to enter the room right as she decides to slide through the doorway, and we find ourselves chest to chest in the rapidly shrinking space. I look down as she looks up.

"Oh! Sorry…"

Her words are breathy as she seems to gulp air into her lungs. I shift back so she can go in first.

"No, my bad."

God, give me strength.

I look around Alice's bedroom slowly. Her bed is made with decorative pillows in various shades of blues and greens carefully arranged against the headboard, and the carpet has lines from recent vacuuming, but the top of her dresser is a mountain of pictures, books, jewelry, water bottles, and anything else she could fit on the surface without causing an avalanche. There's a squashy chair with an ottoman on one side of the bed, a throw blanket balled up, and art and pictures on the walls. The space is warm, lived in.

I find Alice standing near the closet, with its sliding mirrored door clearly hanging lopsided. She looks at me like she's waiting for my evaluation of her space.

"I really like your room," I say honestly. It feels juvenile to say, but it's the truth. I like the space and everything else about her.

She visibly sighs with relief and blushes when she murmurs her thanks. Maybe it's not so juvenile after all to just tell the nice girl when you like something about her.

"Hopefully, this won't taint your opinion of the space." Alice moves aside to give me access to the door. I take a flashlight from the toolbox and click it on to get a better look at what's happening on the tracks overhead. The inside door seems to have gotten jammed half on the track for the outside door. I give the door a firm shake, but neither one will budge and there's only a narrow opening where you can get into the closet right now.

"I've basically been squeezing in there and finding my clothes by flashlight," Alice explains.

"Would you mind standing in there now and supporting the door from the inside? I'm going to have to angle the door pretty far to try to dislodge it, and I don't want it to fall in and crack the mirror."

Alice nods and presses herself into the narrow opening. "All set!" she calls from within.

I quickly unscrew the guide on the floor to give me more freedom to move the doors before lifting and angling the inside door, trying to get it to fall back into its own track. It takes some heaving and having Alice push and lift from inside the closet, but it eventually gives and thuds into place. I lower the base of the door so it hangs on its own and tentatively slide it open.

It moves with ease, revealing Alice squished between hangers in the dark space. I feel like I tower over her. Again, I find myself looking down as she's looking up, and I swear her eyes darken at the sight of me even though the light is now washing over her from the room behind me.

The collar of my shirt feels too tight, the scratch of the denim of my jeans too rough. I don't hear the heater going, but it must have just kicked on because I swear the temperature in the room is shooting up.

It's just a second, but her eyes flit from mine to my lips and back. Like earlier, she pulls her bottom lip into her mouth. I swear she's actively *trying* to test me. She moves to take a step back, seemingly forgetting she's in a closet, and her heel catches on a shoe.

She stumbles, the hangers clanging together noisily around her shoulders. My hands dart out, gripping her elbows and pulling her forward until she instead falls against me, her hands on my biceps.

The air rushes out of her in a soft "oh."

Time slows and, unlike in the doorway a few minutes ago, neither of us pulls back. My hands are still on her elbows, with my fingers pinned against her ribcage, and I swear I can feel her heart hammering inside her chest. I hesitantly rub one thumb back and forth on her arm and feel her shudder in response. I release one of her arms and place a finger under her chin, lifting until she looks up at me.

She blinks twice.

Then, her hands are in my hair, and she's pulling me down to meet her lips.

Thank fuck.

CHAPTER 24

Jake

It feels like my soul falls into her as we crash together, the smell of her drowning my senses when I breathe in sharply through my nose. She inches forward, ushering me back. I gladly relent, taking her with me until the back of my knees hit the bed, and she pushes against my chest harder. I sit roughly, pulling her down with me, and one of her knees comes to rest on each side of my hips.

She rolls her hips against me, long and slow. My fingertips press into her soft thigh and the hard muscle beneath. My other hand moves to her waist and slides up her side, bunching the material of her shirt as I go.

Alice breaks our kiss, throwing her head back as she arches into me, and her hands find my shoulders. She's ticklish. I run my thumb against her ribs just beneath her breast, and she bucks against me, eyes like fire.

"Quit stalling," she hisses, and I grin.

"I've already told you, Ace. No miscommunication here. I want to be sure you're sure about this. I don't want to rush you after everything with—"

"I'm sure. Trust me."

"I need you to tell me what you want."

"You, Jake. I want you."

She punctuates the request by rolling her hips again, hard. My hands tighten further as I clench my jaw, but I stay still. I try to go back to listing the states, but I can't think of a single one. Her writhing body pressed against mine is short-circuiting every thought in my brain. I focus hard just to be able to speak.

"Specifics, Ace. I want to hear the words. Now, tell me what you want." My voice sounds rough and deep in my ears.

"I…" Alice groans dramatically and rolls her eyes. I'm not sure she's ever had to voice it before. Her pupils are blown wide when she finds my gaze again. "Please…"

"I'll help you, but I still need to hear you say it," I offer the compromise, and she nods eagerly. I palm her backside and stand, taking her with me before turning and laying her down on her back. I lean over her, pressing her into the mattress, with the ridiculous pile of pillows haloed above her head.

She releases one hand to weasel it between us and find the button on my jeans, but I press down and trap her there. I have no doubt she can feel how hard I already am, even through my jeans.

I click my tongue like I'm scolding her.

"Not yet," I admonish.

"I want to make you feel good, too."

I want to say that I don't know what messed up partner made her think that taking care of her wouldn't make me feel good, but Reid's face flashes in my mind, and I immediately understand.

"Trust me. I feel incredible."

I lean down and run my nose along her neck up to her ear. She turns her head away and sighs softly, just as responsive as when I'd teased the same spot last time.

"Do you want me to kiss you here, Ace?" My teeth graze her ear as I breathe the words against her skin.

I feel her nod again.

"Use your words, Ace."

"Yes…" The word lazily spills from her lips, like it's a struggle to form the sounds.

I drag my teeth down the column of her throat and kiss the hollow at the base. She squirms wildly beneath me, and it feels like a reward. I press my hips down harder to hold her still because as good as she feels writhing against me, a man can only take so much. I lick across her collarbone until I reach the neckline of her long-sleeved tee. I bite the material and pull it away, so it snaps back when I release it.

"And how do we feel about this shirt?"

"Off. Please, take it off." Her hand, still stuck between us, clenches and pulls at the bottom hem of her shirt. I lift up to follow her instructions, but she rips the shirt over her head before I can.

I take a moment to drink in her curves.

She's wearing a simple nude bra, but she could be wrapped in a strip of ratty old fabric and still look like a goddess. Her skin is smooth and soft, with a few beauty marks dotting across her chest. I want to memorize every single one of them.

I look up and see Alice watching me expectantly like she's again waiting for my evaluation.

"You are perfection, Ace."

She blushes all the way down to her breasts.

"Tell me what you want," I say again.

She giggles and slaps her hands over her face. I swear the redness on her skin darkens. I drag my finger up her side, from the waistband of her jeans to the band of her bra, and she leaps around beneath me. When her skin erupts in goosebumps, I see her nipples pebble underneath the fabric.

"Tell. Me. What. You. Want." The words come out as a demand this time.

Alice peels back her hands.

"Touch me. Kiss me," she whispers the command, but I'm still proud of her.

"That's my good girl," I praise before placing a kiss against the skin right above the button on her jeans.

I lick up to her belly button, where I kiss again. Her back lifts off the bed as she arches towards me. I slide a hand into the gap beneath her and flick open the clasp on her bra. I slide both of my hands up her body, pressing my thumbs under the fabric between her breasts where I pause.

She lifts her head to look down at me, frustration clear in her expression. I raise my eyebrows because she knows what I'm going to say.

"Tell me what—"

She rips off her bra and grabs both of my hands, pressing them into her soft skin and moving one of my thumbs to brush against her hard nipple.

"I *want* you to touch me, Jake," she nearly growls the order at me, and I can't help but grin.

"*There* you are."

I roll her nipple under my thumb, relishing the moan that breaks from her lips. I slide up her body to flick the other with my tongue, and she tightens the grip she still has on my hands. She's warm and responsive, twisting and molding against me. One hand flies back to my hair and grips into a tight fist. I feel it like a jolt of electricity through my body.

I think I might be obsessed with this woman.

"Jake—" My name is a plea on her lips. "Jake. I need more."

I give a sharp nip to the skin under her breast before kissing it after.

"Shh," I murmur against her skin. "My needy girl. Whatever you want."

"Please, Jake," she begs. "I— I need you…"

"You never need to beg," I assure her softly. I pinch both of her nipples, tugging them just a bit before releasing them. I work my way down until she sucks in a sharp breath, and my thumbs slip under the waistband of her jeans.

"Just ask. Do you want me between these pretty thighs?" I kiss that spot above my thumbs, and she groans.

She opens her mouth but says nothing. I nip the skin, not enough to hurt, and her head flies back against the bed.

"Yes!" The answer bursts from her.

As a reward, I pop open the button on her pants and drag down the zipper without further teasing. I stand to remove her jeans completely. She props her feet on the bed to lift her hips and shimmy them down. I pull the material off her legs, catching her socks and removing those, too, leaving her in a pair of charcoal cotton panties with a lace band around the top. She snaps her legs together as soon as her jeans are off, pressing her thighs against one another for some relief.

"Perfect," I whisper again, reverently. "You are perfect."

I take one delicate ankle in each hand and persuade her legs to separate so I can reclaim my place between them. I run my hands along her calves until I'm cupping the back of her knees. I feel unworthy with my calluses catching on her soft legs, running my thumb over a scar on her left knee.

"I fall down a lot. It's fine." Alice is impatient, and I love it. I press a kiss to the mark anyway.

I squeeze her legs and roughly yank her down until her ass is right at the edge of the bed. She squeals at the sudden change of position and props herself on her elbows in time to see me sink to my knees and drape one of her legs over each of my shoulders.

I turn my head to kiss the inside of her thigh and feel her shudder beneath my touch. A flush immediately stains her skin from my beard. I touch the spot softly, and her leg twitches.

"Ace… does that hurt?"

"I like it," she breathes. "Don't stop."

I brush my face against her leg again, and she repeats her shudder, murmuring softly.

"You're teasing again," she complains. "I want you to touch me, *please*."

I move my hands up her thighs and press my fingers under her panties until I can splay my fingers across her abdomen.

"Fingers or mouth?"

"Huh?" Even the confused sound is music to my ears as she sinks into her bliss.

"Fingers or mouth, Ace?"

"Mmmmmmm…" For a moment I don't think Alice will respond, but she delights me again. "Both."

I run my thumb down her center, pressing into her to my first knuckle.

"You're so ready for me, Ace." I withdraw my finger, spreading her wetness around her opening, and slide back in.

Alice throws her arm over her face, turning so she can bury her eyes in the crook of her elbow.

That won't do at all.

I press a kiss against the cloth of her panties, just above my thumb still inside her. She is divine.

I remove my finger and yank her panties down her legs before resuming my position with one of her legs thrown over each of my shoulders. She whimpers in anticipation, and her need urges me on.

Before the sound from her has stopped, my mouth is back on her with the flat of my tongue tasting her, bottom to top. She cries out when I drag my teeth over her clit and then suck. Her ankles cross behind my back, but I hold her thighs apart. I start rubbing my hands up over her thighs while my tongue works between her legs, dragging up and down, pressing into her.

I look up and see her chest heaving, but her arm still covers her face.

I sit back.

"Come on, Ace. Let me see your beautiful face."

She violently shakes her head. I move my fingers between her legs, tracing around her opening but barely touching her.

"Please?"

She raises her shaking arm just enough to peer down at me. I press a kiss to her clit as my fingers keep teasing her.

"More."

I run my middle finger through her wetness, sliding up and down. She flings her arm down to her side, where her fingers immediately tangle in the comforter and clench.

"That's my girl."

I slip my middle finger into her and pump it twice before adding a second finger and lowering my mouth back to her clit. Clamping my lips over her, I suck, hard.

She tries to thrash, but my other arm is banded across her abdomen, determined to keep her in place.

"Oh *GOD!*" she cries, and I'm grateful the only house nearby is my own empty one. Her sounds are mine and mine alone.

"It's just me, baby girl," I say against her skin before turning to kiss her inner thigh.

I slow my pace with my fingers, curling them slowly inside her, rotating my wrist to find exactly what she needs. My thumb moves to her clit, and I press in patient circles, shifting my finger so I can drag my tongue along the sensitive bud.

Alice hums a content sound, but her breath hitches partway through. I repeat the motion, and she gasps again.

"Do you want to come for me, Ace?"

"Yes, please. Yes."

"What did I say about begging, pretty girl?"

I gradually speed up my movements, pressing more purposefully against her clit with the heel of my hand, and Alice's breathing picks up speed.

"Your tongue, please."

I doubt Alice is fully aware of what she's saying, but I'm happy to oblige nonetheless, moving my tongue against her, biting and sucking as she cries out. One hand finds my hair yet again, and that pulse runs down my spine. My cock presses uncomfortably against the rough material of my jeans.

It would seem I have a thing for having my hair pulled. I take a deep breath through my nose to compose myself.

Alice's ankles are still hooked behind my back, and she tenses again as her thighs press around my ears, squeezing my head. If this is how I go, I'll die a happy man.

I feel it the second Alice comes. Her fingers on my head splay wide before she drags her nails along my scalp. Her walls clamp around my fingers as I keep moving them, letting her ride this out.

Soon, she stills, and the only sounds in the room are her panting breaths. I withdraw my fingers and run the pad of my thumb along the outside of her opening. Her whole body shivers. I wipe my other hand down my mouth and kiss her stomach, just below her belly button.

"You did so well, Ace. So, so well."

I unhook her legs and move up the bed to lie next to her, dragging her further onto the mattress. She immediately turns towards me, nuzzling her face into my neck and flinging a leg over my hip. I slide an arm under her and grab the comforter to wrap around her.

Her hand begins moving down my chest, toward the hardness she must feel pressed against her leg, but I gently twist her fingers with mine and still her movement.

"Not today, Ace."

She lifts her head slowly from my shoulder like it weighs a thousand pounds.

"But I want to do something for you" she protests.

I shake my head and smile at her.

"Trust me, that was incredible for me. *You* are incredible for me."

CHAPTER 25

Alice

I feel boneless and blissful curled against Jake. There's a chance he finger fucked my brain right out of my head, and I'm ok with that. I nuzzle against him for one more moment before leaning up to kiss his lips. I can taste myself there, and it makes me feel a little slutty in the best way possible.

I smile against his lips, give him another peck, and drag myself up. I'm extremely aware of my nakedness when I slip out from under the folded comforter, but the look of appreciation in Jake's eyes when I glance back over my shoulder at him gives me confidence.

"I'll be right back," I assure him before scurrying quickly to the bathroom. As I wash my hands after, I *know* he won't have bailed, but I feel an urgency to get back to my room anyway.

Relief washes over me when I get to my doorway and see him sprawled across my bed, with his hands folded behind his head, looking awfully pleased with himself. I flush at his pride, even though he earned it.

It's been a while since I've had an orgasm that satisfying or an orgasm from somebody else at all. Reid was… selfish, and I never really had the urge to encourage him to keep trying. The sex with him ending sooner rather than later was just fine by me.

Jake, on the other hand, had played my body like his own personal instrument, seemingly content to continue working me as long as it took. The effort did not go unnoticed.

I pad over to the bed, flop on my stomach beside Jake, and scooch over until I'm fused with his side and absorbing his heat. I drag the edge of the comforter back over me, creating a cozy place for me to burrow. In spite of Jake's assurances, I feel guilty not reciprocating. He looks over at me and a line appears on his forehead when he furrows his brow.

"Hey, stop thinking like that. I'm *extremely* happy," he says, reading my mind.

"After all of *that*," I vaguely wave my hand around. "I feel like I owe you."

Jake quickly rolls onto his side, facing me and catching my chin so I look directly at him.

"Please hear me when I say this. You *never* owe anybody anything in bed. *Ever.*"

His tone is serious, and his insistence encourages me to believe him.

"I mean it. There will be *plenty* of time for more later, but this was about me appreciating you, and I am so grateful for the privilege."

He pauses again, and his words settle.

"Do you understand?"

I smile and nod. "Yeah."

"Good girl."

I shiver again, and he pulls me against him again, engulfing me and the bunched-up comforter in his enormous arms.

I wake up the next morning with a smile on my face, but alone in my bed. Yesterday, after enjoying some a-plus cuddling from Jake, I reluctantly dressed so we could go downstairs for some food. It was blissfully ordinary to share my space with him.

Unfortunately, Jake had to go back to the nursery for a couple of hours in the evening. He stayed at his house after that because he wanted to get up with the sun to go in early, and he didn't want to wake me. He promised that would give him leeway to take another half day, and he planned to be back in the early afternoon.

I head over to Barefoot Bake to see Hannah. I've been texting her a bit, but I think an in-person visit is due, even though it's cold as crap outside.

Hannah looks up when I enter the bakery, and her eyes narrow.

Play it cool, Alice.

I trust Hannah and believe she would keep anything I tell her to herself, but I haven't told Piper about the new progress with Jake yet, and she needs to be my first confidant.

"You good?" Hannah asks vaguely when I get to the counter.

"I'm great," I say honestly.

"You'll tell me sometime?"

"Yup."

"Alright. I'm here when you're ready."

I told you. It's easy being friends with Hannah.

Leslie is trying to pick her winter sport of choice for the year, and Hannah is terrified of all the options, so I happily listen to her unload while I sip some cinnamon apple herbal tea. Then, I water all the plants, read some, and head home.

By lunch, I'm eager to see Jake again, and I'm trying not to let myself worry that he will blow me off and stay at work because "something came up" the way Reid did time and time again.

At 12:45, my phone buzzes, and my heart sinks. Jake said he would be over by one and the text is from him.

JAKE

> Ace – I'm so sorry. Tim is running late, so I'm stuck here for a few extra minutes.

I flop onto my couch and fall to my side, a little embarrassed by how crushed I feel. I grab the remote and turn on the television, not really seeing what's on the screen. At least he texted with an excuse. Reid rarely did. I still have my phone in my hand, just waiting for the next text saying he can't come over after all.

A bit later, a firm knock on the door makes me jump. I roll off the couch and trudge a few feet to the front door.

"Yeah?" I mumble as I open the door without checking who is there. I guess it didn't take long for the city-girl suspicion to leave me.

"Well, that's hardly the excited 'hello' I'd hoped for." Jake's voice sounds like a laugh, and my eyes jump up to his.

I blink, but Jake's image seems solid — not a hologram. I'm surprised to see him, though. I think I really did prepare myself for him to cancel.

"Jake? What are you doing here? It's only…" I check my watch. "1:04."

"I'm so sorry I'm late. Can I still come in?" He smells like pine and fireplaces, and I notice he's still in his work boots and the thick coat he wore when he helped me select pumpkins. He must have come straight here from the nursery.

"Of course you can!" I hop aside when I realize I'm in his

way and let him through. "I'm sorry. I just thought you said you were going to be late."

"I was. I said I'd be here at one." He cups my face with one of his cold hands. My shiver has nothing to do with the chill. "Forgive me?"

I pop up onto my toes and press my lips to his. "There's nothing to forgive. Thank you for texting me to let me know."

The bar must be in hell, but Jake's concern over being less than five minutes late has my heart singing. He gives me basic consideration, and I'm weak in the knees. I feel ashamed for assuming he'd behave the same as Reid when Jake never gave any indication that he thought Reid was anything other than trash.

Jake has a dazed smile on his face when I lower my heels back to the floor, and I silently promise not to make assumptions like that again. Jake clears his throat and seems to refocus.

"I wanted to come in to say hello first, but I want to head back outside and collect some of your pumpkins. The carved ones are turning, and I don't want any surprise wildlife visitors popping up. Can I have the key to your garage to stack them over there for now?"

I take the key off the hook behind the door and drop it into his awaiting palm.

"I'd offer to come outside and help you, but it's cold, and I don't want to." I grin at him. Being taken care of really is nice.

Jake rolls his eyes at me but drops a kiss on the top of my head before heading back out. I make some hot cocoa, so I'm ready and waiting once he steps back inside. He shudders before taking off his coat and boots and tucking them away.

"You're right. It *is* cold." He greedily reaches for the steaming mug of liquid chocolate that I hold out to him. He takes a big gulp, somehow not burning his whole mouth. Then he takes my mug from my hands and sets it with his on the kitchen table.

He looks down at me with hooded eyes, and I take a step toward him like a moth drawn to a flame. He places his hands on my hips before quickly sliding them under my shirt and pressing his freezing fingers against the warm skin of my lower back.

My eyes fly wide as I squeal and leap forward into him, trying to get away from the sudden cold. He tightens his embrace and even tries to flip over his hands as far as he can to warm the backs, too. I playfully shove at his chest, and he releases me with a full-body laugh.

"Evil!" I jab a finger at him before rubbing my back, trying to encourage the feeling to return.

His feigned innocence is completely foiled by his inability to stop laughing.

"I don't know what you mean. I was just trying to warm my poor, poor hands."

"For that, your work starts with the downstairs toilet today," I huff, scooping back up my cocoa and cradling it against my chest like it's a lifeline.

Even though Jake's trick was a rude surprise, playful Jake is my favorite. From everything I've seen and heard, he seems to spend his life wound as tight as he can stand. I'm proud to be the one to help him let some of that go, even if my warmth is a temporary casualty as a result.

It turns out I need a new rubber doodad to make the downstairs toilet stop running at all hours and a couple of new hinges for the cabinet doors that hang wonky. Jake offers to go to the hardware store alone so I can stay cozy at home, but that makes me feel like a lazy schmuck, so I bundle up to take the ride with him. I smile when I see his truck parked in front of my house like he didn't even want to waste time walking from his house to mine when he got here.

Instead of being a stubborn mule, I gladly accept Jake's chivalry as he hurries to open the passenger side door for me, something I now realize he did whenever he could beat me to it, even when he wanted to shake some sense into me. Once he's shut me in the cab, I scooch over to sit in the middle seat beside him, like a lovestruck teenager. The smile on his face when he climbs behind the wheel tells me that he doesn't mind my silliness one bit.

As soon as Jake turns the car on, I immediately start fiddling with his radio, but he doesn't say a peep about me messing with his stations. He places one giant hand on my thigh and squeezes in the most delicious, possessive way.

We don't talk on the short drive into town, but it's like night and day compared to our previous silent, awkward, awful drives. This time, I'm giddy and unashamed of my joy. I even proudly sing off-key with the radio. At a stop light, Jake leans over to kiss my temple but wisely keeps his mouth shut about my terrible singing.

Once we park outside the hardware store, Jake finally removes his hand from my thigh, just to hook it around both of my legs so he can slide me along the bench seat toward him as he gets out of the truck. He easily lifts me and sets me on my feet before tucking my hair behind my ear. As a tall girl, I'm not used to being so easily moved. I feel manhandled, and I like it.

Jake closes the car door, revealing Tim, the cashier from the nursery, stopped dead in his tracks in the doorway to the hardware store, slack-jawed. He looks much the same as he did the day I met him: kind of dazed, maybe stoned. His face splits into a shit-eating grin.

I look over my shoulder to make sure there isn't something fascinating behind me. No dice. Tim is floored by us. I turn back and awkwardly wave at him. Jake follows my confused gaze over to the doorway and rolls his eyes.

"Nosy busybody," he grumbles. He turns back towards me but gazes vaguely over my shoulder like he's considering something.

"Fuck it," he finally says, taking my hand firmly and leading me to the hardware store.

My stomach swoops yet again at Jake basically declaring us as *something* to his employee and maybe the town. I've been here long enough to know everybody will have this new gossip within the hour. I feel like a prize that Jake is proud of.

As we approach, Tim shuffles out of the store so we can slip past.

Tim opens his mouth, but Jake cuts him off.

"Not. A. Word."

Before the door closes, Jake barks, "Take a picture. It'll last longer."

The second the wooden door clicks shut behind us, Tim erupts in excited laughter. A second later, it sounds like he's on the phone. His voice is clear, even through the shut door.

"You won't believe who I just saw *or* who they were with."

Jake huffs again and pulls me deeper into the store, seemingly knowing exactly where to find what we need. "We live in a town of lunatics," he mutters over his shoulder.

I laugh because the reaction feels so outrageous for something so ordinary. I remain smiling because I like his use of "we."

Jake shops efficiently and, when we approach the front to pay, levels the cashier with a glare that efficiently silences whatever personal question the girl is about to ask. She sticks to the perfunctory, "Did you find everything you need?" and other pleasantries.

Within minutes, we're on our way again. I tell myself I imagined Bets from the post office throwing herself behind a parked car across the street as I looked in her direction. I'm sure she just dropped her phone… that she was pointing at us…

It's fine.

I'm in a fit of laughter, doubled over and resting my forehead on the dashboard by the time Jake closes the passenger door for me, partially because this town *is* seemingly full of lunatics and partially because Jake's face is, yet again, the perfect imitation of the straight-mouthed emoji. I'm surprised he doesn't have a literal storm cloud floating over his head.

Once he's also in the truck and we're driving down the road, I finally compose myself.

"I've never lived *anywhere* like this before," I say, wiping the tears leaking from my eyes. "I can't tell you the number of times I saw something completely outrageous in the Common, and everybody literally just kept going with their day."

"Wilcox Grove is about as different from Boston as you can get," Jake agrees. "Do you… mind that it's different?"

I think about it for a minute.

"You know, I really don't. Making it in the big city makes me feel worthy of all the sacrifices Mom made for me, how hard she worked every day so I could have more than she did. I wanted to check all the boxes for what people consider to be success — college, post-grad, respectable and secure job, respectable and secure partner, family… all of it. And I liked a lot of it. I loved being a student, and when I was still spending most of my time teaching. But I've been really happy in Wilcox Grove, too."

Jake is quiet for my little monologue, but I don't miss the concern on his face when I talk about Boston. I feel concern when I talk about Boston, too. There are very real responsibilities there that I've been avoiding, and it's not right. My life is still there, and we both know it, but he seems to be as keen as I am to pretend my return to the city isn't looming. I beat my guilt back once more and focus on Jake.

A smile lifts the corner of his mouth as he makes the turn that leads to our houses and he says, "I know I wasn't the most welcoming when you got here, but I think Wilcox Grove suits you. I like seeing you in this space, knowing you're right across the yard in this house. Big city success or not, I think you're spectacular."

I think I blush from my hairline to my navel.

Once inside, Jake gets to work replacing the part in the downstairs bathroom, and I decide to start prep for dinner. The sun is only just starting to set, but I can always eat, and I think Jake skipped lunch to get back to me quicker, so nobody's saying no to an early dinner.

I'm making burger patties when Jake joins me in the kitchen.

He makes a noise of appreciation when he looks over my shoulder and sees what's on the menu.

"Oh, just you wait. I'm going to *cook* them, and then they'll really be good!"

I love how easy it is to poke fun with Jake. I also love that he laughs, even when my jokes are awful. I wash my hands and take the plate of patties to the fridge, returning to the sink with tomatoes and lettuce.

"Thank you for making us dinner," he says, pressing a kiss to my hair. Jake is a very affectionate man, and I'm obsessed with every one of his little touches or kisses.

"Would I be in the way if I fix the doors on the lower cabinets?"

He talks around a screw pressed into the corner of his mouth, his hands full with a screwdriver and a handful of the new hinges. He'll be working far enough from food prep, so I shake my head.

I'm washing a tomato at the sink when I hear the first thud from the side of the house. Jake and I look at each other with the same puzzled expression. I dry my hands on a towel when there's another scuffle.

"Let me." Jake stands and moves to check out the disturbance.

"It's ok. I've got it."

It's my house, and I need to learn to handle nature. It's probably just Bambi poking around again.

I walk to the side door and jiggle the handle before unlocking it, something I've found *sometimes* helps the door behave.

I'm pleased when the door swings inward. I step forward to see what the ruckus is and start to lean forward so I can peer my head around the side of the house.

"It worked this time, but we should add this door to the list to —" I'm cut off by a loud huff from outside and a clop from a… hoof? I turn my head toward the garage and see an enormous creature sniffing what looks like a smear of pumpkin on the asphalt.

I yelp loudly and unintentionally draw its attention to me.

I hear Jake scrambling inside behind me.

"Ace! Don't!"

His hand wraps around my biceps and yanks me roughly back, his other arm coming to band around my waist as I fall into him, taking us both to the ground in the vestibule. Less than a second later, a monstrosity the size of a small truck goes barreling across the opening where my head just was and down my driveway.

"What the hell was *that?!*" I screech even though I know exactly what I just saw. My heart is jackhammering in my throat.

I feel Jake tighten his grip around my stomach like he's afraid I might disappear or get dragged off by the beast. Thankfully, the thunderous sound of his hooves fades quickly.

"That…" Jake is breathing as hard as I am. "Was a moose."

CHAPTER 26

Jake

I can feel Alice's heartbeat with her back pressed against my chest, and I focus on the rhythmic thudding. Fast as it is, it's a reminder that she's alive. She's ok.

You shouldn't go outside *expecting* to see a moose around Barefoot Lake, but it has happened once or twice in my lifetime. That doesn't help with the shock or the fear I felt when I heard Alice cry out.

Someone who hasn't seen a full-grown male moose up close and personal might expect it to be fairly similar to a horse, and while a large horse may weigh the same as a moose, moose are taller, and their antlers are things you can't really understand without seeing. Let's just say you *really* don't want a moose to run into you. It's likely the last thing you'd experience.

I shift and begin to lift Alice off of me. She reaches for the door to help pull herself up but finds it wobbling loosely on its hinges. Taking a few hundred pounds of human bodies falling against it was a bit too much for the poor old door.

"I'll fix that, I promise," I say as I heave myself up. "Are you alright?"

Alice looks down at herself as if she needs visual confirmation that she's in one piece. I take in a sweep of her, too.

"There was a *moose* in my *driveway*!!" She still seems a little stunned by the whole ordeal. I don't really blame her. She shakes her head in disbelief before suddenly perking up.

"My *car*!!" Alice launches herself toward the door but stops before stepping onto the driveway, carefully looking both left and right to make sure there aren't any other guests.

"Thank goodness…" Her shoulders sag with relief.

I come up behind Alice to take a look, too. The garage door has a hefty dent and several scratches on it, but the CRV seems ok. Thankfully, Alice parks on the far side of the two-car driveway so she can fully open the driver's side door without squeezing between her car and the house.

She looks over her shoulder at me. "What does one even *do* when a moose nearly runs them down? Do we call the police and tell them there's a moose on the loose? That sounds like a goddamn nursery rhyme. Like, what even caused it to come over here? Is that something I should expect on the regular?"

I rub my hands up and down her arms, feeling goosebumps beneath my touch from a moose-induced adrenaline rush.

"It's very uncommon, I swear. It was probably just curious. There's really nothing to do. It likely just took back off into the woods." I reach over her shoulder and point down her driveway in the direction the moose was headed. "Once you pass the street that goes around the lake, there really isn't any civilization in that direction for miles. I doubt he'll be bothering anybody else."

Her gaze follows my finger, and she nods slowly. I guess she is coming to terms with her moose encounter.

"I think its arrival might have been my fault," I admit. She looks back at me sharply, eyebrows furrowed. "Look at the garage. I think it might have been after the pumpkins I put in there this afternoon.

They wouldn't all fit in the food locker. More likely, it got curious, and there weren't people outside to keep it from checking things out. I'm sorry if the pumpkins somehow drew it out."

Alice turns to face me in the small space and presses a hand to my chest to walk me back into the kitchen. The side door lamely swings once we're not in its way, and Alice needs to wedge a kitchen chair under the knob to keep it shut. Once she does, she faces me again with hands on her hips.

"Jake, you have *nothing* to apologize for. We live in the woods. Animals were here first, and they're going to pop up from time to time." She steps toward me and slips her hands into mine. "You just saved my *life*, and that's frickin amazing. So, *thank you*." She stretches up and places a gentle kiss on my lips.

I back her up until she's leaning against the kitchen counter, and I can grip the edge on either side of her to ground myself. I release her lips but stay leaning forward so I can press my forehead to hers, keeping my eyes closed.

"You just told me, maybe an hour ago, that you might be able to find happiness here. I couldn't lose you so soon. That was fucking terrifying."

For a moment, we just breathe the same air. Then, Alice slips her fingers into my belt loops like she did the first time I kissed her. She tilts her head back so her lips brush against my jaw. I shiver and turn my head to hungrily capture her lips. One of my hands releases the counter and skims against her body as I move it up and place it on her throat, needing her pulse beneath my fingers. I feel the vibration from her groan at the possessive touch, and I cherish her trust in me.

"Jake..." Her voice is steady and calm, but needy as her lips move against mine. "No miscommunication. I want you, Jake, if you'll have me."

The fact that she can still question whether I want her completely blows my mind.

My other hand moves to her waist and pulls her toward me. I palm a fistful of her ass and hoist her up so I can move both of my arms under her. Her legs wrap around me like it's second nature, and her ankles hook behind my back. She digs her nails into my biceps, and I hope they leave marks.

I kiss her again, hard and demanding, hopefully removing any question about how badly I want her. Alice presses her lips against the side of my neck before biting the skin there. I hiss sharply.

"Ace, I'm going to need you to stop that or we're not going to make it out of this kitchen."

I turn, intending to carry her upstairs, but I can feel her smile against my skin as we near the couch, and I know to expect the next bite before it comes. She's going to be the death of me. I prop her on the back of her couch, a spot that's becoming a favorite of mine, and wind my fingers in the tresses of her hair. I pull until she's released my neck and is looking up at me.

"You're being a *tease*," I scold, but nearly fold when she digs her teeth into her bottom lip and scrapes her nails down my chest. Even through my shirt, the feeling is electrifying. I groan, and my mouth is on hers again. I'll never tire of kissing this woman.

I drag myself away from her.

"Stand up," I command and she eagerly hops to her feet, eyes alight with curiosity about what I'll ask her to do next. Her willingness to obey when she's usually so stubborn stirs something inside me.

I catch her gaze and hold it.

"Arms up."

Her arms fly up and she crosses her wrists over her head.

"Now stay still, Ace." I reach forward and play with the hem of her shirt between my fingers. Alice's eyes darken with anticipation, and I brush my fingers against her hipbones. She draws that bottom lip between her teeth again.

I press my thumb into her chin, pulling down until she releases that lip. I kiss her, drawing it into my mouth before releasing it with a pop.

"This is mine, do you understand?" I brush the lip with my thumb again.

She nods sharply, eagerly.

"Then stop biting it."

My hand goes back to the hem of her shirt, and I take her tank top and sweater off in one quick movement. I fall to my knees.

"Arms down."

She places them on my shoulders.

"Now don't move, Ace."

I lean forward and brush a kiss against her sternum, just below the lace of her black bra. I unbutton her jeans and pull the zipper down, separating the material. I see the top of her black lace underwear and peer up at Alice.

"Did you match these for me?" I can hear the scratchiness of my own voice. This woman undoes me.

"Mmhmm…" She nods, and I see her swallow. "Just in case."

"I can't wait to unwrap you," I breathe against her stomach before placing another kiss right above her underwear. She groans, and her hands fly to the back of the couch behind her for support. I begin peeling her jeans off, tapping one ankle and then the other once I reach the floor so she can step out of them. Sitting back on my heels, I look up again at Alice, thanking whatever luck and blessings gave me these moments with her.

"You look…" I grin. "Good enough to eat."

As I rise back up on my knees, I slip one of my hands around her ankle and lift her leg with me, hooking her knee over my shoulder and running my hand up the outside of her thigh.

"Show me you've been listening. What did I tell you to do?"

"Don't move," Alice answers quickly. She did say she loved being a student.

"Good girl. Are you going to hold still for me?"

Alice shakes her head violently, and I grin at her honesty.

"Try."

I lean forward and press my nose into the front of her underwear. The lace scrap of fabric looks like it would fall apart in my hands. Knowing she picked it out just for me makes me glow with pride. I flick my tongue against her, and she jolts, so ready for me.

"I like these," I say as I run a finger under the side of the panties, pulling them away from her skin and letting the elastic snap. She gasps, and I think I feel her standing leg tremble.

I move my hand down between her legs and shift the lace aside. I run my thumb across her opening and *know* I feel her leg tremble this time. The knee on my shoulder squeezes as she digs her heel into my back.

"I haven't stopped thinking of this pretty pussy since yesterday." I press my thumb against her bundle of nerves, and she swallows a squeak. "I might never think of another thing again."

"Jake... please," she breathes. I told her yesterday that she never needed to beg, but the sound of her doing just that is intoxicating. I spot her hands against the couch, knuckles white with how hard she's gripping the material.

I can't say no to her and would never want to. I lean forward and immediately draw her clit between my teeth as I press my finger inside her. I curl it against the front of her walls, shifting until she lets her head fall back, gasping, and I know I've found what I'm looking for. I pull out to add a second finger. She rocks her hips forward against my face, and I press my fingers on my other hand into her thigh, encouraging her to take what she needs.

I feel like a man starved, like I was shown salvation through Alice, and now I cannot get enough. Her breaths sing in my ears as they become short and frantic. I alternate licking and biting, fast and slow until I can feel her ready to snap.

She freely rolls her hips against me, riding my face. I tip my head back and speed up my fingers.

"Come for me, Ace."

She groans deep in her throat like a plea. One of her hands flies to the back of my head, holding me against her as she rides the waves of her orgasm. I hold her up when her knee finally gives out, stroking rhythmically until she comes down from her high.

"Jake…" She's breathing hard. "That was—"

"Just the start."

I straighten her underwear and set her back on her feet, making sure she's steady before letting go. As I stand, I wipe a hand across my chin, a satisfied smile on my lips. The pressure of my jeans against my straining cock is uncomfortable. Alice tracks my every movement with an intense gaze.

She reaches up until she's holding a side of my flannel collar in each hand.

"My turn," she whispers and begins unbuttoning my shirt. Her fingers are still trembling and after struggling with a few buttons, she growls and yanks. I hear at least one button ping off the floor somewhere out of sight.

"I'll fix that, I promise," she echoes my words back at me. I've never cared less about torn buttons in my life.

I'm still shrugging out of the sleeves as Alice starts pulling my t-shirt over my head, ripping both tops off my arms at the same time. Her eagerness is like fire in my veins. There's nothing like being wanted by Alice.

Her eyes rake down my torso before settling back on my tattoo. She reaches out and ghosts her fingers over the ink, tracing the line of the mountains.

She smiles softly but looks up at me with hesitancy in her eyes. I run a knuckle across her cheekbone.

"Do you want to stop, Ace?"

Her eyes dart to mine.

"No! God no!" She shakes her head to punctuate the denial. "I'm… nervous. You look like…" She gestures at my upper half.

"And *you* look like that." I gesture to all of her. "You have no clue how lucky I feel to be here with you. But you say the word, and we stop."

"Please don't stop, Jake," she begs. "Show me what you like."

"You've never…?"

"I have, but…" She still looks shy. "I like it when you tell me what to do."

"I've got you, Ace."

I take her hands and place them on the button of my pants.

"On your knees."

She smiles and gently thuds to her knees, finding comfort in the instruction.

"Take off my pants."

As she undoes the button and zipper, the backs of her fingers brush against me, and I jolt. Now I'm the one squeezing the back of the couch over Alice's shoulders.

She looks up at me through her lashes.

"Good girl. Keep going."

She pushes my pants down so I can step out of them and rubs her hands up my legs until they meet the bottoms of my boxers. She hikes one side up when she sees more ink peeking out and drags her nails across the broken clock face tattooed there.

I hum a content sound. I'd let her touch me all day.

She looks up at me quickly, like she's asking for permission to explore.

"Go ahead," I urge. "Touch me."

She spreads her fingers across my thigh and slips her hand under the fabric of my boxers. Suddenly, she shifts so her finger brushes against my length.

I think my heart stops.

"Jesus, Ace," I choke out.

She smirks, quite pleased with herself.

"Take off my boxers."

She withdraws and reaches for the waistband with steady hands.

Please.

I swear my nerve endings are completely wrecked because I feel every millimeter of movement like it's in slow motion. I'm aching for her and spring free the second the material is pulled down far enough.

She doesn't wait for my instruction this time, leaving my boxers at my knees and wrapping a hand around me. She tests me with a tight stroke.

I think I see stars.

I watch her explore more of me, relishing the way her eyes consistently darken, pupils blown wide. Her uptick in confidence is fucking incredible to witness.

"Wow," she breathes, and I preen with male pride before she tightens her grip, and I jerk into her hand.

"Alice," I hiss. I take a deep breath through my nose, attempting to hold on to the illusion that I have any control. "Tighter."

She dutifully obeys, holding a firm grip and leaning forward, eyes jumping up to mine for just a second.

"Yes..." The word comes out through my teeth when I feel her tongue flick against the head.

She looks up at me again, and it's a fucking miracle I don't blow at the sight of her sitting on her knees with my length in her hand.

"Open your mouth, Alice."

She does as she's told and takes me along her flat tongue, eyes still trained on me. Closing her lips around me, her cheeks hollow out. She twists her hand around the part of me that doesn't fit in her mouth.

I'm a goner.

One of my hands falls to the back of her head, where I stroke once before I start guiding her.

I willingly praise.

"That's my girl."

She takes more of me and increases her pressure. She gradually speeds up and hums. I can feel the rumble in her throat everywhere.

I bump against the back of her throat, and I have to stop her. She pulls back and touches her fingers to her lips.

"Jesus Christ, Alice." I'm breathing hard. "Stand up."

She smiles widely and rises to her feet, reaching behind her to unhook her bra. She slips her panties down, kicking them off, all bashfulness gone. I push my boxers all the way off, and Alice hops up onto the back of the couch.

I push Alice's knees open and step forward until I'm between them. I grip her ribs on both sides, pressing my fingers into her back and running my thumbs on the undersides of her breasts, these perfect breasts. I slide my hand up to palm the right one and bend to place a kiss atop the left. Alice murmurs a satisfied hum, letting her head roll back and pushing her chest toward me.

I drag my tongue down until I capture her nipple, pulling it into my mouth and flicking the bud with the tip of my tongue. I roll her right breast in my hand, teasing the nipple with light brushes that have it pebbling. I switch sides, dragging my teeth over the sensitive peak before sucking it further into my mouth.

Her groan rings in my ears.

I release her breast, blowing cool air across the wet skin,

enjoying seeing her react. I slide my hands to Alice's thighs as I bend down, letting go only when I have to.

I pull my wallet from my jeans pocket and take out a condom. I tear open the packet as I stand and roll the condom on. Alice reaches for my sides, pulling me forward and back between her knees. She glances down between us, and her eyes widen.

"Go slow."

I lift her chin so she's looking at my face and nod before capturing her lips and notching myself just inside her. Her mouth opens at the contact, and I sweep my tongue inside. She rolls her hips toward me, and I put a hand behind her for stability, sliding further in.

Alice breaks our kiss, pressing our temples together,

"Jake, yes." She drags the word out.

"You're doing so well," I huff between breaths because she is doing so well.

I pull back and roll further into her, earning myself a groan, her breath hot against my ear. I repeat the action.

She's tight as fuck, and I think I've found heaven being inside her. She scoots toward me, propped right on the edge of the couch, hooks her ankles behind me, and pulls me in. I lick my thumb and reach between us, pressing slow circles into her clit.

"I need you to relax for me, baby."

She hums in my ear, and I roll my hips slowly into her as her muscles begin to unclench. My muscles tremble, but I move slowly and evenly until I'm fully seated. Alice gasps when our hips meet. I pause, letting her adjust to the new sensation before I pull back and slide back in.

"More."

Her request nearly destroys me. I roll my hips against her slowly.

"More. Faster."

Her voice has an edge of desperation to it.

I wrap my arm around her waist and lift her so she sinks down onto my cock. Her hands squeeze my biceps, and her heels press against the couch beside my knees. She braces herself as she lifts up again and again, driving down onto me while I lift my hips to meet her. My other hand is still between us, giving her delicious pressure every time she moves down.

Alice rolls her head down to my shoulder and cries out. I feel her tighten around me, and I know I won't last much longer. I feel pressure building at the base of my spine, and my pace increases. She bites down hard on the skin between my neck and my shoulder, and I explode. She rides me hard through my orgasm, breathing as hard as I am when we slow.

I set her back on the couch before pulling out of her gently. She whimpers softly. Everything is sensitive. I move my hand slowly against her slick opening, and her hips buck toward me.

"Again, Alice."

She mumbles incoherently. She's close. I press two fingers inside of her, curling them toward me and pressing the heel of my hand against her clit. She rolls her hips again and again, hard against my hand.

"That's my girl. Take it."

Within seconds, she's spasming around my fingers, and digging her nails into my arms. I kiss her slowly and extract my fingers. She looks sleepy.

I remove the condom and step away, wrapping it in a paper towel to throw it away.

I return and lift her back off the couch, gathering her in my arms and holding her on my lap as I walk around the couch to sit. I pull a blanket over us both, and she nuzzles her face against my chest.

"God, Alice. You are fucking magnificent."

I feel her smile, and I might be the Grinch because I swear my heart grows three times in size.

CHAPTER 27

Alice

As I sink into the couch with Jake, I think that I could spend all my time in his arms and never tire of it. I want to fall asleep here, with him, but his stomach grumbles loudly. I peel an eye open to peek up at him.

Even after what we just did, this man has the nerve to blush.

"Sorry…" he mutters, and I can't help but laugh.

I unwind myself from his limbs and press a kiss on his cheek.

"I'll be right back," I promise, standing. I snatch Jake's flannel from its landing spot on the arm of the couch and, once I untangle his t-shirt from it, slip it on. It barely has any functioning buttons left and stops just barely below my bottom, but I deem that good enough and head to the bathroom.

When I emerge and come around the corner to the kitchen, I freeze at the sight before me. Jake has put his boxers back on — bummer — and is standing in front of my stove, cooking our burgers. He looks over at me and smiles. The importance of these ordinary moments sends a tingle all the way down to my toes.

I spot my underwear and retrieve them, noting Jake raises his eyebrows when I put them on. He disapproves but smirks with some level of satisfaction when I move gingerly. I'm already deliciously sore. I roll my eyes and make my way to the sink so I can finish cleaning the lettuce and tomatoes.

It's not until I'm digging into my stacked burger with cheese, lettuce, tomato, bacon, avocado, and barbecue sauce that I realize I'm starving. After the first bite, I can't help the little happy food dance I do in my seat before I inhale the rest of my food.

I spot Jake, also finished and leaning back in his chair, and he's looking at me like I'm the greatest thing since sliced bread. He reaches over and plucks at his sleeve on my arm.

"I like this," he says simply. I don't know if he means seeing me in his shirt, eating dinner together, or enjoying a post-sex glow, but I like all of it, too.

After we clean up together — so domestic! — Jake lays back on the couch, and I crawl over him like a cat until I find the perfect spot to wrap around him. He turns on the television but keeps the volume low like anything louder would disrupt the calm in the room.

"Tell me something about you." I've known this man biblically, but I still want more. I want to know what makes him smile, his pet peeves, embarrassing moments, and dreams. I want to know the big things and the little things.

"Like what?" His chest rumbles beneath me when he speaks, and it feels intimate.

"Anything, really. What's…" I try to think of anything. "Your favorite food?"

"Easy. Sushi. What's yours?"

"Cheese."

Jake barks out a laugh. "Cheese?"

"Yes! And don't you dare disrespect the sanctity of cheese." I laugh with him, but I mean it.

We continue like that for what feels like hours, sharing whatever we can think of. His favorite movie is surprisingly *Mean Girls* ("It makes me laugh!"), and I tell him mine is *My Cousin Vinny*. He tells me he broke his leg while snowboarding when he was ten and has refused to try again, even though he lives in New Hampshire. I tell him about my irrational fear in high school that the email chains threatening to curse me if I didn't keep it going were real.

It's silly, and it's open, and it's easy.

We talk about some deeper things, too. Owning Wilcox Nursery wasn't a lifelong dream of Jake's, but he's always had a green thumb and loves being able to work with his hands and his best friend now.

I tell him about my dream of visiting Paris someday. Money was tight growing up, so Mom and I didn't travel much, and we never went abroad. I've always had this picture in my head of me sitting at a wrought iron table on a narrow cobblestone street in the city of love, reading a novel, drinking a glass of wine, and snacking on bread and cheese. It feels magical.

Eventually, Jake asks about my father again.

"You never wanted to find him?" he asks.

"Nope!" I know I answer too quickly and hope he doesn't pick up on it. I don't like lying to him, especially since the whole point of this conversation is to get to know one another better, but this is a secret I haven't told anybody, not even Mom.

I want to move off the subject as quickly as possible and shut down the prickling guilt at the back of my mind. I shift so I can see Jake's thigh tattoo and tap a finger on the ink.

"Tell me about this."

The image covers most of the front of his left thigh with a large antique clock face that looks like it's been shattered in the center. Where pieces of the glass have fallen away, there's an old compass behind that peeks through. Between the twelve and three, there are bits of frost on the clock face. Between three and six, some vines grow around the numbers. Between six and nine, the sun shines a glare on the broken shards, and between nine and twelve, leaves flutter through the cracks, swirling toward the compass.

"Scott's always been good at drawing, but he used to be embarrassed about it. I'm guessing some asshole probably picked on him for it. I found this on his desk one day, and I dunno, I think I just really liked it. He was thrilled when I asked if he'd be ok with me getting the tattoo." Jake shrugs. "He was in high school at the time, and so many kids are just absolute shits at that age. He always stayed kind. But it was just the two of us by then, and I wanted him to know I was proud of him and his talents."

"It's perfect," I say, tracing different lines across his skin. "I don't think tattoos need to always have some deep purpose or back story, but I think for my first one, I want to pick something really meaningful, like this. Did I tell you Reid basically forbade me from getting one?"

I gag at the memory.

He looks down at me. "You know how fucked up that is, right?"

"Yeah." I nod.

"Well, if you decide on something, I'll take you to Ila in town. She's the best and is especially good with first-timers."

That's a project for another day. Tonight, Jake takes me upstairs and draws me a steaming bath in the separate claw-foot tub. I pout when he takes back his shirt, settling me in the water.

"I'm going to run next door to grab a few things, but I'll be right back." His expression becomes stern, and he uses what I've deemed his bossy sex voice. "I expect to find you right here. You got it?"

I nod, and he turns to leave.

"Yes, sir," I say to his retreating back.

He freezes before grumbling, shaking his head, and continuing his way back downstairs.

I sink into the decadent warmth, resting my head on the towel Jake propped on the edge of the tub for me and closing my eyes.

I wake with a start to a hand trailing lazy lines up and down the inside of one of my calves.

"Hi, sleepy," Jake says from his spot kneeling beside the tub. He's still in the same clothes as before, and I notice for the first time that his hair is sticking up in every direction. That's likely my fault, but I'm not the slightest bit sorry.

"I'm not sleepy!" I insist, but my yawn betrays me.

Jake shakes the water from his wet hand and begins undressing. I prop my hands behind my head and enjoy the show.

"You're ridiculous," Jake says once he's naked, rolling his eyes, but I just shrug. I'm not going to pretend I don't like looking at him.

He bends to unplug the drain in the tub and holds out his hand for me. The shower is already on behind him. He must have turned it on before waking me.

"Let's shower and then get you to bed."

I raise my eyebrows suggestively.

"To sleep," Jake corrects, but his cock noticeably twitches.

I take Jake's hand and step out of the tub, hopping from one bathmat to the next to minimize the likelihood of leaving a massive puddle in my wake.

The shower is warm, but I turn it up to "fires of hell" hot. Jake hisses as the water beating against him heats up, but beyond a glare, he doesn't object.

His body blocks most of the spray, but water is dripping from his hair, making rivulets down his body, and I'm reminded of him standing in my doorway after falling in the lake. This time, though, nothing stops me from touching him.

I step forward, pressing my hands to his ribs and licking one of the droplets running down his chest. Jake captures my face between his hands and tips my head back so he can kiss me deeply. I melt into him, pressing my body completely against his.

He slowly turns us until I'm under the water and starts running his fingers through my hair. He keeps turning us until he's blocking the water again. I like our little shower dance.

He breaks the kiss, and I pout when his warmth moves away until his hands return to my hair with shampoo, and his fingers begin massaging my scalp. The sound I make is filthy. I would do anything this man asked of me so long as he kept this up.

I drop my head bonelessly against Jake's chest, and he turns us again so he can rinse my hair.

Forget being an independent woman. I need to be pampered like this forever.

Kidding! Mostly.

He holds me against him when he reaches for the conditioner. As he works it into the ends of my hair, avoiding my scalp, I frown, wondering where he learned that. As if reading my mind, he chuckles.

"I condition, Ace."

I smile up at him, and he collects my hair over my shoulder so the conditioner won't get rinsed out yet.

"I even had a phase when I refused to cut my hair short. It was…" He grimaces. "Bad. Very bad."

"Tell me there are pictures."

"I've destroyed any I could find."

His face is so serious that I can't tell if he's joking or not. He picks up the shampoo again and begins washing his own hair.

I go back to ogling him, watching his muscles shift as he moves. Looking further down his body, I feel suddenly bold.

While Jake's rinsing his hair, once the water has run clear, I sneak to my knees and take his length in my hands.

His eyes fly open, and his hand slaps against the shower wall as he looks down at me. The shower floor is hard on my knees, but it's worth it for his reaction. I've never felt more powerful.

"Ace," he croaks. "You don't have to…"

His voice trails off as I drag my tongue across the head of his quickly hardening cock.

"I want to." I pause. "If I may?"

"Fuck yes, you may."

I lick him slowly from base to tip, and his entire body jerks.

"I was interrupted earlier by a distraction."

"A distraction, huh? Is that all—"

I cut him off before he can sass me by taking him in my mouth, swift and deep. I think it's possible he also stopped breathing.

I pull back and make eye contact.

"Tell me how you like it."

"Tighter," he grits out like before, and I tighten my hands around him. I move forward to take him in my mouth again. "And keep your eyes on me."

His fingers flex before clenching in a fist like he's looking for something to hold on to. I look back up at him as instructed.

"You can guide me if you'd like," I say, guessing what else he might like. His eyes flare. I was right.

"Tap my thigh if it's too much." He runs his fingers down my cheek before moving them to the back of my head and shifting so his body fully blocks the water from hitting me.

"Ok." I nod and twist my hands around him, maintaining the pressure he asked for. "But it won't be."

Jake takes a steadying breath before encouraging me forward. I focus on breathing consistently through my nose and pop my mouth open when he presses against my lips. I keep my eyes on

Jake's as he slides in easily. When he pauses, I close my lips around him and suck, sliding further toward him.

His fingers clench in my hair.

"Ace, fuck!"

I'd grin if I could.

He eases me back before sliding into my mouth again, but he pauses, holding back. Still keeping eye contact, I nod, trying to urge him on with my minimal range of movement.

He sides out and back into my mouth, again and again, finding a rhythm. I move one hand to the front of his hips and scrape my nails over the sensitive skin while I twist the other around his length.

He jerks forward and picks up the pace. I repeat the movement. He hits the back of my throat, and my eyes start to water. I move my hand from his hip to cup his balls and walk the delicate line between perfect pressure and pain. I read Jake right because he begins driving into my mouth now. He's breathing hard, and he squeezes his eyes shut.

"Ace, I'm —"

He releases my head, but I keep moving, working my hands and head in tandem until I feel all of him clench as he releases down my throat. I've never swallowed before, but I feel empowered as I continue to work him, swallowing, slowing my pace, and eventually releasing him.

Jake slumps sideways against the shower wall but holds out his hand to help me up. Ever the gentleman. Once I'm standing, he pulls me against him, cradling my head in his hand.

"You're extraordinary," he murmurs before kissing my temple.

Jake heaves off the wall and shuffles us back under the water, softly running his fingers through my hair as he rinses out the conditioner. My hair is going to be soft as fuck tomorrow.

I see the reverence in Jake's gaze and know this is how a partner is supposed to make me feel.

He hands me the bar of soap so I can wash myself before he efficiently does the same for himself. I turn off the water while he grabs two towels from the counter. He slings one over his shoulder and wraps the other around me, squeezing my hair out in one end. Only after I'm taken care of does he dry himself.

We silently brush our teeth and drag ourselves to bed, shutting off the light on the way. Barely dried, we fall on my bed and twist about until we're under the covers. Jake gathers me in his arms, and I blissfully fall asleep tangled in his limbs.

CHAPTER 28

Jake

When I wake up, I'm surrounded by the smell of bacon, but that's not what has my attention. That honor is held by the knuckle dragging slowly down my spine.

"Jake…" Alice's voice is soft, but it sounds like it might not be the first time she's said my name this morning.

My head is turned away from her, pressed into several pillows, so I smile even though I haven't opened my eyes yet. I hope if I pretend to be asleep for at least another minute, she'll keep running her finger over my skin. It's a damn good deal, waking up to her.

I jolt when a swift smack connects with my ass, still a powerful force even through the blanket, and flip my head to glare at Alice.

"I knew you were awake!" Alice's tone is mock accusatory, but her eyes are sparkling with delight. She's in my flannel again. I can't be sure, but it might be all she's wearing.

"And if I wasn't?"

"Well, then that should have done the trick." She smiles, and all is forgiven. As long as she smiled at me like that, I'd help this girl bury a body.

She bends down to press a kiss to my lips like it's something she's been doing her whole life.

"Flip over. I brought breakfast."

Alice jerks her head toward her dresser, where a tray stands over her scattered knickknacks. As I roll over, I notice the bright sun fighting through a crack in the window curtains. I never sleep this late, even without alarms.

"What time is it?" I ask.

"Almost nine. Do you need to go?" Alice tries to sound casual, but I can hear the disappointment in her voice.

"A benefit of owning the nursery is that I don't. The team can open the place even if Eli and I aren't there. I don't need to be anywhere but here. I'm just not used to sleeping this late."

"Yeah, I thought you were Mr. Early Bird," Alice says as she retrieves the breakfast tray. It's filled with three glasses of different kinds of juice, two mugs of coffee (one normal and one that looks like a glass of light brown milk), a stack of waffles, bacon, fruit, a cup of yogurt, and a couple of hard-boiled eggs. She sets it over my thighs before circling the bed to crawl in on her side and sit on her knees facing me.

"Are we expecting company?" I tease but then pointedly look across the bed as I growl, "Because there are some aspects of my life where I do not share."

Alice's eyes dart to my lips before she licks her own bottom lip. I pick up a piece of the crispy bacon.

"Breakfast is one of them," I say, my voice returning to its normal tone.

Alice snatches the bacon from my hand.

"You suck, you know that?"

I just smile at her.

Despite thinking Alice had brought too much food, we finish every bite. I guess certain activities really build an appetite. Rested and fed, I set the tray with the empty dishes on the floor beside the bed before rolling toward Alice and pinning her to the mattress. I swallow her squeal and discover that she is, in fact, just wearing my shirt.

It's late morning when I look up at Alice from where I'm crouched on the floor by the side door and shake my head, frowning.

"Time of death… sometime yesterday." Alice sighs and places a hand on the open door. "It's been real, door. You — Well, you fucking sucked."

There's no way I'd be comfortable just repairing an external door after the beating it took when we fell on it, so it'll need to be replaced.

She looks back at me. "I blame the damn moose for this."

I scoff as I stand, picking up some pieces of splintered wood and chucking them outside.

"I don't know. Fall on a door once, shame on the door. Fall on a door twice… maybe it's you."

"That's not at all how the saying goes! And what do you even mean, twice?" Alice looks outraged.

"Do I need to remind you what happened to that poor shed out back?" I close the dilapidated door and wedge the chair back under it to keep it in place.

"That was the spiders!!"

"Sounds like somebody's putting a lot of blame on nature."

Alice huffs and crosses her arms. I put my arm around her shoulders and pull her against me, kissing the top of her head.

"We can replace both today and then I'll teach you how to walk."

Her elbow quickly jabs into my solar plexus. I deserved that.

Fifteen minutes later, we're in my truck on our way to the nearest Home Depot several towns over. Alice insists on having the heat up so she can crack the windows. The radio is also turned up so she can hear it over the wind. I don't dare suggest that we close the windows so we can lower both the heat and the radio volume. I'm not a complete moron.

Alice spends the drive in the middle seat, leaning her head on my shoulder and holding my hand between hers.

Our shopping excursion is efficient, and we're back on the road with two new doors, handles, hardware, and paint in no time. We stop for fast food on the way back, a necessity for road trips, according to Alice. I also don't tell her that a forty-minute drive each way is hardly a road trip. These fries are a simple joy, and I'll always accept those.

"Do you have Thanksgiving plans?" I blurt the question before I can talk myself out of asking.

The holiday is still over three weeks away, and it's a big one for such a new… whatever we have. Relationship, I guess? But I want to spend it with her anyway.

She hasn't given any indication that she isn't going back to Boston in January, so I don't know what I'm doing here except setting myself up for pain. Best case scenario is a relationship across state lines. I must be a glutton for punishment because I can't stay away.

Instead, I keep getting in deeper.

"Not really. I was thinking of asking Piper if I could invade hers," Alice answers.

"Would you like to come with me and Eli to his parents'?"

She looks up at me.

"Really?"

She has no clue how tightly she's already got me wrapped around her finger.

"Yeah. What do you say?"

"I say 'yes.'"

She nuzzles against my shoulder again and adds, "I can't wait to get all the dirt on you from Eli."

It's possible I didn't think this through fully.

Once we get back home, Alice hops out to move her car so I can back the truck up close to the garage. By the time I get out, she's already in the open garage, unfolding two plastic tables in the center of the open space.

She comes to meet me at the back of the truck a moment later.

"Are you sure you don't need to go to work?"

I remember what she said about Reid always putting her at the bottom of his priorities, well below work, and I assure her again.

"I'm positive. I'll go in tomorrow, but for today, the team can call me if they need me. Like you once said, 'everything in this town is only five minutes away,' or something like that." I bump her shoulder.

She smiles, but it doesn't touch her eyes.

Again, I find myself wishing I'd hit Reid harder for making her think so little of herself. I silently promise I'll do whatever I can to make sure she never questions her worth again.

"It's about balance, Ace. You're a priority here. I promise I'd tell you if something came up."

"Yeah?"

"Yeah."

She takes a breath to reset and focus on our job.

"I figure we can prime and paint them tonight and put them up tomorrow."

I don't know if it's her easy use of "we" or the fact that she's taking charge of the project, but something about the whole situation is extremely attractive. She grips the handle to lower the tailgate.

"Yes, ma'am." I see a pleased smirk play on her lips at the title. I'll gladly play second fiddle for her any day.

We unload the doors together and place them on the tables. Thankfully, we were able to find pre-drilled doors that matched the measurements we'd taken of the existing door frames, so we don't have to deal with that nonsense.

Alice holds up the can of quick-dry primer and two small rollers. "One door each?"

I nod in agreement, and we get to work.

Alice does home improvement projects just as I'd imagined she would, by dancing to music from her phone and seemingly following a plan of chaos. But even though she jumped around from section to section on the door, the color covered evenly. Maybe there's a method to the madness.

After what feels like no time at all, the doors are painted and propped up to dry.

I look over at Alice, about to congratulate her on a job well done, when I see that there's little of her *not* splattered with paint. There's even a large stripe in her hair, like she pushed it out of her face with a fully loaded paintbrush in her hand.

I think about it for a second. That's almost certainly exactly what she did.

"Ace, what the heck *happened*?"

She looks down at herself before grinning broadly, quite pleased with herself and entirely unbothered with the paint on her body, jeans, and long-sleeved top. The brush she used is still in her hand.

"I painted!"

I stand before her and shake my head.

"Time to clean you up."

In the time it takes me to blink, her expression turns purely mischievous.

"Or it's time for you to get messy."

Before I can leap away from my little demon, she swipes paint across my forearm and bolts down the driveway. She's quick and has a few seconds head start, but I catch up easily enough and grab her around her middle. She squeals when I fling her over my shoulder and band an arm over her legs to hold her in place.

The maneuver gets even more paint on me from her and the brush still clutched in her hand, but I find that I don't care. She squirms and kicks, but I've got a good hold on her. I smack her ass beside my head.

"Behave."

"Never!" she hisses, and I'm ninety-nine percent sure she begins to paint as much of my butt as she can reach.

This woman.

I hike her further up on my shoulder and head back toward the garage, pulling the door closed and locking it with my free hand before grabbing her keys and bag from the back of my truck.

It's a bit tricky taking the steps to the front door and unlocking it with a whole-ass human on my shoulder, but Alice's wisecrack of "You could just put me down if this is too difficult for you," means I'd rather slip a disk than admit defeat.

As I kick the door closed, she quips again.

"Are you pleased with yourself, caveman?"

I drop her bag and kick off my shoes.

"No, but I will be soon." And I charge up the stairs to drop her fully clothed into the shower under an icy spray.

I hold Alice across my lap and play with the ends of her damp hair. The wet spot it makes on my shoulder is a nice contrast to the warmth from the fire bowl in front of us and the large blanket wrapped around us. We're quietly watching the sun disappear behind the mountains on the far side of Barefoot Lake and making s'mores on Alice's back patio. She holds the skewer for toasting marshmallows. I hold her. It's a good setup.

"I know you're a morning person," Alice whispers against my skin, consistently turning the marshmallow in the flames like a s'mores pro. "But this is my favorite time of day. It's like the world is telling us that it's ok to rest, now."

I hum in agreement against her hair, feeling more relaxed with her than I have in a long, long time.

A breeze lifts some crisping leaves from where they were barely hanging on to a tree, and we watch them float down to the lake's surface.

"I think I came here at the right time, too," Alice continues. "I know it was too cold to go in the water, but it's impossible not to fall in love with Barefoot Lake in the fall. I mean, look at it all."

The trees have lost some of their foliage, but there are still sizable patches of vibrant yellows, reds, and oranges in the trees and blanketing the ground. In the setting sun, they look like painted fire.

The actual fire before us pops loudly, drawing Alice's attention back to it. She removes the metal skewer from the flames and sandwiches the charred marshmallow between the graham crackers and chocolate she prepared. She holds it up before me, and I take a bite before she does. Her technique to blacken the outside while keeping the inside gooey was worth it.

"Perfect," she murmurs as she does her happy food shimmy. She's right. Everything about this night is perfect.

"So did you? Fall in love with Barefoot Lake, I mean?" I ask tentatively.

"I really think I did." She sighs sadly, though.

"But you have to go back to Boston?" I know the answer, but I ask anyway. Hopeful.

"I think I do." Alice opens her mouth to say something else but seems to reconsider. After a pause, she says, "Moving up in the department took a lot of work and sacrifice. I owe it to Mom not to abandon it."

She sounds sad, but I'm unsure if she's sad thinking about Rain or her own future.

My bite of s'mores suddenly feels like a rock in my stomach.

Just a few hours ago, we were planning Thanksgiving together. How is it possible that we're talking about her leaving now?

Would it be temporary? Would she come back? Would *we* last? Do I even have a right to ask these questions?

My first instinct is to tell her not to go, to stay here. But I stop myself. External factors pulled me back to Wilcox Grove and kept me here. If she stays, it has to be her decision. I don't know *what* to say.

I tighten my arms around her and press my cheek against her hair, like if I can get her close enough, I can keep her.

Alice spears another marshmallow and shoves it into the flames before looking back out over the lake.

She points up.

"First star of the night. Make a wish."

She whispers it to preserve the magic.

I won't ask her to stay, but I'll be damned if I don't wish for her to want it on her own.

CHAPTER 29

Jake

I wake up the next morning wrapped around a very naked Alice. We're sweaty from clinging to one another, and my arm is dead asleep, but I can't remember having woken up happier, even considering the nagging uncertainty of our future.

A man could get used to this. And for now, I'm determined to enjoy Alice's company as much as possible.

I carefully disentangle us and head to the bathroom for a quick shower. After I'm dressed, I kneel beside the nightstand. I know Alice and I had discussed my heading to work today, but I still don't want her to wake up alone.

I gently run a hand over her hair and whisper.

"Alice?"

She hums and scrunches her face like she doesn't want to wake.

"Ace? Baby?"

Her eyes flutter open, and she blinks a few times before a sleepy grin spreads across her face. "Hi, Jake."

"Hi, pretty girl."

I kiss her nose. She's adorable. Sue me.

"I'm going to head to the nursery for a few hours. I'll be back this afternoon to help you put up the doors."

"Mmhmm."

She's still resisting being awake.

I drop a quick kiss to her cheek and stand.

"I'll be back this afternoon. Text me if you're bored."

She gives me a wave before I step into the hallway and head downstairs. As I'm putting on my first shoe, my phone buzzes in my pocket.

I unlock and nearly drop it when I see the picture of Alice, sleep-tangled hair sprawled across her pillow and that damn thin sheet *barely* covering her. There's an accompanying text.

ACE

So you don't forget me.

I kick off the shoe and take the stairs two at a time. Alice is still lying on that pillow, looking just like her picture. I stride to the bed and take her face between my hands, kissing her fiercely.

"There's no chance I'll forget you, Ace. You're going to be the damn death of me."

She smiles, and her giggles follow me all the way out of her house.

I make a pit stop on the way to the nursery to pick up donuts for Eli and our team. After seeing Alice's face when I told her I could stay home with her yesterday, I especially appreciate the people I work with.

Even though it's early, the bakery is buzzing. Despite the chilly morning outside, it's cozy and warm within.

Small towns have many early risers, opening their own stores, working fields or with livestock, and heading to school. Some-how, Barefoot Bake still beats us all. Leslie and Hannah must wake up at an ungodly hour to have already filled the display with freshly made pastries every morning by the time the whole town comes knocking.

I step up to the counter when it's my turn.

"Jake! What can I get for you?"

Hannah is always a ball of energy. It's impossible to tell she's already been up for hours. She's always ready to go and has a constant gleam in her eye that makes you think she's up to some-thing. Most of the time, she is.

Even if Alice hasn't talked to her about me yet, I expect she heard that we were out together yesterday. I wonder if she's going to say something.

"Morning, Hannah. Can I get a dozen donuts — mix it up with whatever speaks to you — and a hot coffee, light cream, no sugar, to go?"

"I've got some maple bacon ones coming out in a few minutes that are to *die* for if you can wait."

"For maple bacon? I'll wait. Thank you."

I pay, and she holds out my coffee cup. I go to take it, but she doesn't let go.

"Do anything fun around town these last few days?" she asks.

There it is.

"Just some projects. You know how some of those old houses need regular upkeep." I try to be vague without being rude.

"Mmhmm," she hums. "Just make sure you don't do more harm than good."

The thinly veiled threat is gone in a second and replaced with Hannah's usual smile.

I warily step out of the way and lean against the archway to the bookstore. While it isn't technically open yet, a few people are sitting in the armchairs within, either enjoying their breakfasts or waiting for their orders to be ready.

I spot Grateful Bob drinking out of a mug topped with a mountain of whipped cream. I raise a hand in greeting, but he waves me over.

"Come give me a proper hello, boy."

I push off the wall and head toward him as somebody vacates the chair beside his. I'm happy to put more space between me and the baker who might stab me.

He gestures for me to sit, and I clap a hand on his shoulder as I sink down.

"Good morning, Grateful Bob."

"Don't you 'Good morning' me." He fixes me with a fierce glare, and I suddenly realize him happily calling me over was a trap. I've been ambushed twice, and it's barely even light out.

I hesitantly take a sip of my coffee, awaiting whatever smackdown seems to be coming.

"What are your intentions with Alice?"

I sputter into my coffee, choking on the burning liquid. I have to pound a fist against my chest a few times before I'm able to speak.

"What?!"

"Alice McDermott. Your neighbor. I believe you're familiar with her?" There isn't even a hint of a smile on Grateful Bob's lips.

"Yes, I know her."

"She came to see me on Halloween, asking for advice about your dumb ass, so I'd like to know what you did to fix things."

I blink at him stupidly. She asked about me? Obviously *now* I know I'd been on her mind, but hearing how she went out of her way to talk to Grateful Bob about me makes me feel a certain kind of way.

I don't realize Grateful Bob is still waiting for me to answer until he says, basically growling at me, "Boy, you *did* fix it, didn't you? Because I heard you two were buying hardware yesterday, and if you didn't..."

The threat at the end of that sentence doesn't need to be spoken. Also, how did he make "buying hardware" sound so scandalous?

There's a good chance this man might kick my ass.

Alarmed by Grateful Bob or not, I still feel myself flush scarlet, thinking of my post "fixing it" activities with Alice.

"I— uh— Yes. Things are good with Alice."

He narrows his eyes at me, scrutinizing my face. I lean away, just a bit afraid of this old man. He's not about to let me off as easily as Hannah did.

"And you intend to..." He gestures like he'd like me to finish the sentence.

"Make her as happy as I can for as long as I can." It's an easy answer.

His face stays serious as he nods.

I'm holding my breath. Is this where I die? In a bakery-slash-bookstore?

He cracks a smile, and a wave of relief washes over me.

"You're a good one, Jakey." He pats my knee. "That's what I told her, too."

Hannah calls my name from the counter, and I look up to see her holding up my box of donuts. I'm extremely grateful for her timing, so maybe Grateful Bob won't see the fear in my eyes. I just need a second to fix my face.

I set my coffee in the chair's armrest cup holder and retrieve my donuts.

I return to Grateful Bob's chair but stand beside it, tapping a finger against the side of the box in my hands. Before this conversation, Grateful Bob had always been a good source of support and advice. Unlike Eli, he's a commitment man. He was married for decades. And while he's a gossip about trivial stuff, we've always had an understanding about my need for privacy.

"Could I…" I hesitate, hoping he's not about to bite my head off. "Could I actually ask for advice about Alice?"

He pats the chair I'd been sitting in. "Have a seat, kid."

I sink down, slouching in the chair.

"I think she might leave," I mutter.

"Might?"

"Plans to," I correct.

"I'm sure you know she works at a college back in Boston. She said she has to go back for the spring semester. Her leave was just for fall. I was avoiding her when she first got here because I figured she'd leave soon enough, so it's not like her plans to go back are a surprise. But now that things are good, I don't know what it means for us. Is this just it?"

"Have you asked her about it?"

"Not yet. Things are… new. I don't want to jump the gun or overstep."

"Asking isn't overstepping. It's communicating."

"I know. I just —" I look down.

"Go on…"

"I love Scott, and you know I don't regret any of the choices I made for him."

Grateful Bob raises his eyebrows like he's saying "Duh."

"But I stayed in Wilcox Grove because I had to. I'm not sure I would have come back otherwise, not permanently. That decision was made *for* me. I want Alice to stay, but I don't want to ask her to. I don't even want her to *think* I'm asking her to stay for me."

"So don't ask her to stay," he says like it's the simplest thing. "If she left, would you try distance? Would you be willing for things to be a little difficult to keep her?"

"Of course." I start, surprised by my answer. The words are out of my mouth before I realize I've even thought of them.

"Yeah… I'd at least try to keep things going. I don't think distance works long term, but Boston isn't *so* far away while we figure it out."

"And if it continues to work, what is she worth?" Grateful Bob asks.

I pause. It feels rash to think it already, but Alice feels like home.

"Maybe everything," I admit.

"Then I'm not seeing much of an issue. Life is hard, and you might be at one of the hard parts. It could get complicated, but maybe it won't."

"I think she's special. I don't want to mess up."

"It sounds like you don't need my advice, Jake."

Tim and Marty (short for Martine), another high schooler we have working at the nursery, are thrilled by my benevolent gift of donuts. They take two each and scurry off with quick shouts of "thanks!" thrown over their shoulders. Eli, on the other hand, eyes me suspiciously from where he leans against my desk, beside the pastries. I sit in my chair and try to ignore him, but he stares me down.

"What now?" I finally cave.

"Three days ago, you hightail it out of here because you can't stop thinking about your sexy neighbor, then you take off two days and come back with donuts? Word on the street is that the two of you were canoodling around town yesterday. What's the deal?"

"Maybe I just took two days off, and there isn't more to it."

I shrug. I know there's no way Eli lets me off the hook here, and I'm certainly not trying to hide Alice, but it's fun to jerk his chain anyway.

"And maybe people in this town need to mind their own business," I continue, looking around for Tim. It seems like he took his donuts and fled.

"Of course they should. That's not the point. You didn't just take two days off and there is more to it. I know there is," Eli persists.

I take a bite of the maple bacon donut I'd snagged. Hannah was right. These were worth the wait.

"Have you tried the maple bacon donuts? Hannah made them this morning and they are fire," I deflect.

Eli turns to look at me head-on and smacks his palms down on the desk, making everything shake.

"You've gotta tell me what happened with Alice!"

"You've gotta be more gentle around the donuts. They're precious cargo." I slide the box toward me and give Eli my best "serious" face.

Eli huffs and crumples against my desk, exasperated. I take mercy on him, though the dramatics are entertaining.

"I spent the last two days with Alice."

Eli perks up immediately.

"I *knew* it!" he shouts.

I quickly shush him and lean forward to look into the greenhouse space to make sure Tim and Marty haven't reappeared to eavesdrop. I finally spot them pretending to straighten potted plants, but really just shooting the shit.

Eli lowers his voice and continues.

"And what were you doing for two whole days?"

"We were... *not* fighting." I can't keep the corner of my lips from ticking up at the memory. Thinking about those moments without Grateful Bob glaring daggers at me is much more pleasant.

Eli holds up his hand for a high-five. I smack it aside, but grin, nonetheless.

"I like how I feel when I'm with her, Eli. She's incredible." There's no shame or embarrassment here. Alice *is* incredible and I'll tell that to anybody who will listen.

"I'm happy for you, man." He starts walking around my desk. "I'm going to hug you now. Don't make it weird."

I laugh as I stand to accept the hug. Eli is a dork, but I love him.

"I hope it's cool that I invited her to Thanksgiving," I say as we separate.

"Oooh, so it's serious!" Eli is grinning as widely as I am, and his support means the world. "Of course it's cool. I've told you for ages that you could always bring somebody. Mom is going to be *thrilled*."

"Thanks. I'm hoping it *could* be serious. We'll see."

"I can't *wait* to give her all the dirt on you."

His expression has become downright maniacal.

"You know, Alice said the exact same thing when I invited her?"

I suddenly think of the many stories from our decades-long friendship he could share.

I think I may have made a grave error.

Being with Alice is easy, natural.

That evening, I return to Alice's place to find her seated in her driveway beside one of the new doors, which she had moved about three feet.

"What happened here?" I ask with my hands on my hips.

She looks up at me sheepishly.

"It's heavier than I remember from yesterday."

She eyes the door like it might attack.

"That's as far as I got before I gave up."

Together, we eventually get both doors replaced. I'll admit that carrying one all the way down to the shed wasn't the most fun, but Alice batting her eyelashes like a cartoon and thanking me for being a "big, strong man" made it all worth it.

As the day progresses, I think more and more about my conversation with Grateful Bob and become less and less worried about things with Alice. Assuming she wants this to continue, and I think she does, it'll be ok. I may not know exactly how yet, but it will.

For the next two weeks, I feel like I'm walking on air. Even the hard days aren't so bad when I can spend my evenings with Alice in my arms. She's compassionate, funny, clever. She keeps me on my toes.

I expect the whole town has an idea that something is going on between us, even though we haven't been out together since the hardware store excursion. For some reason, nobody has harassed me about it since Hannah and Grateful Bob threatened me. I expect it's out of respect for Alice's privacy and her lack of familiarity with small-town gossip.

I think the same courtesy should be awarded to everybody, but I'll take my victories where I can. As long as they protect Alice, I'm on board.

One afternoon, as I'm finishing up at the nursery for the day, I feel my phone buzz in my pocket. I fish it out and see a text from Alice.

ACE

What do you say to picking up Italian for tonight?

The idea of a carb-filled night with Alice is enticing, but another thought pops into my mind.

ME

A good offer, but I've got another idea if you're game?

Her response is almost instantaneous.

ACE

I'm intrigued… count me in.

ME

Excellent. I'll be there soon.

ACE

I'll be waiting.

My heart leaps in my chest, a feeling that's become familiar over the last few days. The drive feels like it takes years, especially since I make a quick pit stop, but it's only about fifteen minutes later when I park in front of my house. I want to leave access to the garage free for later. I quickly run inside to drop some things off before I jog over to Alice's house, and she opens the door when I get near.

"I heard your truck," she explains as I climb the stairs.

As soon as I'm close enough, she takes my hand and pulls me inside, wrapping her arms around my neck and pulling me down for a kiss before the door is even closed. My hands find her hips while my heart leaps around inside my chest. Touching her breathes new life into me.

"Hi, Ace," I say, my lips still brushing against hers.

"Hi, mountain man." She breathes in deeply. "You smell like trees."

I take a deep breath, suddenly nervous.

"What do you say to going out for dinner tonight?"

Her eyebrows jump as she leans back to fully see my face.

"Jake Preston, are you asking me out on a date?"

"I am. As much as I love keeping you all to myself, what do you think?"

I swallow and wait for her response.

She lights up.

"I would *love* to."

She kisses me again, and my heart finds its normal rhythm. She gestures to the couch.

"Hang until then?"

"As much as I would love to stay, I'm going to head home so I can come back in a couple of hours to pick you up properly."

"Ok, then." Her eyes sparkle. "Woo me."

I drop a peck to her lips. "I'll see you at seven-thirty."

CHAPTER 30

Alice

"Jake and I had sex," I blurt the second Piper answers my video call.

I don't even wait to see if she's in private — whoops. Thankfully, it looks like she's alone in her bedroom.

Piper's face freezes on my screen, and I momentarily wonder if the connection died. Then, she begins screaming.

I let her work through whatever she's feeling and plug in my flat iron to heat up. Ever since Piper taught me how to curl my hair with it instead of a curling iron, it's all I've used. Best curls ever — I swear.

"I knew it. I knew it. I *knew it*!!!" Piper squeals and rolls around on her bed. She stops just to shout at me. "I told you so!"

"Ok, okaaaaaaay! You were right," I huff out the words.

"Say it again."

"You. Were. Right." I smile.

She was.

"Was it amazing? I know it was amazing."

"It *was*, in fact, amazing. Also, it's been multiple times. For like the last two weeks."

"What?!" she screeches, just like I knew she would. "We've texted daily, and you've been holding out on me!"

I section my hair and begin curling it.

"I know, and I'm sorry. I think I just wanted to be sure first?"

Piper smiles sweetly at me.

"So, are you?"

"I might be." I know I'm smiling stupidly, and I don't care.

"I'm SO happy for you, but I need details. Immediately." Her face is split into an enormous grin on my screen, and I love how much of a girl's girl she is.

Even though Piper is on a screen and not beside me, I'm reminded of when we would sit on my dorm room floor gossiping and eating junk food. Those were the days.

I walk her through the last couple of weeks as I finish my hair, but I gloss over some of the more… intimate details. I also leave out the entirety of Reid's little visit. Telling her would introduce too many questions that need a much longer discussion.

Instead, I focus on Jake. I tell her about how good he is and how good I feel when I'm with him.

I rake my fingers through my bouncy curls and turn to show her the back.

"How's it look?"

"Alice, you look stunning, but you didn't give a single one of the *important* details. Now, dish!" Her impatience echoes around the bathroom.

She holds up her two pointer fingers and begins slowly moving them apart.

"Just tell me when to stop," she says.

"Piper!"

"What? It's a fair question!"

"Well, I'm *not* answering it."

I try to think of what I can say without dying on the spot while I collect my makeup.

"He's a big boy."

My face is on fire.

"He's, uh, also very not selfish." I'm so red that it's impossible to determine how much blush I should put on.

"Again, I *knew* it!" Piper bounces around on my screen, and I know she's literally kicking her feet. "And he saved you from a charging moose? Like, are we joking right now?"

"No joke. He did do that. And he's cooked and fixed things and *communicated* about his day. It's been wonderful. He's picking me up at seven-thirty for a real date." I sigh and lean toward the mirror to put on my eyeliner.

"Is this something serious?"

I stop and lean back. Is it? It could be, but it's still so new. Plus, I can't exactly stay here, can I? My job — my life — is in Boston. I have obligations. I should be attending to some of those soon, too. I don't like to go too long…

"I'm not sure, but I'm also not sure I'd mind if it were. After everything with Reid, I don't want to jump into another relationship, but I also don't want to push away a great guy because some arbitrary expectation says I need to wait, you know?"

"You've got to go with your gut. But what are you going to do about things back here? Don't you have to be back here in a few weeks for work? Would you do distance with Jake? Have you even found an apartment here?"

She's asking me questions I don't want to answer, some that I *can't* answer. I've been telling myself I still have time, but I'm not sure that's still true.

"I don't know! I — it's — I don't need to be back until January. It's fine."

That last part is a lie, and Piper can tell. She gives me a look that says so.

"I've been actively avoiding thinking about Boston. I've liked it here. And now I'm actively avoiding thinking about what it means for me and Jake when I do come back."

"You know I can't tell you what to do, but I'm here to listen. You don't need to figure it all out tonight. Enjoy your date with someone who sounds like a good man."

"Thank you, bestie."

I shimmy into a high-neck, backless, black cocktail dress with long sleeves that each have a slit from the shoulder to the cuffs at my wrist. I hook the delicate rhinestone chain across the back at my shoulders and give a twirl in front of my phone for Piper.

"What do you think?"

Piper whistles in response.

"Walk him like a dog, sis. Walk him like a dog."

I roll my eyes at her and carry my phone into my bedroom so I can sit on the bed.

"Enough about me. What's new with you, Pipe?"

"Nothing new. There's just more of the same old bullshit. New boss *Bernard* is still a demeaning, arrogant piece of crap. The other day, I was seriously tempted to see if I could push one of the shelves on him, but I didn't want to hurt the books."

"I think the books would understand in this case," I say, making a face.

Piper has always loved working at the library, and it hurts to see her so miserable because of one nasty, poisonous seed.

"You're a bad influence! You're supposed to say things like 'No, Piper. Murdering your boss would be bad!'"

"My mama taught me that lying was bad."

We're both laughing when I hear a knock downstairs. Piper glances at her clock.

"Oh! And he's punctual, too? You found a rare gem."

"I really think I did…" I smile and squeal. "We'll be finishing this chat soon, though, ok?"

"Ok, but you've got to go now! I love you!"

"Bye! Love you, too!"

I disconnect the call and drop my phone and essentials in a small cross-body bag. I slip on a pair of heels before scurrying down the stairs and opening the door. The dress is worthy of fudging my "no shoes indoors" rule.

My eyes land on Jake, and I have to actively remind myself to keep my mouth from falling open. My worry about our future momentarily flies out of my head. He's in gray slacks, a white button-up with the top couple of buttons undone, and a gray blazer. He's trimmed his beard close and tamed his beautiful curls so they stay out of his eyes. Now that I've seen scruffy Jake, casual Jake, naked Jake, and suave Jake, I can say with absolute certainty that they're all gorgeous.

"I — uh — you — Damn." Jake clears his throat. "You've broken me. You look stunning."

I smile and look down, catching sight of the roses in his hand. I'd been so distracted by all of *him* that I hadn't seen them at first. Jake holds them out to me.

"These are for you."

"They're beautiful," I say honestly. The dozen red roses are blooming and full. It should feel like a cheesy old movie, but it doesn't. It's a man trying to make me feel special.

Once empty, Jake's hand flies to the back of his neck. The poor man is nervous.

I hold up one finger.

"One second."

I leave the door open as I scurry inside to put the flowers in a vase and set them in the center of the table. Burying my face among the blooms, I take a deep breath before hurrying back to Jake. He holds my coat in his hands so I can slip it on. I turn to accept his help and let this wonderful man woo me, just as I requested earlier.

Outside, I freeze on my top step, and my mouth does fall open this time. On the other side of my lawn sits a vintage black Trans Am. I'd recognize the firebird stretched across the hood anywhere. I'm not a car expert, but I like them, and I know that one is sexy as fuck.

I glance at Jake and realize he's waiting at the bottom of the steps with his hand outstretched to help me down. He doesn't seem at all surprised by the presence of the shiny vehicle.

"Where did *that* come from?" I ask as I take his hand and come down the steps.

"*She* is why I never park my truck in my garage and why I pay to store my boat at the marina. I'd rather have a cold truck than even risk parking next to her."

He leads me to the passenger door.

"She was my father's, and I hardly ever take her out, but this is a special occasion."

He places his other hand on the roof of the car and tenderly pats it — her. Obviously, this vehicle is one of his most prized possessions, and I do not overlook the significance of him taking her out for me.

"Well, she's beautiful."

"So are you."

I've blushed so many times this evening that I'm afraid it'll be permanent.

He opens the car door, and I slide into the smooth leather seat. The interior, like the exterior, is pristine. A second later, Jake is in the driver's seat. He turns on the car, and the engine growls. I can't help but smile. This car is *cool*.

Jake looks at me, gently turning my face to him with his fingers on my cheek.

"I almost forgot to do this."

He kisses my lips hungrily, and I know foregoing lipstick was the right choice. I grip the lapel of his jacket as he starts to pull away, tempted to say, "fuck dinner" so we can have sex in this car.

I feel Jake grin against my lips.

"Another time, Ace." He must be able to read my mind.

I groan but sit back in my seat. I still fold my arms like someone denied her treat.

"I'm holding you to that."

The smile on his face is devilish.

I'm loving the closeness of everything in a small town because, in no time at all, we're pulling into the parking lot for a restaurant called Papa's. Jake catches me looking at the sign.

"Have you been here before?"

I shake my head.

"I haven't. I feel like there's so much more in this little town for me to discover."

"Well, let me show you."

I reach across the front seat and squeeze his hand. It's dangerous how much I like this man, especially considering the uncertainty of our feasibility. My heart swoops with unease.

"I'll drop you off up front," Jake offers. I expect he wants to park away from other cars to protect the Trans Am.

"Nah. Park in the boonies. I'd rather walk with you."

I want to soak up every second I can with him.

He squeezes my hand back and parks in an empty part of the lot. I know by now to wait for him to come around the car and open my door. I am fully capable of opening my own door, but I won't lie. I like it when he does it.

I take his offered hand and swivel so I can slide both of my feet out of the car at the same time. The cocktail dress maneuver, am I right? I see Jake's gaze catch at my ankles and slowly work its way up my legs, his throat working when he reaches where my skirt has slid up my thighs.

It takes Jake a second to realize that I've stopped my progress and he's been caught staring. He presses his lips together and shakes his head like he's trying to refocus himself.

"Are you *sure* you don't want to head back home and spend some time in this car with me?"

"You know, I'm really questioning that decision at this precise moment."

His eyes jump to mine before falling back to my legs, and I part my knees ever so slightly. He swallows again.

I snap my legs together and continue sliding out of the car.

"Well, now I'm hungry, so we're going inside. And whatever you're thinking about will have to wait."

I know torturing him just a little bit now will pay off later, so I tug on his hand to heft myself out of the low-riding car. Once I'm standing directly in front of him, I look up, brushing my nose against the underside of his jaw. He tips his head down and likely sees the mischievous look in my eyes.

"Evil woman," he grumbles under his breath. He closes the car door and leads me to the restaurant.

We're immediately seated at a booth with a rounded bench in the corner of the dining room. I like it because it makes me feel like a mob boss and I get to sit beside Jake.

I flip through the menu, giddy as hell to be on a real date with Jake. We're just out and about for the world to see instead of left home, hidden.

I soon realize that there are a lot of eyes on us, and it makes me nervous. It seems like everybody knows Jake, from the hostess to the servers milling about to just about every single other patron who waves as they pass by our table. And he's just sitting here, shoulder-to-shoulder with me, beaming.

I *really* don't want to fuck this up. I think about Boston again, and my smile slips.

Our waiter comes by and asks if we'd like anything to drink besides water. I'm distracted and don't know what to order.

"Um… wine? Red?"

Jake smiles kindly at me and selects a bottle like his brain is still fully functioning. That makes one of us.

My leg is bouncing a mile a minute under the table as I try to focus on the menu. There's a sudden weight on my thigh when Jake places his warm palm there, gently stroking my skin with his thumb. My leg stills, and I look sheepishly at him.

He leans over and whispers, "What's wrong?"

"I feel like everybody is looking at us." I start with the easier of my worries.

"They probably are. I know I wouldn't be able to resist looking at you."

I crack a smile, but it's half-hearted.

"That was extremely smooth, sir."

He chuckles.

"I mean it, though. Being here with you? This night is already perfect. So, you don't need to be nervous."

"It really *is* perfect. Everything with you these last few days has felt… perfect."

"But…?"

"I'm leaving in January. I have to go back to Boston, and I don't know what that means for us."

"This thing we have? It's important to me, and we'll figure it out."

He says it so simply, like there really is nothing to worry about. I look at him perplexed. After what I've learned about Jake's abandonment issues, I expected a lot more panic.

"What makes you so sure?"

"I talked to Grateful Bob this morning. And while he was

basically threatening my life and asking about my intentions, he also made me realize that it doesn't matter where your life takes you. If you want me in it with you, I'm in."

It warms my heart to know I've got Grateful Bob looking out for me, but my train of thought catches on the mention of threats.

"He what?"

Jake waves me off. "The point is, I'm in. I want you to decide what's best for you and know I will work around it. Certain decisions in my life were made for me, and I don't want you to ever feel like you're 'stuck' or that I'm making any for you. If you want to try distance, we will. Boston isn't so far, you know."

He makes it sound so simple, but it feels selfish that I get to decide what I want and have it guide both of our lives. Wouldn't I be doing to Jake exactly what he said he doesn't want to do to me? I think back to the things tying me to Boston, and I feel even worse because I haven't told him the whole story.

"I…" I'm not sure what to say.

"You don't have to decide now. I'd prefer it if you didn't. This is new. Take some time. I'm here to talk about it if you want to. And if you don't, I'll still be here once you make a choice."

I nod slowly, feeling a tightness in the bridge of my nose.

I will __not__ cry.

Jake's promises are what any girl would dream of hearing. They're perfect. He's perfect. But he has a home here, people who care about him, memories, and the nursery. He says things will work out, but I can't take him away from here, not just for me. Long distance isn't a permanent answer, and I don't see a way I can leave Boston permanently.

It feels hard to rally after such an important decision. It also feels soon to talk about changing our lives. I'm off-balance.

Our server returns with our wine, and I take a big gulp once they walk away again.

Jake's hand tightens on my leg.

I look up at him.

"Pull out of that spiral for me, Ace."

He rests his palm against the side of my throat and slides his fingers into my hair. His thumb presses slow circles into the nape of my neck. I think again that he feels so sturdy. I take two slow breaths.

"I promise to think about everything you said, but not tonight. Tonight, I want to be here with you and eat a ridiculous amount of parmesan cheese."

"Deal."

I lift my wine glass.

"Cheers, Ace," Jake says, clinking his glass against mine.

"Cheers."

The drink of wine I take is likely (definitely) larger than is ladylike, but oh well. Jake raises his eyebrows at me but smiles. There's no judgment in his eyes, only curiosity.

"It's to calm my nerves. I don't know if you know this, but I'm on a date with the cutest boy in town."

I bat my eyelashes and pull out my best high school girly voice.

He barks a laugh. "What a lucky bastard."

Dinner is delicious, and I make a mental note to come back here enough times to try everything on the menu. I really do my best to forget our geographic issues and enjoy this night with Jake, but I resolve to come clean with him tomorrow.

CHAPTER 31

Alice

As Jake drives us home, in the silence of the dark car, I slide deeper and deeper into my thoughts, battling between the ties I have in Boston and the joy I've found living on Barefoot Lake. I'm quiet, and Jake keeps stealing glances at me. I don't need to look at him to know his brow is furrowed.

After he stops the car in front of my house, Jake reaches over to touch my cheek like he did when we first got in the car a few hours ago. Again, he kisses me.

"Do you want me to come inside?" he asks softly.

"Yes, please," I admit. I feel vulnerable, and I want him to hold me.

He gets out and comes around to open my door for me.

"I'm just going to put her back in the garage and then I'll come back over," Jake explains, jerking his head back to the car.

Still, he walks me up to my door and waits until I've unlocked it and stepped inside before returning to the driver's seat. Minutes later, he's back by my side, and I quietly lead him upstairs.

Jake helps me out of my dress before stripping down to his boxers and draping his clothes over the chair in my room. He picks up one of his white t-shirts from that same chair — the last few days have resulted in a little stockpile of Jake's clothes at my house — and slides it over my head.

We brush our teeth in silence before crawling into bed. Without a word, Jake collects me in his arms, pulling my back flush against his chest and slipping one of his legs between mine. I'm completely consumed by him.

It feels safe.

We stay quiet, but neither of us falls asleep anytime soon.

Jake's speech at dinner was full of assurances, and I want to say yes to him, but the guilt I feel over the idea of upending his life threatens to crush me.

With Jake's breath on the back of my neck, this moment feels like goodbye. And I'm not sure if that's worse.

I wake up still wrapped in Jake. I can see the glow of the early sun peeking around the curtains. I couldn't have slept very long, but I still feel wide awake.

I keep thinking of my return to Boston with dread. I haven't prepared at all. I don't have a place to live in the city, and I haven't spoken to work since finalizing my fall sabbatical. The mere idea of falling back into the bustle and the noise of city life is daunting. But I'm wildly behind, and I can't put it off any longer. Even without housing and work concerns, I need to get back to Boston for a visit soon. Today.

My mind keeps running through the mountain of things I have to do in a relatively short period of time. The semester starts in a month and a half. I'm out of time.

I text Piper to ask if I can stay with her for a couple of days while I sort things out with work and look for apartments. Thankfully, she answers quickly and says yes. She must be opening at the library today to be awake this early.

Jake is lazily twirling the ends of my hair between the fingers on one of his hands, so I know he's awake too. He lifts himself so he can press a kiss to the side of my head.

"Morning, Ace."

I plaster on a smile that doesn't feel authentic, turn over in his arms, and press tighter against him, nuzzling my face under his chin.

"Would you like me to stay home today?" Jake's morning voice is gravelly, and I'm irritated that my sour mood prevents me from fully appreciating it.

I don't see how I can win when it comes to my future with him. I take a deep breath.

"Actually, could you take a drive with me to Boston? I need to show you something."

I feel Jake trying to pull back from me, but I squeeze him tightly.

"Is something wrong?" he asks.

"It's –" I don't know how to answer him. "It'll make more sense when we get there."

He sinks back against me.

"I'll go anywhere with you."

As we drive away from Wilcox Grove a couple hours later, I can't help but compare it to my drive up in September. The trees that were just beginning to change color then are now vibrant and the road is littered with scattered leaves. The late summer sunshine is gone, and gray clouds chase me back to Boston.

Jake is driving his truck, and I'm occupying my usual spot in the middle of the bench seat. I try to put on music to clear my head, but everything just feels like noise. So, we drive in silence.

Several hours later, I'm directing Jake to take an exit just north of Boston. I give him directions that I've got committed to memory, and soon, we're pulling into a parking lot for a large three-story building. The sign out front reads "Willow Acres."

Jake parks and turns off the truck. I'm impressed that he resisted asking any questions about our destination all morning and for the several-hour-long drive, but the time has come.

"Ace, where are we?"

I can't meet his gaze, so I stare at my hands in my lap.

"I lied to you when you asked if I was ever curious about my father. For most of my life, I really wasn't. But a few years ago, after Mom got sick, I did some digging. I had a name on my birth certificate, and I guess at some point, he participated in a genetic matching service. I've never told anybody, not even Mom, but I found him."

Jake places his hand over mine. I didn't realize I'd been picking at my nails, but his touch stills me.

"There's nothing wrong with looking for him. It's natural to want to know."

I shake my head.

"It's not that. Willow Acres is a facility for people who need full-time care. My father lives here, and he has dementia. He doesn't know who I am, but I'm all he has left."

CHAPTER 32

Jake

I don't know what to expect when we approach William Davis's room, but the door swings open to reveal a clean-cut man in a three-piece grey suit who looks like he's in his sixties sitting behind a desk reading a book. The right side of the room has a bed pressed up against the wall, a chest of drawers, and a closet, with the door slightly ajar. But the left side of the room looks like an office, with a wall of overfull bookcases and two leather chairs before the desk.

Alice's father looks up as we enter and closes his book.

"Come in, come in. Please, have a seat," he says warmly and gestures to the two chairs. He begins shuffling papers on the desk. "You must be here to ask about the grades on the papers. I'm sure I have yours here somewhere."

I follow Alice's lead and sit down, but I don't know what's happening.

"Actually, we're not, Professor Davis," Alice speaks up.

William stills and looks kindly at us.

"Thank goodness. Your classmates have been hounding me all day. I'll be returning papers in class tomorrow, anyway. What can I do for you?"

It seems like he thinks he's a professor and we're his students, visiting during office hours.

"Well, Sir, I was hoping to get your advice. I think I'd like to become an English professor, like you. I was hoping you could tell me about the path you took to get to where you are." Alice accepts her role. Before we came inside, she told me she typically participates in his delusions during her visits to be able to spend time with him without distressing him.

"Ah, an academic mind," William says, leaning back in his chair. He clasps his hands in his lap and begins repeatedly rubbing his finger with his other thumb. It's the *exact* same motion I've seen Alice do a dozen times when she's not sure what to say.

"Teaching wasn't always the goal for me," he continues. "I began my studies as a theater major, determined to become a world-famous actor. I wanted to familiarize myself with as many characters as possible, so I became consumed by reading. It started with plays, but I quickly moved on to other genres, devouring anything I could get my hands on. I think the story-telling abilities of the authors became an obsession of mine.

"Eventually, I transitioned to English, so I could make a profession of learning and sharing the worlds I'd walked in. Being in the classroom with new students is the best part of the job. The bureaucracy is rubbish, but as long as you love working with the students, it's a really good gig."

He gestures to his bookcases, and I turn to look at them. I catch a glimpse of Alice's face before she turns, too, and her eyes are shining. I can't imagine how difficult it is for her to sit before this man, with whom she shares so much, and not have him know.

Alice asks him about his favorite books to teach – the American classics – and they excitedly talk about different books, but I can't take my eyes off Alice. She's animated and engaged, but her hands are tightly clenched in her lap, and her thumb presses hard into her finger as it rubs back and forth.

About an hour later, William's eyes slide to the clock on his desk, and he starts.

"My goodness! Look at the time. You're going to be late for your next class!" he exclaims and stands.

Alice's face falls.

"It's alright. I don't have an afternoon class today. I can stay," she protests.

"No, no. You're young. You should be outdoors, not cooped up in an old man's stuffy office. You've let me prattle on far too long. Besides, I must get back to work." William steps around his desk and walks to his door.

I follow Alice when she reluctantly stands up. When she stands in front of him, I see physical similarities between them, in his smile and his blue-grey eyes.

"Thank you for your time, Sir. It was very helpful," Alice says quietly.

"Of course! It's always a pleasure to speak with someone as clever as you are," William answers, holding out his hand. I don't think he notices Alice's hesitation before she takes it to shake.

William turns to me.

"Good man, coming along to listen to us go on and on."

"I was happy to listen, Professor. It was good to meet you," I say honestly. He shakes my hand, too, and we leave.

We sign out at the front office before walking to the car in silence.

Once we're in the car and back on the highway toward Boston, Alice says, "He's why I can't leave Boston, Jake."

I don't know what to say. I really have no idea what it would feel like to be in her shoes.

"He's a kind man," I awkwardly shift the conversation instead.

"This was a good visit. Sometimes, I can't pick up on who I'm supposed to be to him, and I say or do something wrong, and he gets frustrated. It's easier when he thinks I'm one of his students, though. He seems most comfortable when he's a professor. He taught for decades. I think it was his true love in life. It was his colleagues who noticed he wasn't well."

"Did you know he was an English professor before you met?"

"I didn't. My Mom told me my dad was in theater. I don't know if he lied to her because acting sounded cooler to a pretty girl in a bar, or if she changed the story for me. It was a surprising discovery, though. Funny how the world works sometimes."

She leans her head on my shoulder, and I hold her hand. Her breathing is even, but every few seconds, I feel a tear drop land on the back of my hand.

CHAPTER 33

Alice

I texted Piper when Jake and I were five minutes from her place, so she's standing outside her apartment building when we pull up.

When Jake gets out of his truck to get my bag from the back, Piper fixes him with a suspicious look, and I hastily wipe my face again. I've cleaned myself up as best as I can, and I hope my eyes aren't red from crying. I don't need Piper to misinterpret and punch Jake on the street.

I take my bag from Jake, and he pulls me tight against him, pressing his lips to my hair.

"I'll see you in a few days," I say into his shirt.

"Are you sure you don't want me to come down and get you?" he offers for the umpteenth time.

"Thank you, but I'm sure. You're allowed to get me from the bus station, but that's all."

"Alright. You two." He releases me and pauses before uncomfortably finishing. "Have fun."

While I'm thrilled to be seeing Piper, there's nothing fun about starting the process of returning to a job I don't like or finding an apartment in a city that I don't want to live in anymore. I think Jake knows that.

Jake and Piper exchange waves before Jake gets back in his truck. He waits until Piper and I are in her building before pulling away.

Piper shares a small two-bedroom apartment in the western part of Boston with a girl she met through friends from undergrad. The fifth-floor walk-up is awful and the building, like most in Boston, is ancient, but it's safe, has good access to the T, and is the perfect location for Piper's job.

"Do I need to kill him?" Piper asks, taking my bag from me and leading the way back upstairs.

"Huh?"

"You show up with same-day notice, the morning after your date. Do I need to kill him?" she repeats.

I smile because I'm reminded that I'll have Piper always, no matter what.

"No."

She looks skeptical.

"Really, no. He's still perfect. I just *really* wanted to finish our conversation about your boss."

She closes the door to her apartment behind us and then turns on me.

"What's going on?"

I flop on her couch.

"I need to talk to the college and find an apartment. Also, I wanted to see you, so here I am."

"You don't sound too excited about coming back to Boston," she keenly observes.

"I'm not. But here we are."

Piper squints her eyes at me like she's trying to see if there's more to the story. She collapses on the couch next to me, and it seems like I've passed her evaluation.

"Do you want to dive right in, or should I order all the fried food I can think of first?"

"Fried food first." It's mid-afternoon already, and I haven't eaten since breakfast back at home. I lean sideways and put my head on her shoulder. Sometimes, you just need to ignore life with your best friend for a while.

I do shoot quick texts to Hannah and Grateful Bob, letting them know I'm in Boston, sorting things out for my return. They both wish me luck and ask for an update once I'm back.

Half an hour later, we're carrying our take-out haul back up the stairs in Piper's building while she fills me in on the seemingly endless list of terrible things her boss has done since he started.

"He calls them 'uniform inspections,' but we have no uniform! So, he's just judging our clothes, making snide remarks, and even commenting on peoples' weight. I don't know who he's related to, but only nepotism could be keeping this asshat from getting fired."

"I mean, it sounds like he's creating a hostile work environment. Is he even legally *allowed* to say the crap he says? Have you reported him?"

"There's no *way* it's legal. And I want to, but when Jared tried to a few weeks ago, Bernard somehow twisted everything, so Jared sounded like a lazy piece of crap who was making trouble, and then Bernard literally bullied him until he couldn't take it anymore and quit."

"Have *you* considered quitting?"

I huff as we climb the third flight. I don't know how Piper can talk while taking these stairs without running out of air. But she just keeps going.

"Every damn day. But I really like this place. Or I *did* before Bernard came around. It's so close to here, and I'm getting to know a lot of the people that come in. I don't want to abandon it and watch assface completely ruin it."

We finally reach Piper's floor, and I lean against the wall while she unlocks the door. I need to figure out a cardio routine or something. This is embarrassing. I'm sure the two pounds of mozzarella sticks that I'm carrying will help.

May, Piper's roommate, is nice but usually does her own thing and is out for the day. She's been spending most of her time at her new boyfriend's place lately, so she was totally cool with me staying with Piper for a few days.

The apartment isn't big enough for a kitchen table, but we cover her TV trays with the many take-out boxes we brought back. Piper queues up *Gossip Girl*. We still share a Netflix account, so she picks up right where we left off when she visited me at Barefoot Lake. We would *never* keep watching without the other. We settle into the couch and dive in. At one point, I open my laptop to vaguely scroll through apartment listings and email the head of the English department to set up a meeting, but I slam it shut after barely ten minutes.

Piper and I blissfully avoid reality for the rest of the afternoon, reheating leftovers when we get hungry again, reciting lines along with our show, and shouting in dismay every time Dan shows up on the screen.

Later that night, when we're sitting on her bed, Piper finally gives me a look that says she's not letting me hide anymore.

"Not that I'm not thrilled to have you here, but what happened on this date that had you running back here? Did Jake freak out about your job?"

I stare up at the ceiling, a smile on my lips at the mere mention of his name.

"The opposite. He said all the right things. He told me that if I want something with him, he'll be there. He's willing to try long distance, and if things continue to go well, we'll figure it out."

"Are you sure he's real?"

I look over at her and nod. "He's *very* real."

"So, what's the problem?"

"I don't really want to come back to Boston. I wasn't happy here, and that wasn't just because of Reid."

My heart is beating fast like I just did fifty jumping jacks. Looking back at my Boston life, it would seem like I have no reason to be displeased. I was successful at my job, paid well, and respected at a reputable university. I was trusted with big decisions and got along well with my coworkers. I'd "made it" in a huge city, and that city gave me access to incredible restaurants, shows, pop-up art fairs, farmer's markets, sports teams, music venues, and more.

I feel like I'm waiting for Piper to laugh at me or question whether I'm a moron.

Piper doesn't laugh, though. And she doesn't insult me.

"What do you mean?"

She says it gently like she's coaxing a scared animal out of a corner.

"Maybe it started because Reid made me feel so small and alone, but you're really the only person I have in Boston. I haven't spoken to anyone from work since I went on leave. None of them are real friends, even if some are nice work acquaintances. And…"

I pause for a steeling breath.

"I hate my job," I blurt.

Piper does start at that one.

"What are you talking about? You *love* teaching!"

"But that's the problem. I don't *teach* anymore. I only have one class in the spring. I've almost fully transferred to a department lead role."

"So why don't you go back to teaching?" Piper says it like it's a simple solution, but nothing feels simple about it.

"I'm not sure that I can, or that I should. This is supposed to be the dream. I'm getting very close to being a department head, and it's happening so much earlier than I ever expected. I feel… guilty for hating it. But I *hate* it."

"But why? Why do you feel guilty?" Piper looks truly perplexed, and I question for the first time whether I might be being too hard on myself.

"I feel like I'm not feeling what I'm supposed to. I should be grateful that the school trusts me so much. It also feels like I want to quit because I can't hack it. Like I can't handle the pressure or responsibilities, so I'm running back to what was easier."

Piper furrows her brow.

"But that isn't what's happening at all. You *can* hack it. You just don't *want* to. And I'm here to tell you that that's completely alright."

I look at her sheepishly.

"Is it, though?"

She throws her arms up.

"Of course it is!"

"I feel like a failure, like a disappointment." My stomach is twisting itself in knots. Maybe fried food wasn't such a good idea.

"To who?"

I pause.

"To Mom."

Piper's face splits into an enormous grin. I pull the pillow from behind me and smack her with it.

"I'm glad my failure amuses you!!"

She takes the pillow from me, puts it on my lap, and lies on it. She reaches over to lace her fingers with mine.

"I'm smiling because you're ridiculous. There is nothing about what you want that sounds like failure, and you're insane if you think you could disappoint Rain."

"She sacrificed so much for me to get what I have, and now I want to just walk away from it."

"She sacrificed for you to be *happy*, Alice. And you're not walking away. If you go back to teaching, you're walking toward what you love."

Well, when she says it like that…

"And if you're not happy in Boston at all, why are you coming back?"

When I first found William Davis, I decided not to tell my mom about it. I still don't know if that was the right choice, and I likely never will, but she was already sick, and I didn't want to risk her thinking that I was disappointed with my life with her as my sole parent. Finding out about his illness only solidified my decision.

Since I kept him a secret from Mom, I didn't tell anybody else. It felt wrong to tell even Piper without Mom knowing. Now, though…

"I found my father just over two years ago, and he's living with dementia north of the city in a full-time care facility."

Piper launches back up from my lap, and her mouth slowly opens as she stares at me, completely speechless. After a few beats, she launches across the bed and throws herself on me, squeezing me in a tight hug.

"You know that's a big bomb to drop, hun," Piper says squished against me.

"Yeah…" is all I can think to say. "So, I can't exactly leave."

Piper pulls back, holding me at arm's length.

"I'm sure there are options you could explore," she suggests, but I just shake my head.

"Not this time."

She doesn't push things. Eventually, we lay down and fall asleep side by side.

CHAPTER 34

Alice

I spend most of the next day looking at overpriced, cramped, ancient apartments around Boston. I for sure waited too long to start my search, and the pickings are slim. The biggest moving day in Boston is September 1st, when students attending the hundreds of colleges and universities in Boston and the surrounding towns come back to school. There aren't many apartments with January 1st move-in dates as it is, and looking only a month and a half in advance is sheer idiocy on my part.

Cold and with sore feet, I end the day with photos of some places that don't look completely diseased and links to several invasive applications in my inbox. Great.

The following day is my meeting with the head of the English department at my university. She's a kind and reasonable woman. Inspired by my conversation with Piper, I have a whole plan for telling her that I want more time in the classroom and less admin work.

Sitting across from her, I can see I'm failing to convince her why I'm unhappy with my current work path. She doesn't understand why I'm not thrilled with the oversight opportunities I'm being presented with. In fact, she informs me that my one teaching opportunity for the spring semester has been transitioned into a hybrid class, so only five sessions are in person, and the rest will be taught via video conference. *And*, after the spring semester, she wants to get me on track for an associate dean position without any teaching obligations at all. I think I'm supposed to be elated, but I feel like I've been punched, instead.

After an hour, I stumble out of her office, unsure how I ended up even further away from my goal. I run through the conversation over and over in my head as I walk to the little park where I planned to meet Piper. We're going out for dinner tonight.

I'm so deep in my own thoughts that I don't realize precisely where I'm sitting until I hear my name.

"Alice, Alice, Alice." The cool voice is cruel in its mocking. "Coming to my work to get me back?"

My head snaps up, and my heart sinks even further. Reid is quickly approaching my bench from across the street. He kept work so separate from me that I'd completely forgotten where his office building was located. Reid isn't a factor in my life anymore, and I really wasn't thinking about him at all. I'm cursing my own stupidity when he comes to a stop in front of me.

I look up at him, holding that snakelike gaze and resisting the urge to vomit on his shiny shoes.

"I'm not here for you, Reid. Please go away."

His expression turns sour. He looks twisted and nasty. I don't know how I never saw it before. I really thought this man was attractive?

He looks up and down the street.

"Where's your bodyguard, then? He going to jump out and sucker punch me again?"

Sick of Reid literally talking down to me, I get to my feet.

"He defended me against an ambush outside my home," I snap at him. "Don't rewrite history."

Unlike when Reid showed up in Wilcox Grove, I'm not afraid.

I'm furious that he is trying to bully me *again,* and that he seems to be coming for Jake. I've lost too many battles today, and I will not lose to Reid, too. I squeeze my hands into fists when I feel my fingers start shaking.

Reid steps forward and points a finger in my face, but I hold my ground.

I can feel his breath on my cheeks when he hisses, "You'd better watch your fucking mouth. Because *I* remember your little boy toy attacking me, and I'd bet the police would *love* to hear all about that dangerous brute. You're lucky I haven't already said something."

"Alice?"

Both Reid and I turn and see Piper approaching us, her phone in her hand. She makes a face like she smells something nasty when she sees Reid is the person in front of me.

Reid lowers his hand, and I move to stand with Piper. Her eyes dart between us.

"You remember what I said," he snarls.

I spin back toward him.

"No. *You* remember what you've done. You treated me like shit for years and couldn't handle it when I left your sorry ass. You came to *my* house to bully me into coming back, and you failed. You're pathetic, Reid, and your threats are bullshit. We both know it."

"You're lucky I took pity on you as long as I did. I was slumming it with you." Reid's voice rises as he steadily loses his grip on his temper. Some people on the street have turned to look at us.

"Crawl back in the hole you came from. I'm done being torn down by you," I practically snarl.

Reid steps toward me again and raises his hand like he might grab me.

"I wouldn't." Piper's voice is like ice.

Reid slowly turns to her, and she's holding up her phone screen. 911 is already dialed.

"Give me a reason to call. I *dare* you."

Reid's eyes dart to the screen, and he seems to be considering whether Piper would follow through on her threat.

He steps back, and his arm falls to his side.

"You're not worth my time," he hisses.

"Tell yourself whatever you need to, buddy."

I loop arms with Piper, and we walk away together. I keep my head held high, and I don't look back.

Once we're a few blocks away, Piper slows and pulls my arm to stop me. I'm still shaking from anger, and I'm sure she can feel it.

"Alice, what was that? Are you ok?"

"I'm ok." I take a deep breath. *I'm ok.*

"That was a grown man throwing a tantrum because somebody told him 'no,'" I continue.

"Has he been like that before? And did I hear you say he came to Barefoot Lake?" Piper's face shows a mix of shock and concern.

Reid's words fly through my mind again, and I feel a wave of nausea when I remember how he threatened to report Jake.

"I'll tell you everything, but I need to call Jake quickly."

Piper looks like she might object for a second, but she nods instead and ushers me to a bench.

"I'll give you a minute," she says before stepping away. She doesn't go far, and her head is on a swivel, probably keeping an eye out for Reid. She's my faithful guard, and I love her.

I dial Jake's number, and he answers on the first ring.

"Ace – Hey! What's up?" He sounds honestly happy to hear from me, and my heart sinks with the knowledge that I'm about to ruin his day, maybe more.

"Hey." My voice is unsteady.

"What's wrong?" His tone immediately shifts. I hear shuffling like he's standing up and pushing his chair back.

"I ran into Reid."

"What happened? Are you ok?"

"I'm ok."

I then recount the argument, including Reid's threat.

"I'm so sorry. I don't know what he's going to do," I finish.

"Ace, we've talked about this. You have nothing to apologize for. And I'm not sorry for hitting him. From what I know about him, I doubt somebody with an ego like his will admit to having his ass handed to him. If he does, we'll deal with it."

"I feel awful,"

"I don't. I'm so proud of you. Are you sure you're ok?" I haven't heard Jake sound this worried since the last time we encountered Reid.

"Yeah. I'm ok."

"I can be there in a few hours."

"It's ok. You don't need to. I'm coming home tomorrow."

"I don't like that you ran into him. It's too wild to be a coincidence."

"I really think that's all it was, and I'm ok. I promise." The line is quiet, and I'm not sure what to say. "I owe Piper an explanation, so I should probably go."

"You're incredible, Ace," he says reverently. "Can I talk to Piper quickly, though?"

I figure he wants another person to assure him I'm ok, so I get up and hand Piper the phone, letting her know it's Jake. She's quiet at first, listening to something Jake's saying.

"Yeah, she's alright," Piper says.

I don't want to hover, so I go back to the bench. She comes to sit beside me after another minute on the phone. She takes my hand, and we sit quietly together for a little while.

Piper and I bail on going out, opting to pick up wine and more take-out and heading back to her place. We suddenly both feel exhausted.

We sit on her couch, and she immediately tackles me in a bear hug. I tell her about how things really were with Reid, and about his little visit to New Hampshire.

"You didn't have to carry this alone, Alice," she sputters with difficulty.

"I know. I just… I thought it was my fault, that maybe he was right. It was embarrassing."

"You know this says nothing about you and everything about him, right?"

"I do. And I did then, too. But it didn't make it easier."

"I'm so sorry, babe."

We just lay there for a while, holding one another. We eventually pick at food and sip our wine, neither of us is too hungry. Piper puts on *Dumbo* and has me sit on a pillow on the floor in front of her so she can braid my hair. Our evening becomes a marathon of old Disney movies. We're about to put on another when Piper suddenly stands, checking her phone. She goes to the door and hits the button that unlocks the door downstairs.

I look at her confused, but she just shrugs, like nothing weird is going on at all.

There's a knock on her door.

"It's for you," she says, even though she's standing right by the door.

I give her a suspicious look but get up and pass her to open it.

Out of breath from running up five flights of stairs stands Jake.

CHAPTER 35

Jake

The second Alice has the door open far enough for me to fit through, I step forward and sweep her into my arms.

"Jake?" Her voice is muffled by her face pressing into my chest.

I try to pull back, but her arms wrap around my back, and she squeezes me. I look over her shoulder and lock eyes with Piper.

Thank you, I mouth at her.

She gives me a dignified nod before tiptoeing into another room and quietly closing the door.

I slowly scoot myself and Alice further into the apartment so I can close the front door behind me, but I keep her in my arms, willing to hold her as long as she needs. She can be the first one to end this hug.

I press my cheek against her hair and breathe in her smell. I just saw her two days ago, but it already feels like too long, especially with Reid's ambush.

After a few minutes, she shifts and pulls back. I hold her shoulders and look into her eyes, which hold a deep sadness and exhaustion from more than just physical tiredness. I want to hit Reid again.

One of my hands slides down Alice's arm to grasp her hand, and she leads me to the couch.

"What are you doing here?" she asks.

"You've got to be out of your mind if you thought I would just sit home tonight. I had to see you, to make sure you're alright. Maybe I was hoping to bump into Reid on my way through the city… with my front bumper."

She chuckles at that.

"I'm not here to be some overbearing caveman, though, and I can go back right now if you want me to."

She vigorously shakes her head.

"Or Piper said I could crash on the couch if you'd prefer I stay."

She nods just as furiously.

"But isn't this disrupting your life? Work? Something?"

"You're more important. You were attacked today."

"I wasn't—"

"You were. Even if he didn't hit you. Don't downplay how he came at you or what he's been doing to you."

"No, I won't," she agrees.

I wrap an arm around her shoulders and tip her toward me for another hug. She said she was ok on the phone, but it's still comforting to feel her breathing against me.

"So, you'll stay tonight? We're watching Disney movies and eating things that are bad for us."

"I'll stay."

Alice smiles, and I think my heart could burst out of my chest.

"It's safe to come back out now!" Alice hollers toward the door Piper hid behind, and I unwrap my arm from around her.

The speed with which Piper pops open that door makes me think she was sitting right behind it with her ear plastered to the wood. I don't blame her, though. She's always looking out for

Alice, and I love that these two women have one another. Besides, she did me a solid, letting me come down and crash tonight, so she can eavesdrop all she wants.

Piper drops down on Alice's other side and wordlessly hands me a Styrofoam box with buffalo wings inside. Alice recounts the rest of her trip down to Boston, including the unsanitary apartments and the discouraging discussion with her university. Piper sufficiently expresses her outrage over the situation, and we jointly support Alice for a while before she asks that we press play and watch over a hundred dogs cover themselves in soot. She says we can worry about her living situation and job another day.

Halfway through a film about a kitten trio and the alley cat father who stepped up, I look down and realize Alice has fallen asleep on my shoulder.

"Psst!" I hiss to get Piper's attention, pointing to Alice when Piper looks over at me.

Piper carefully holds Alice up while I stand so I can carry her to Piper's room. Once Alice is settled in the bed, I turn to see Piper holding out some black basketball shorts.

"From the former hookup pile. Don't worry. They've been washed," she whispers.

I'd literally gotten in my car and come straight here, so I didn't bring anything with me. I take the shorts and follow Piper back into the hallway. She shows me to the bathroom and tells me there are new toothbrushes under the sink.

"Thanks. For the shorts and toothbrush, but also for letting me come down here."

"Thanks for wanting to come." She pauses. "You seem good for her. Don't fuck this up."

"I won't."

"Good." Piper narrows her eyes at me, and I know this woman will look out for her best friend for the rest of her life.

"Good night, Jake. I like you," she says as she moves toward her room.

"I like you, too, Piper. Good night."

In the morning, the three of us have breakfast together before Piper leaves for work. Alice and I wish her strength to handle Bernard, who I understand is basically a disease. There are hugs all around.

Now that I'm here, I get to drive Alice back to Wilcox Grove. I know she would have been fine on the bus, but I'll take any chance I get to spend time with her. Once we're in the truck, Alice looks at me.

"There's somewhere I'd like to take you before we head back. It's not far. Is that ok?"

"Of course it's ok."

She leans toward me, tilts her head, and kisses my cheek.

"Thank you," she says softly.

Alice gives me directions, and after a short drive, I park at the back of a sandy beach. Nobody else is around.

Once we're out of the truck, Alice leans against the fender to slip off her shoes, so I follow suit. Holding her shoes in one hand, she laces the fingers of her other with mine.

Silently, we walk across the chilly sand, stopping where the foam from the waves just kisses our toes.

"This is where I spread Mom's ashes," Alice says, barely above a whisper.

A lump immediately forms in my throat. I squeeze Alice's hand and step closer as her head falls against my shoulder.

We stand silently side by side for close to fifteen minutes

while I say a silent goodbye to my friend. I breathe out a slow, shaky breath.

Alice lifts her head and turns toward me.

"Are you ready?" she asks.

"Yeah," I reply, nodding. "Thank you for bringing me here."

"I am sorry I didn't think to invite anybody from Wilcox Grove to her service. I should have done better for her."

I give her hand another squeeze.

"You're the best she could have asked for."

And I mean it.

As we near the truck, Alice gets a call. She looks concerned when she sees the number on her screen.

"It's Willow Acres," she explains before answering.

I only hear her side of the conversation.

"Hello?… Speaking… He is?... No, I'm not far." She covers the speaker of the phone and turns to me, excitement all over her face. "They say he's lucid. He hasn't had a day like this since I found him. Do we have time to go there?"

I nod and immediately unlock and open the door.

"Get in," I direct. "Let's go."

"Enter," William's voice calls from inside his room after we knock. He's sitting behind his desk, as he was last time, furiously shuffling papers. He looks more disheveled than he did last time. He isn't wearing a vest or suit jacket, and his shirt is rumpled like it was hastily thrown on. A facility employee, maybe a doctor, is standing beside him and the concerned look on her face gives me a bad feeling.

William glances up at us before glaring at the doctor.

"I have students," he snaps. "Like I told you, you need to go."

I can almost feel the disappointment washing over Alice.

"I'm sorry, Professor," Alice's voice cracks. "We can come back later if you're busy."

"No," William answers, still stern. "I am here for *students*, not for pointless meetings with unnecessary doctors."

The doctor clenches her jaw but acquiesces.

"Fine, I'll go."

On her way out, she pauses beside me and Alice, gently placing a hand on Alice's arm.

"I'm sorry," she says and leaves.

William had gone back to his papers but looks up again.

"Well? Sit!" He's still agitated, and I expect this is what would be considered a bad day.

We tentatively move further into the room and sit.

"I can't find— I don't know—" William is mostly muttering to himself again. I'm not sure he knows what he's looking for. "What do you want?" he barks at Alice, and she jumps.

"I'm sorry, I—" she struggles to think of a lie that will soothe him. "Can we discuss what you're currently reading?"

"Miss, office hours are for legitimate questions about course material, not for mindless chit-chat. I am a respected Professor here and a very busy man. If you're interested in yammering on about new books, might I suggest joining a book club?"

Alice looks cowed, and I want to yell at the brute of a man berating her, but I remember he's sick, and I can't. Alice opens and closes her mouth a couple of times, clearly searching for something to say.

"We apologize, Professor. We didn't mean to disturb you. We'll go." I stand and reach for Alice's hand. Her chin is quivering when she walks with me to the door.

My hand is on the doorknob when the room becomes suddenly silent.

"Rain?" William's voice is gentle. "Rain McDermott?"

Alice and I spin toward him. His face has become soft, his expression tender.

"I've missed you every single day," he barely whispers.

"What did you say?" Alice's voice cracks.

William blinks a few times, and his brow furrows again.

"I thought we were finished here," he says angrily. "Out with you!"

We leave, and I gently close the door behind us. The doctor from earlier is waiting in the hall.

"Are you his daughter?" she asks Alice.

Alice nods. "What just happened in there? He said my mom's name right before I left. He's never done that before. He doesn't even know who I am."

Alice is hugging herself, but her voice is steady.

The doctor lays her hand on Alice's arm again with a sympathetic touch.

"We may never know what he saw. Dementia is a very complicated and cruel condition. His status can change wildly very quickly. He was doing well just a few minutes before you arrived. Then, like a switch went off, he was locked in his mind again. I know it can be very distressing to see, but it's not uncommon," the doctor explains.

Alice nods again, but it's unclear how much she's processing. Her father just called her by her dead mother's name. I place a hand on her back, and she leans into it.

"Is he ok now?"

"He's safe, and he will be well cared for."

"Ok… Ok, good. Let me know if there's any change. I'll be back as soon as I can."

I wrap an arm around Alice's shoulders and pull her close to me as we walk out.

In the truck, Alice still sits in the middle beside me, but she keeps her hands in her lap and stares blankly out the front windshield as we drive north. The silence stretches five minutes, ten, twenty.

"Alice?" I finally crack, feeling helpless while she faces whatever she's feeling after that very difficult visit.

"I'm going to end up just like him," she vaguely replies.

"You don't know that," I protest. "There's no guarantee…"

"I don't mean the dementia, though I guess that is possible, too. I don't have the gene. I got checked. No, I mean the regret."

I quickly glance over at her, but her position hasn't changed.

"He knew what he said when he called me Rain. I know it. I might never get to hear their story or why he wasn't around, but I can feel it in my bones that he was being honest. He's missed her every single day. And he'll never know he now has me. I'm not even sure he knows I exist. It's utterly heartbreaking."

The English language hasn't created words that are appropriate to say to somebody in Alice's position. The ones I settle on are pathetic.

"I'm so sorry."

She reaches for my arm, and I release the wheel with my right hand to hold her.

"I don't want to be in Boston. I don't want to be an administrator. I don't want to be away from you and Grateful Bob and Hannah and Wilcox Grove. I've felt peace in Wilcox Grove that I never had in Boston. I never thought I would, but I've loved recognizing familiar faces on each grocery run, getting to know people and their families around town. I feel supported. When I got to Boston and texted Hannah and Grateful Bob to let people know I'd be away, I realized I had more people to check in with, more people who would notice my absence, than I had when I left Boston. I love the nature, the quiet, and the comradery of crazy flag football fans. I finally understand why Mom decided to go there when she got sick, and I wish we could have enjoyed it together.

"But I can't leave William, and I won't let you leave your life for me. I'm afraid I'm going to have decades of regrets, just like he does."

I feel worthless, without a single answer for her. Her voice is so small, and she sounds broken.

"We'll figure it out. I promise." Even in my own ears, the vow feels hollow. I have to figure this out.

CHAPTER 36

Alice

I've been back in Wilcox Grove for a few days, but I feel like a ghost watching somebody else go through the motions of my life. The visit with my father keeps playing on repeat in my head. I swear I hear him call for my mother every time I close my eyes. It was chilling for him to be there for one moment and gone again so quickly.

Tomorrow is Thanksgiving, and I keep debating whether I should cancel on Jake and his invitation to spend the holiday with Eli's family. I'm no fun at all right now, and I'm not sure I have the emotional capacity for an evening surrounded by people.

While I've appreciated Jake's company every day since the Boston trip, we've mostly sat in silence. I think he's been really busy with work planning stuff, maybe for the holidays, because he's hardly been off his laptop, and he's regularly stepping into another room for phone calls, even after he comes back from the nursery.

I highly doubt Eli's family is planning on an evening of silence and existential crises.

I put on my shoes and walk outside when I hear Jake's truck pull into our little space. We've been alternating spending time at my house and his, and it's his turn tonight. He meets me at his front door after parking the truck, just beaming.

We've been equally somber for the last several days, so I briefly wonder if he's cracked. He catches my face with both of his hands and sweeps me into a deep kiss, very unlike the hello peck we typically share when he gets home or when I visit him at work. He's cracked.

He grips my hand tightly while he fumbles to unlock his front door. I've never seen him this excited. I pause when he gets the door open, but he tugs my arm.

"Get in, get in. I have something to show you."

Once I'm inside, he gently takes me by my upper arms and guides me backward to sit on his couch.

He stands in front of me and pulls a small stack of folded pages out of the inside pocket of his jacket. He separates it into two piles and hands them both to me.

"Go on, look," he says eagerly.

I begin leafing through the pages. The first pile has page after page listing different care facilities, along with doctor bios and qualifications, reviews, pricing lists, insurance plans accepted, and printed directions from my house. The second pile has at least a dozen different English teaching positions at universities and community colleges around New Hampshire.

"Jake, what are these?" I ask even though it's clear what they are.

"Stay," he says simply.

"You deserve to have a life without regret. I can't promise that, but I want to try. I've done some research and spoken to people at each of these facilities. I think they could all be great options for your father if you'd like to look at moving him. If not, I'll drive down to see him with you whenever you'd like. Or you can go alone, maybe visit with Piper. I also looked up some teaching opportunities within forty minutes of here. I don't want to overstep, but I want you to know that you have options. If you want to stay in Wilcox Grove, I want to help you be here."

I stare at him in disbelief.

"Is this what you've been doing on your computer every night?"

"I wanted to be thorough." He shrugs.

I look back at the pages in my lap.

"I don't know if moving William is a good idea, though."

"That's ok. Talk to his doctors. See what they say."

"And I'm committed to my old job at least for the spring semester. I couldn't bail on them this close to the end of the year."

"That's ok, too. You said your class is almost all remote anyway. I bet there's a lot you could do from here if you wanted to. If the university had to choose between you leaving entirely or working primarily remotely from New Hampshire, I'm betting they'd figure something out for you."

"There's no guarantee I would get one of these other jobs for the fall."

"There's not, but I have faith in you. And if it takes some more time to get you back in the classroom, so be it. I'll hire you at the nursery in the meantime if you're bored."

He really has been thorough, and the realization barrels into me like a freight train.

"I can stay?"

"You can stay."

CHAPTER 37

Jake

The next day, I try to keep a straight face as Alice squirms like a noodle in the passenger seat. Her leg bounces up and down at over a hundred beats a minute, and she keeps glancing at me every few seconds. We're on our way to Thanksgiving dinner at Eli's parents' house, and she's nervous as all holy hell. I find it hilarious because we're about to spend the evening with a group of the least intimidating people ever.

"Ace, you've got to stop bouncing around so much. I'm going to get pulled over for hosting a rave while driving."

She stills for about four seconds before her leg starts bobbing up and down again.

"I can't help it! I'm nervous!"

"That's what I don't get. *Why*? You've already met Eli and Scott, and you get along better with Grateful Bob than I do, and I promise you Eli's parents are the nicest people on the planet. So, what's got you so tied up?"

"These are your people, and I'm the interloper! What if they hate me?"

"They don't hate you. You already know four of the people

there like you."

"Four? Eli, Scott, Grateful Bob, and..."

"Me, you dingbat. I like you."

"You like me?"

"A whole fucking lot."

She goes quiet, and her leg stills. I look over at her, and she's staring back at me like she wants to say something. I look back at the road giving her time to work through it.

When I pull over in front of Eli's parent's house, she's still struggling.

I put the car in park, turning fully to face her.

"Ace, what is it?"

She takes a deep breath.

"I more than like you, Jake."

I feel her words like a zing to every atom in my body.

I smile before leaning over to kiss her.

"I more than like you, too, Ace."

She smiles back at me.

As I walk around the front of the car to open Alice's door for her, I'm hit with the realization that I probably just fucked up the "I love you" moment, and I immediately feel nauseous.

I do love her and must have almost said it at least fifty times, but I haven't been able to get it out. I haven't said those words to a woman in over a decade, and the last time I did, I certainly didn't feel this way about the woman. I'm not sure I even knew what love was at the time if this is what it's supposed to feel like.

I look through the windshield and see Alice gazing at me expectantly because, apparently, I've stopped dead in my tracks. I hurry over to her door.

"What's up?" she asks.

"I, uh, couldn't remember if we brought the cranberry sauce." The excuse is awful, but Alice doesn't seem to notice.

She holds up the can in her fist. "Fear not. I've got it right here!"

I take the can from her since she's also carrying an apple pie she baked. Halfway up the walkway, I grab Alice's free hand and feel slightly better, being able to touch her, even though all I can think about is my missed moment.

I try to plaster a neutral look on my face. I think it's working.

I release Alice's hand to ring the doorbell before scooping it back up.

Through the glass panel beside the door, I see Helen, Eli's mom, rushing to greet us. She's a short woman, all soft and warm, and always trying to load me up with food to take back home. Her short silver hair is swaying around her ears, and her eyes are nearly shut with how big she's grinning. She swings open the door, and the smile on her face falls.

"Are you feeling ok, Jake?"

My neutral look is, in fact, not working.

"Yeah, Ma. I'm fine."

I lean forward and give her a one-armed hug.

"This is Alice," I say, releasing Helen.

Alice drops my hand to hold out hers, and I can see it trembling.

"It's so nice to meet you, Mrs. Chambers. Thank you so much for having me today."

Helen's face warms instantly and the creases from a life of smiling are deep-set beside her eyes. She takes Alice's hand in both of hers, squeezing it before stepping forward and enveloping her.

"You sweet girl, it's my pleasure. And, please, it's Helen."

Alice tentatively wraps her arm around Helen's back and glances sideways at me from where her face sits above Helen's shoulder. Her eyes have welled with tears, and I realize this is probably the first mom hug she's gotten since Rain died. Alice closes her eyes and sinks into Helen's embrace.

I blink furiously to clear the moisture in my own eyes. I know how safe that hug feels.

Alice quickly wipes at her eyes when she steps back, and my heart squeezes at the tender moment.

Then, Scott comes barreling around the corner, sliding on the tile in his socks.

"Alice! What's up! Welcome to the family, sis!" he exclaims, scooping Alice up in a bear hug that lifts her feet off the ground as he affectionately crushes the life out of her.

Scott has never been chill a single moment in his entire life, and he's been acting like Alice and I are married since I told him she'd be at Thanksgiving.

I try to catch his eye to glare at him for attacking Alice when she's already nervous, but as he releases her, Scott immediately asks about Piper and shuffles Alice into the house, completely ignoring me.

Helen laughs.

"I'm sure he's thrilled to see you, too."

"I don't mind," I say honestly. "I don't notice anybody else when Alice is around either."

"I'm so happy for you, Jake," Helen says sweetly.

She ushers me inside and closes the door.

There's already chaos in the great room. Eli and his father, Richard, are arguing over the best way to carve the turkey, both with gigantic knives in their hands. This is particularly amusing since Eli is basically a clone of his father, besides the shocks of silver hair at Richard's temples. Grateful Bob is loudly watching football and frequently shouting at the television. Scott is taking Alice from picture to picture, which Helen and Richard have displayed, showing her all of the horrible, awkward stages of my childhood as I stand beside Eli in many of the shots.

I'm home.

Alice somehow escapes Scott and slides up beside me, but the Cheshire Cat grin on her face isn't reassuring.

"Should I be worried?"

"You missed at least one of the photos from your long hair phase."

My eyes jump to the row of picture frames lining the mantle, remembering the exact photo she's talking about. I move to go steal it, but Alice puts a hand on my arm.

"Don't bother. I already took a picture of it." She pats her phone in her pocket.

I groan and drag a hand down my face. "Any chance you want to forget you saw that?"

"Not for all the money in the world."

She's smiling and seems much more at ease now. I look around and realize all of the important people in my life are in one place. This is a really good day, even with Eli deciding to share the most embarrassing stories he can think of.

The entire day is perfect. Alice fits right in, not that I doubted she would, and we all eat a stupid amount of delicious food. It's loud and messy, and Richard almost loses a toe when Eli drops a knife, but it's perfect.

We even step into a quiet room to call Hannah and Leslie and then Piper to wish them a Happy Thanksgiving. It's a small moment, but sharing it feels immeasurably important.

We've finished eating but are all sitting around the table, listening to Eli recount the latest story of our youth.

"And then," Eli wheezes in between laughs. "And *then*, he

basically tackles somebody's mom because he refused to move his legs."

Alice flashes me a sympathetic look but fails to hold in her laughter.

"I'm so sorry, Jake, but it's a *really* funny mental image."

I lean back in my chair and cover my face with my hands. Eli decided to share the story of the time I ripped my pants ice skating in front of our entire class and then spectacularly crashed into a very understanding woman.

I peel back my hands and point an accusatory finger at Eli.

"You failed to mention the fact that I was *seven*." My shout is barely audible over the laughter around the whole table.

"Details, details." Eli waves me off and takes a gulp of his water.

"Here I was, thinking it would be nice for you two to get to know one another. I must be insane."

I move my finger between him and Alice. They're quite the duo, but it's all in good fun. Plus, I don't entirely hate sharing more of my life with Alice.

"Aw, no. It is nice! We're bonding over how much we like you," Alice insists, bumping her shoulder against mine.

She likes me. She more than likes me.

I smile down at her.

"Alright, fine." I look to Eli. "Let's have another story, then."

Later that night, Alice and I follow behind Scott as he drives back to our house. He came straight to Helen and Richard's from work but will stay for the weekend before returning to New York.

Like she often does, Alice slid into the middle seat so she can rest her head on my shoulder. She's crashing the second we get back.

"You have a good day, Ace?" I ask as I pull up next to Scott's car in front of my garage.

"I had the best day, Jake. Thank you for sharing your people with me."

"They're your people now, too, Ace. You know that, right?"

"Yeah," she says very sleepily.

"Let's get you to bed."

"Mmhmm."

Her eyes are fluttering closed, so I scoop her up and carry her inside.

Scott mouths "good night" at me before settling onto the couch. He waits until I've shut my bedroom door to turn on the television.

I pull off Alice's coat, boots, tights, dress, and bra, and maneuver her uncooperative arms into one of my t-shirts. She's maybe half-conscious, but zero percent helpful.

I get her situated under the blanket before changing and brushing my teeth. As soon as I lie beside her, Alice turns toward me and curls against my side. Everything feels right.

I brush her hair from her forehead.

"You still up, Ace?" I ask softly.

"Mmhmm," she mumbles.

"Alice?" I try again.

She opens her eyes and smiles.

"Hey, Jake."

"Hey, Ace. I just need you to know I love you."

She props herself up, more alert now.

"Yeah?"

"Yeah."

My heart is thudding.

"I love you, too, Jake."

I squeeze Alice tight against me and fall into the most peaceful sleep of my life.

CHAPTER 38

Jake

A week after Thanksgiving, I make the turn toward my and Alice's houses and spot Alice sitting on the steps outside of my house. She stands when she sees the truck and points to the gravel on the other side of my lawn.

I quickly park and step out of the truck.

"Is something wrong?" I ask.

"Does your friend Ila take walk-ins?" she answers my question with a question – one completely out of left field.

"What? Ila? Unless it's a big piece, she only takes walk-ins or appointments a few days in advance. She loves the excitement of spontaneous art. Why?"

"Will you take me to see her?"

I can hear the excitement in her voice like she's bursting to say something. The worry I felt seeing her waiting on my stoop leaves me.

"I'd love to."

"Thank you! And Jake?"

"Mmhmm?"

"Let's take the Trans Am."

I laugh with my whole body. That explains why she wanted me to park in front of the grass instead of in front of my garage. My girl is hot for vintage sports cars. I back it out of the garage but still stop and get out to open Alice's door for her.

"What are you up to?" I ask once I get back in the car.

"It's a surprise," she answers, the gleam in her eyes vibrant.

Alice and Ila immediately take a liking to one another. Ila shuffles Alice off to the back of the tattoo studio so they can secretly discuss whatever Alice wants to get. She says I'm not allowed to know yet. They've been back there for over half an hour.

I don't *need* to know, but not being *allowed* to know makes me painfully curious.

I peek toward the back of the studio and see the women with their heads bent over Ila's iPad, but I can't hear a word they're saying. As if they can feel my gaze, they snap around and pin me with a death stare simultaneously. I shuffle back over to a chair and take a seat.

At five feet, Ila is small but fierce. Her long, straight brown hair spills over her hunched shoulders as she draws, but if it's in her way, she doesn't seem to notice. It's hard to tell from my place in time-out up front, but she might have added to the ink trailing down her arms since I last saw her.

After a few more minutes, Alice squeals with delight. I guess Ila's come up with something that Alice likes.

"Alright, Jacob, you can come on back!" Ila calls. She's the only one who ever calls me by my full name.

I head back and see Alice seated in a chair with her left arm on a saran-wrapped cushioned platform, palm up. Ila is collecting the stencil from the printer. Alice points to a stool on her other side.

"You can stay back here with me, but you have to sit there and face away from me. And no peeking! I don't want you to see it before it's done."

"Yes, ma'am," I huff as I take my seat, grumpy over being left out of the secret these girls now share. Alice places her right hand on my leg.

"But please hold my hand."

I thaw instantly.

I turn my head slightly, so I can see a bit of her face and smile.

Taking her hand in both of mine, I gently repeat, "Yes, ma'am."

Ila finishes setting up her equipment and placing the stencil. A low buzzing sound fills the room, and Alice squeezes my fingers. I rub my thumb across the back of her hand and keep doing so until the buzzing stops almost two hours later.

Alice sits very well, especially for a first-timer, but she still lets out a big sigh and takes a second to loosen her stiff fingers from where they've been clenching my hands. She's quiet for a second before gasping.

"Oh my god, they're *perfect*," she breathes.

The anticipation is killing me. I just about shout, "Can I look now?!"

I hear the sound of ripping medical tape and expect Ila is taping plastic wrap over the new tattoo.

"Nope!" Alice says cheerfully. "Not yet."

I turn my head just enough for her to see me glaring at her. Her smile grows wider. Alice sits up, keeping her left arm tucked beside her leg so I can't see anything.

Ila links her arm through Alice's right and leads her to the front of the studio, explaining aftercare and making sure Alice has Ila's number in case she has any questions.

Alice pays Ila and asks, "Could I also use your number if I

don't have questions? Maybe we could hang out, get coffee sometime?"

Ila grins at Alice. "You'd better!"

The women hug, and we're off. Alice had taken off her sweater before getting her tattoo and has now draped it over her left arm. I drop my coat over Alice's shoulders, so she isn't cold while we walk to the far back of the parking lot, where I left the Trans Am all by itself. She shifts the sweater as she's getting in the car, but it's already dark out, and I don't even get a glimpse of the ink on her arm.

Alice laughs at my obvious frustration.

"Patience, Jake," she whispers once I'm in the car. It's only a few minutes before I'm driving between the trees to get to our houses.

"Park it in front of your garage," Alice says, pointing to the darkened alcove.

I catch the mischievous look on her face and do as I'm told. Alice reaches up to click on the interior light and uncovers her arm. Through the transparent bandage, I can clearly see three leaves that look like they're carried on the wind, wrapping around her delicate wrist. I remember sitting on Alice's back patio, watching brightly-colored leaves falling from the trees and into the lake, and I see those leaves inked into her skin, with brilliant splashes of orange, yellow, and red.

Alice lets me silently examine her arm, carefully turning it over to see the third leaf curling over the inside of her forearm. I look up to find her watching me.

"Barefoot Lake feels more like home than any other place I've ever been," she explains, still speaking softly.

"I've spoken with the head of the English department at the university, and she's agreed to allow me to work primarily remotely for the spring semester. I only need to go down to

Boston for the five weeks when I have in-person classes. She tried to convince me to stay but was finally understanding when I told her point blank that I do not want what she can offer me."

She takes a deep breath and continues.

"I've also spoken with William's doctors, and they feel confident it would not be too disruptive to move him to a facility closer to Wilcox Grove. They're even familiar with a few of the facilities you found and have made some calls to begin the transfer process to the one they believe will be the best fit for his circumstances."

I'm a reasonably intelligent adult human. I hear the words Alice is saying and understand what each one means, but I'm not quite letting myself believe the conclusion.

That is, until Alice says, "I'm staying in Wilcox Grove. I want to be here, I want to be with you, and in the fall, I want to be back in a classroom teaching full-time. I'll need to work hard, but I'm going to convince somebody that they need me in their English department."

I release a breath I didn't realize I'd been holding. It's only been a week, but I feel like I've been waiting my whole life for her answer. Maybe I've just been waiting for her.

"You're staying?" I ask, just to be sure.

"I'm staying."

I slide my hand up her arm and cup her cheek. I lean forward and press my lips to hers, breathing in deeply through my nose, until her cinnamon apple scent consumes me.

Alice places her hand on my chest and presses further into me. My hand slides behind her head and my fingers lace with her hair. Her hand clenches, fingers twisting in the fabric of my top.

I need her.

As if she can hear my thoughts, Alice breaks the kiss, twisting and sliding over the center console. She's in my lap, pressed close to me and crouching low so she doesn't hit her head on the ceiling.

I look up at her and find that mischievous look back on her face. She reaches between my seat and the door, and I suddenly lurch backward as the seat lies flat. She reaches up and flicks off the interior light, plunging us into darkness.

"I think it's 'later' now, Jake."

CHAPTER 39

Alice

For a moment, there's only darkness, but as my vision adjusts, I see Jake looking up at me with intrigue.

"In the car?" he asks.

I nod.

"Outside?"

I nod again.

I'm vanilla, always have been, so this little change of scenery feels thrilling. I don't care how impractical car sex is. I want Jake *now*.

He slides his fingers up my bare arms, the coat he'd draped over me discarded in the passenger seat. Heat still blasts from the air vents behind me, but my skin erupts in goosebumps. I press my palms into his shoulders for leverage and purposefully grind my hips against his, telling him I'm in charge.

Jake's eyes flutter closed, and his chest rumbles with a groan, his fingers tightening around my arms. I can feel him growing hard beneath me.

I release his shoulders and reach for the hem of his top, lifting off him enough to tug the material up. I slip my hands beneath the fabric and scrape my nails along his abdomen. Jake squeezes his eyes tighter shut and pushes his head back into the seat beneath him. I've noticed he's very sensitive here.

I grind against him again, my hands pressed against his hot skin between us, but am careful not to rub my brand-new tattoo. I bring my lips to his neck, licking up to his ear where I lightly bite the shell.

I don't know if it's the tattoo or the rush of taking control of my life, but I feel bold.

"Tell me what you want, Jake," I hiss, reminiscent of the first time we were together in my bedroom.

Jake's eyes fly open, but unlike I was when he asked me the same question, he is not shy.

"I want to be deep inside you. And I want you to ride me."

I breathe in sharply, and it takes me a second to restart my brain.

Oh.

I grin.

Ok then.

I reach behind myself to pull off my shoes and toss them on the passenger floor. Jake's hands find my sides to steady me, and his thumbs begin rubbing circles on the front of my hip bones. He abruptly presses me down and drags me forward while lifting his hips, a promise of what's to come.

He hooks his thumbs under the waistband of my leggings, pulling the material down as far as he can. I lean forward so I can lift my hips off him, and he drags the material and my underwear over my ass, spreading his fingers to knead my skin as he does.

I clumsily extract my legs, one at a time, and settle back over Jake's lap, hands flying to his belt and quickly unhooking it. The ice-cold buckle hits my thigh, and I gasp. Jake's hand covers the spot, rubbing deliciously further up my leg. My fingers move to the button on his pants, but it's becoming harder and harder to concentrate the closer his thumb gets to the apex of my thighs.

I force myself to focus while I draw down his zipper, so nobody gets hurt, and the second my hand slips under his jeans and wraps around him through his boxers, he presses his thumb to my clit.

I nearly launch myself into the back seat, but Jake's other hand is back on my hip, holding me down.

I take a few breaths in through my nose, steadying myself, as he slides his fingers between my legs, feeling how wet I am for him.

I need him now.

I run the heel of my palm along his length and enjoy the way he bucks against me. I want him to be as undone as I am. I extract my hand and rise on my knees, my thighs already shaking. It's awkward and cramped, but neither of us cares. I hold myself off him as he yanks his pants and boxers down to his mid-thighs. I basically fall back against him. I can't help but stare when he springs free, and his cock bumps against my stomach.

Jake's hand stills on me when I wrap my fingers around him again, this time without any barrier between us. I pump him slowly a few times, and Jake breathes out heavily. He watches my hand move before his eyes dart up to mine.

"*Deep* inside you, Ace," he reminds me.

He presses a finger all the way inside me before extracting it and spreading my wetness on my skin, teasing me.

I love that he wants me as badly as I want him.

I reach over and grab my purse, digging around until I find the condoms I'd shoved inside earlier. I came prepared for this moment. I rip one open and roll it onto him.

Now, both of his hands are on my hips, and he helps me rise up as I position him at my opening and slowly begin to sink down. I close my eyes, relishing in the fullness as gravity helps me take him inside of me. My weight falls forward again, and I catch myself with my palms on his chest. My thighs shudder hard.

"That's it, Ace. Let go. I've got you."

Jake's hands move down to cup under my thighs, and he literally holds my weight for me, lowering me onto him.

We groan together when I'm fully seated. He hisses when I roll my hips against him, giving myself more friction. I drop my forehead to his, and we stay still for a moment, breathing each other's air.

Then, Jake lifts me and presses me back down. He repeats the motion, and I force my legs to help him. Again. Again. Again.

Jake keeps one hand on me, guiding me, but he licks the fingers on his other hand before returning them to my clit, pressing, teasing, and flicking the sensitive nerve bundle. Somehow, without disrupting our pace at all.

I'm moving more quickly now, and Jake raises his hips to meet me, thrust for thrust.

"Alice— fuck— I love you so damn much."

I silence him by pressing my lips to his. Those words make this feel like so much *more*. His hand stills between us as I ride him harder. He licks at my bottom lip, and I unravel for him. I'd lay every part of my soul bare for this man.

Jake thrusts up hard into me, and I feel him shudder through his release. I slow my hips, letting him ride this out.

He kisses the side of my mouth, my cheek, under my chin. His beard is rough on my neck, and it makes me feel alive. I roll my hips against him, and he presses his fingers against me again. I grind down harder.

His other hand leaves my hip and slides up my torso under my tight tank top. He roughly shoves my bra above my breast and cups me, pinching my sensitive nipple. I gasp, and he bites the skin where my neck meets my shoulder. The rush of feeling zips down my body, and I want to squeeze my legs together, but there is still a large man between my thighs.

Jake kisses over the stinging spot on my shoulder before licking and biting his way up my neck. He's still inside me, and his fingers continue to work between my legs. He rolls his hips up, and every place he's touching me feels like it's charged with electricity. He rolls my nipple between his thumb and forefinger and drags my earlobe between his teeth.

It's overwhelming. I feel him everywhere on my body, breathing in my ear, his heart pounding in time with my own, his fingers drawing pleasure from my body like he *needs* it, his length filling me completely.

It's sudden, and I'm freefalling over that edge once more. My nails dig into his chest, and I roll my head until his temple is pressed against mine. My orgasm crashes into me again and again.

I feel like I've run a marathon, out of breath, heart hammering. My bones have obviously been replaced with Jell-O.

"I love you, too, Jake," I breathe.

Jake must feel me drifting because he slowly removes his hand from under my shirt, shifts my bra and top back into place, and pulls his other hand from between us.

"Come on, let's go inside," he whispers.

I force myself to lift and shift back into the passenger seat, whimpering when Jake slides out of me.

We should get this car detailed.

Jake efficiently lifts his hips to slide his pants back up and promptly hops out of the car. I realize his top is still on the seat under me. I'm trying to sort out my leggings since one leg got pulled inside out while Jake darts to the side door of his house to unlock it and then comes back to the passenger side of the car.

I squeal when he pulls open the door because I am *not* decent, but he just laughs, bending over me to wrap his sweater around my lap and then scoop me up. I snatch up my bag as I'm being lifted from the car, but my shoes and other clothes are left behind.

"Jake!" I yelp. I lower my voice even though there's nobody within earshot in any direction and our homes are completely secluded in their little clearing. "My pants!"

Jake just adjusts me against his chest, nudges the car door closed, and walks to the house.

"You don't need them. I'd just be taking them back off anyway."

He carries me inside and right up to his bedroom, where he lays me out on his bed like his own personal feast.

Jake

EPILOGUE

THE FOLLOWING MAY

"Jake…" I vaguely recognize the voice calling my name, but it sounds distant. My brain doesn't want to wake up yet, but the voice is persistent.

"Jaaaaaaake. Wake up, honey."

Honey…

A smile spreads across my lips when I realize the voice belongs to Alice. She must have let herself in with the key I gave her months ago.

Today is her first day officially living full-time in Wilcox Grove after going back and forth to Boston for the spring semester. While she was in Boston, Alice was thankfully able to stay with Piper. Since Piper's actual roommate was almost always at her new boyfriend's house, as long as Alice contributed to the upkeep of the apartment and occasionally filled the fridge, the other girl was ok with Alice crashing from time to time.

We visited William frequently. He had settled in well at the new facility, and even though he still nearly always thought Alice was a student, they've been able to share a lot of good days.

For the weeks Alice was in Wilcox Grove, we spent almost all our free time together. Sometimes, she would help at the nursery. Other times, I would watch her teach her remote class. Wilcox Grove's flag football team wrapped up and made room for softball. Alice was adamant about remaining only as a spectator, but it felt damn good to look over and see her on the bleachers.

A few weeks ago, Alice accepted a position teaching English and writing full-time at a small college near Wilcox Grove, and she couldn't be happier at the prospect of being back in the classroom come fall. I've been counting down the days until the semester ended, and I can hardly believe we're finally here.

I slowly open my eyes, reaching up to grab Alice around her waist and pull her down beside me. I wrap her in a full-body hug, even hooking a leg over hers, bundling her in the comforter smashed between us. She laughs as I latch onto her like an octopus and kiss her temple.

"Good morning, birthday boy," she gets out between laughs.

"Mmmmm," I hum. "Thank you. Are you here to give me a present?"

My tone is dripping with innuendo.

"I am…" she replies, with an equal amount of innuendo.

Best birthday ever.

I move to roll on top of her and rip the comforter out of the way, but Alice looks pointedly at the ground beside my bed. I glance over the edge of the mattress and find a sizable, wrapped box sitting on the floor with an enormous bow on top.

The box jolts.

I sit up, still straddling Alice.

"Did that box just move?"

Alice just shrugs at me, pure innocence on her face.

I untangle myself from Alice and practically fall out of bed, my curiosity at an all-time high. There's no way Alice would know, would she?

I reach out tentatively toward the box and it *definitely* jolts now.

I rip off the bow and paper, and the lid of the box pops up. I pull it off and find a small, wiggly bundle of fur inside.

I'm in shock. I look between Alice and the little puppy several times before I remember how my arms work. I scoop the dog up, and he immediately begins showering my face with kisses.

I've wanted a golden retriever for as long as I can remember, and holding this little fella doesn't feel real.

"I—how—how did you know?"

Alice shrugs again. "I'll never reveal my sources."

I stand, taking the puppy with me, and sit beside Alice on the bed.

"Hi, buddy! Hi—" I look at Alice. "Does he… she have a name?"

"His name is Waffles."

I feel so overwhelmed that I don't know what to do.

He's too small to know his name, but at the sound of it coming from Alice, the puppy launches out of my arms toward her. She catches his tiny body and flops back on the bed, taking him with her.

"When I spend *all* of my time over here, I want you to know it's for him," she says, laughing again as Waffles stomps all over her torso with zero concept of personal space.

An idea sparks in my head. I lie back beside her on my side and prop my head up on my hand.

"You know, you could see him all the time if you moved in here."

Alice freezes, even though Waffles continues climbing all over her.

"Are you asking me to move in?"

I shrug. "Why not? I want to spend every minute with you anyway. Plus, Scott and I talked on the phone yesterday, and he said he wants to move back up here. Why not rent him your house and move in here? It would give us some privacy. Or we could move into your house, and Scott could stay here. Whatever you want, really."

She blinks at me, and I'm worried I've asked too soon.

Then her eyes light up. "Yes! Absolutely, yes!"

Acknowledgments

I have so many people to thank for helping me get to this point – actually publishing a whole damn book! Writing this might be more stressful than telling Alice and Jake's story.

First, I need to thank my husband, Ben, without whose support, this never would have happened. He's patiently sat through countless bouts of rambling nonsense about this little world and has comforted me time and time again when I insisted my becoming an author was impossible, convincing me to keep on writing. You're my best friend, Ben. Thank you. I love you.

Next, the biggest thank you to my family for over thirty years of never-ending support for this silly little dream of publishing a book. Mom, you also spent many years as my teacher fostering a life-long love of reading and always ensuring I had the resources to keep on writing. Dad, your pride in my accomplishments has taught me to believe in myself. Without these things, there'd be no book.

Georgianna – I can't count how many hairbrained ideas I've come to you with, and when it came to my writing ideas, you always encouraged me to go for it. Well, big sis, I really went for it this time. Each time I leapt, thank you for jumping with me.

To my alpha and beta readers, Lexy, Emily, Jamie, Carissa, and Jack, thank you for taking a chance on a new writer, just making it up as she went. Your support has meant the world.

To the creative women I am so blessed to be surrounded by, Sam, Nicole, Maribeth, and Grace Elena, thank you for bringing my vision of this book to life and sharing it with the world. *Barefoot Lake* was a labor of love, and it means so much to me that you put some of your love into bringing Wilcox Grove to life.

To my editors, Megan and Cassidy, thank you for your encouragement, honesty, and listening ears. Megan, without, this book simply would not exist. I know I would have put it down at some point and never picked it up again, but you didn't let that happen. Cassidy, you helped make *Barefoot Lake* ready to go out on its own, and I am so grateful for your time and attention.

To my ARC readers and street team, I am so happy to have welcomed each and every one of you to Wilcox Grove. I'm still shocked people want to read something I wrote, and I'm so thankful for the time you've put into going on this journey with me. I wish we could all make s'mores on Alice's back patio together. Thank you.

Always to Mrs. Prisco, Miss Price, and Mrs. Andrews, my kindergarten and first grade teachers, and the first cheerleaders I had outside of my family for my writing. You showed a little girl how to love learning.

To the first third of three children in a trench coat, Mads, our giggling, kicking, and screaming over the sweetest romance book moments make me fall in love with love over and over again. You are light, even when you're your most sassy, and I have loved screaming into the void with you over how impossible writing can sometimes be. You've followed this little baby book from the very beginning, and I'm so glad to have you by my side.

Lastly, to my sister author and my soulmate, Ila (and the last third of three children in a trench coat) – there is nobody I'd rather be on this authoring roller coaster with. I have no clue where I'd be without you, and I have no interest in finding out. Your love, chaos, loyalty, and wit have made every day I've known you better than those when I didn't. You are part of me and part of this story. From *Wicked*, "So much of me is made of what I learned from you. You'll be with me like a handprint on my heart. And now whatever way our stories end, I know you have re-written mine by being my friend." Weasel snakes forever <3

Content Warnings and Spice Guide

Barefoot Lake includes references to the following topics:

Emotional manipulation
Off-page parent death (one from cancer and another couple from
a sudden, violent accident)
On-page parent with dementia

Explicit sexual scenes can be found in the following chapters:

Chapter 24 Chapter 26 Chapter 27 Chapter 39

After nearly half a decade of practicing law, Kim Swizz is now a recovering attorney, living her best life writing small-town romance. Kim has always had a passion for creative writing but has never published a novel (unless you count the book she wrote and had bound in first grade, a titillating story entitled "The Cat is Eating") — until now. She is excited to leave behind the days of drafting contracts and start this new chapter.

A forever Jersey girl turned former Arizona resident, Kim now calls Boston home with her husband, though they love to travel together.

When she is not writing spicy scenes or making her readers cry, you can find her crocheting tiny things, knitting, embroidering, cross-stitching, bullet journaling — you get the point.

Kim is never without her emotional support Kindle and is an avid F1 fan, keeping up with news on all of the drivers, but mostly Carlos Sainz.

Kim is an unapologetic Disney adult who loves the smell of fall, small animals, and dancing her heart out (and Carlos Sainz).

Barefoot Lake is Kim's debut romance novel.

www.ingramcontent.com/pod-product-compliance
Lightning Source LLC
Chambersburg PA
CBHW022024310726
48972CB00006B/1799